ANYA
AND THE
DRAGON

ANYA
AND THE
DRAGON

By Sofiya Pasternack

VERSIFY
HOUGHTON MIFFLIN HARCOURT
BOSTON   NEW YORK

hmhbooks.com

The text was set in Berling LT Std.

Interior illustrations by Celeste Knudsen

Library of Congress Cataloging-in-Publication Data
Names: Pasternack, Sofiya, author.
Title: Anya and the dragon / by Sofiya Pasternack.
Description: Boston ; New York : Houghton Mifflin Harcourt, [2020] |
Summary: In an alternate ninth century, twelve-year-old Anya and a new
friend face a Viking and a tsar to protect the water dragon that saved her life,
putting her family's home at risk.
Identifiers: LCCN 2018052139 | ISBN 9780358006077 (hardcover)
ISBN 9780358379058 (paperback) | ISBN 9780358438540 (Grinspoon paperback)
Subjects: | CYAC: Magic—Fiction. | Dragons—Fiction. | Vikings—Fiction. |
Kings, queens, rulers, etc.—Fiction. | Jews—Fiction. | Fantasy.
Classification: LCC PZ.1.P3753 An 2020 | DDC [Fic]—dc23
LC record available at https://lccn.loc.gov/2018052139

Printed in the United States of America
DOC 10 9 8 7 6 5 4 3 2 1
4500812289

To C—
I love you.

To Mom—
For letting me be weird
and grow up with goats
in the house.

CHAPTER ONE

A NYA WAS NOT a good goatherd.

The sun had barely broken over the trees as she pulled Zvezda back to the barn by his horns for the third time. The stupid goat had broken his leg two weeks earlier, and Anya's grandfather wanted him to stay in the barn and rest for at least a month. But the goat had chewed off his splint and, apparently bored with the comfort of the barn, pushed through the doors and followed Anya out to the onion fields.

Her grandfather, Dyedka, sat in the barn on a stool and milked a goat. When Anya pulled the door open, all the goats swiveled their heads toward her, and Dyedka said, "Back already?"

She shoved Zvezda inside. "Can you make him stay?"

Dyedka shrugged. "He's not my goat."

"They're all your goats," Anya said.

He shook his head. "That one's yours. He doesn't listen to me, either."

"But you have animal magic, Dyedka." Zvezda nibbled on her dress, and she pushed him away. "You're a bad goat!"

Dyedka patted the goat he was done milking on her rump, and she walked away. He turned his head to Anya so he could study her with his good eye. He had lost his other eye, plus both of his legs at the knee, in a past war against the tree people—who Anya was disappointed to find out weren't actually people made of trees but just people who lived in the forest—before she had been born. He had wooden legs that he got around on with the help of his walking stick, which leaned against the wall nearby.

Another goat stepped in front of him and bleated, ready to be milked. Dyedka scratched the top of her head and said to Anya, "You know no one is allowed to use magic, Annushka."

She snorted and watched the line of goats waiting patiently to be milked. "You're using magic," she said. The goats didn't behave this well for anyone but Dyedka and Papa, because both of them used animal magic.

Dyedka nodded. "Because I'm old and missing too many things. The tsar makes his laws in Kiev, but they don't always apply to us out here away from the cities."

Anya quoted a sentiment she'd heard a lot in the village when people decided to break the law: "'God is far up high, and the tsar is far away'?"

"Exactly." Dyedka milked the goat. "Besides, magic won't solve all your problems."

She wouldn't know. Anya still didn't have the ability to see the threads that were the key to performing magic. She was hoping that ability would make its appearance in a month, when she became a bat mitzvah. If she was old enough to be responsible for all her own actions, she was for sure old enough to use magic, right?

Zvezda nibbled on her dress again, and she pushed his head away. This time he didn't let go as easily, and she groaned at the sharp *rrrrip* of her dress tearing.

"Zvezda!" She grabbed at the torn fabric. "Now I have to harvest the onions *and* bake challah *and* mend this before sundown."

"Just mend it tonight," Dyedka said.

"It's Shabbat, Dyedka."

He shrugged as he milked the goat. "I don't remember all your rules."

She pushed Zvezda at the milling herd in the barn. Talking about Shabbat rekindled her urgency to get the onions brought in from the field so Mama could take them to the Friday market. If she didn't sell enough onions, they wouldn't be able to get the fish they needed for dinner, and they wouldn't have enough to eat that night and the next day.

"Stay," she said to Zvezda.

He blinked. *"Myah."*

Anya slammed the wooden barn doors shut, and as she took a step away, she heard Zvezda bleat inside.

"Oh no, you don't!" She backed against the barn doors and held them closed. Nothing happened. Maybe Zvezda was finally going to stay—

Thump! The door shuddered as the goat rammed it with his head.

Anya rolled her eyes. Maybe not. "Stay there!"

She heard Dyedka laugh. Papa would have known how to make the goat listen, and he would have helped her. But Papa was gone. The tsar's conscription officers had come through months ago and taken inventory of every able-bodied man in the village. Now they were all away fighting against the forces of Sultan Suleiman to the south.

Zvezda bleated again and bumped the door with his head.

Anya scowled. "If I catch you out of the barn again, I'll break your other legs!" She wouldn't really. Dyedka had said Zvezda was her goat, and she supposed that was true. Even though he was annoying, she still liked him, and he seemed to like her. She had named him for the star-shaped black smudge on his white face, ignoring that he was a boy and "Zvezda" was a girl's name. He was a goat. He didn't know he had a girl's name.

Zvezda snorted from inside, as if challenging her threat.

Anya stepped away from the door, waiting to see if Zvezda would escape. The shadows of his little goat legs moved back and forth under the barn door. He bumped the door again with his horns, the dull thud less enthusiastic than before.

With an open palm, Anya smacked the wood of the door.

The goat stopped pacing, letting out a little bleat.

Anya grinned and hurried east toward the road. She passed her family's tiny home: sturdy wood and stone with a half-tidy garden of potatoes, radishes, and leeks around the front and left side. The rest of the house was covered with rosebushes so thick, they looked as though they would crush the house at any moment. But they wouldn't. Anya's blind grandmother, Babulya, whose snores managed to reach Anya as she made her way to the road, made sure of that. Papa's side, the Kozlovs, had animal magic. But Mama's side had plant magic.

The onion fields on the other side of the road were the most in need of harvest. Onions were best gathered in the cooler morning, but if Zvezda kept delaying her, it would be midday before she finished.

As soon as her feet hit the packed dirt of the road, a bleat from behind made her halt. She turned, shoulders slumped with resignation, and stared Zvezda in his black-smudged face. The little white goat flicked his tail and stared at her, then bleated again.

Anya sighed and knelt. Zvezda stretched his neck out and sniffed her nose.

"Listen to me," Anya said. "You can come, but you have to behave. Mama needs the onions done. She's already got enough to worry about. She doesn't need this, too."

Zvezda continued sniffing. Anya envied the goat just then. He didn't know about the war that took the men and boys from the village, or understand the magistrate's tax hike. He especially couldn't see how battling the magistrate wore Mama down the same way fat wore the edge off a blade.

Anya trudged across the road, and Zvezda limped a step behind her. They reached the half-full onion cart. Anya pulled a clump of stalks up, bringing an onion out of the dirt, and she tossed it at the cart. The bulb bounced in.

Zvezda chewed on the side of the wooden cart while Anya went about her chore. She moved farther into the field and pulled another onion up.

"Do you think I can make it from here?" she asked him.

Zvezda grunted from where he gnawed.

"Watch me," she said, and threw the onion overhand in his direction.

The bulb hit the far edge of the cart and then bounced onto the pile of onions inside. Anya shot her arms above her head.

"Yes!" she hollered.

Zvezda bleated loudly.

"I told you I could do it!" Anya pointed at the goat. "You naysayer."

"*Myah,*" Zvezda said.

Anya grinned to herself as she reached for another onion stalk. She saw and heard the serpent coiled within the stalks at the same time, and she yelped as she jerked her hand back. The serpent struck at her retreating fingers, snapping shut on empty air where her hand had been a moment before.

Anya stumbled backwards, tripping over the uneven dirt and landing hard on her behind. Her fingers tingled from the near miss.

The serpent-creature coiled again, displaying a blood-red mouth as it hissed at her. That red mouth, plus tiny curled horns on its head, identified it as a *zmeyok*, so named because people a long time ago thought they were baby dragons. But they weren't. They were just snakes. Bothersome horned snakes that ate anything they could get their mouths around —including, local gossip said, small children.

Anya was small for her age, and this *zmeyok* was enormous.

Its body was thicker than Anya's arm, and its wide head was as big as one of her fists. A fine crest of reddish-brown fur ran along its back from its head to the tip of its tail. The sides of its face were furry, like it was trying to grow a beard, and out of this short bed of hair, its two tiny curled horns grew.

The *zmeyok* flicked a searching tongue in her direction, and its reptilian eyes focused right on her. It shifted, tightening itself into a more compact coil, looking more like it was defending territory than getting ready to leave.

Anya looked up at the field of onions behind the serpent and noted the brightening sunshine. Mama needed the onions, and Anya needed to get rid of the *zmeyok*.

Something winked in the air before her, and she squinted at it. It could have been a strand of spider silk, or it could have been something better, and more dangerous.

She struggled to find the gossamer thread again, and as she was about to give up, it flashed at her.

Magic.

Anya looked toward the road. The unspoken rule of magic in Zmeyreka—and maybe all of Kievan Rus'—was that if you were going to use it, make sure no one saw you.

That rule hadn't ever been a big issue for Anya. Using magic was like playing a *gusli:* anyone could pick up the instrument and strum the strings, but only a talented or trained bard could make real music with it. And since Tsar Kazimir had made magic use illegal ten years ago, magic training had become extinct. The only way to use *real* magic was to have the talent for it.

Her breath caught in her throat, and her stomach fluttered. Maybe this was it, her talent emerging. Maybe it had taken being scared by the *zmeyok* to bring it out. She followed its trajectory toward its end: the ground.

Dirt magic. Elemental. She sighed. Even babies could catch a string of elemental magic and tug on it. This wasn't her talent. But she could still use it.

She pinched the strand carefully as it shimmered close to her fingers. The ground in front of the *zmeyok* rumbled, a miniature earthquake confined to a square inch. The *zmeyok* flicked its tongue out toward the trembling earth.

Sweat broke on Anya's brow. The magic was dusty and brittle, and if she put too much pressure on it, it would snap. She had to be gentle with it, and so, so careful . . .

Her finger slipped on the thread, yanking it down too hard. The thread vanished. As it splintered away, it pulled a little puff of dirt from the ground, spraying it into the *zmeyok*'s eyes. The creature blinked hard and whipped its head around. It thrashed its long body along the onions. Stalks snapped. Exposed bulbs crunched as the serpent's body hit them.

The *zmeyok* turned its bloodshot eyes right to Anya. It opened its red mouth and hissed. Anya went cold, and then the cold turned to ice when the *zmeyok* burst toward her.

She scrambled to find another thread of dirt magic. The air was clear. She lifted a booted foot instead, ready to kick at the serpent before it could bite her.

"I'll save you!" a voice called from the direction of the road.

Anya looked toward the voice, and the *zmeyok* struck at her just as a boy stumbled between them. He went careening by, and Anya heard a dull *whack* as the serpent struck the side of the newcomer's boot. The boy landed face-first in the dirt.

The *zmeyok* hissed and struck at Anya again.

Zvezda charged with his little horned head lowered, and he slammed against Anya's side. She yelped and ended up with a mouthful of dirt as she sprawled next to the boy on the ground.

"No!" Anya gasped, spitting out dirt as she turned toward her goat. A broken leg was one thing, but a *zmeyok*'s bite was completely different. One of the fishermen had been bitten by a *zmeyok* years ago, and the bite got infected. He had nearly lost his hand.

Zvezda brought his head up with some effort. The *zmeyok* hung on to his horn, digging its teeth in viciously. Half of its body trailed along the ground as Zvezda backed around and aimed himself at the handcart.

Zvezda charged. Just before he hit the cart, the snake released his horn and dropped to the ground. Zvezda crashed into the cart, and the *zmeyok* took the opportunity to escape. It vanished into the nearby woods, properly defeated.

CHAPTER TWO

ANYA PUSHED HERSELF UP, breath heaving and still spitting out bits of dirt. The mysterious newcomer sputtered dirt out of his mouth as he shook his head back and forth, and dirt puffed out of his dark hair like a cloud.

Without taking her eyes off him, Anya climbed to her feet and brushed off her dress. She studied the boy. He had skin the color of one of Papa's leather-bound book covers. He was taller than Anya, and wiry. His mismatched socks showed from under his too-short pants. The cloth belt around his tunic was tied in a ridiculous bow rather than a sturdy knot, and the laces at the throat of his tunic were strung through the wrong holes, loose ends flapping in the wind. He picked a stocking cap off the ground and set it askew on his hair, then turned to her with wide blue eyes.

"I can't believe it worked," he said with an accent Anya had never heard before.

"What worked?" she asked.

He pointed down to his boot, where a mark in the shape of the *zmeyok*'s teeth marred the leather. "The magic! It worked!"

Terror hit her then, like a tree dropping snow on top of her. He had seen her using magic. Whoever he was, he had caught her breaking a law. A *big* law.

She hurried to the cart, trembling as she struggled to make some excuse to defend herself. "I don't think . . . I mean, that wasn't really magic. Your boot just—uh, the *zmeyok* didn't account for you being there, and um . . ." She pointed at Zvezda, who had gone back to chewing on the cart. "He did most of it."

The boy's gaze followed her pointing finger to Zvezda and then returned to her. "You think so?"

"Yes." Anya grabbed the cart's handles so she could pull it away from this strange boy. "No magic here."

His shoulders slumped. "Oh. That makes sense. I should have known." He sighed, then shook his head and shoulders like a wet dog. When he stopped, he grinned, stuck his hand out to her, and said, "It's nice to meet you!"

Anya stared at him, hands still clasped securely on the cart's handles. "Who are you?"

The boy's eyes flicked down to his unanswered handshake and then back to Anya. "Ivan Ivanovich. It's fine that you don't know. Father Drozdov is going to introduce my family to the village on Sunday."

Anya's hands tightened on the handles. Her family was the only Jewish one in the village. "We don't go to church."

"Oh," said Ivan. "Are you a heathen, then?" Before she could respond, he grinned wide and exclaimed, "Good Perun to you!"

She blinked once, slowly. "What?"

"Good Perun," he repeated. "Isn't that . . . Do you worship a different god?"

"No," she said, then stammered, "I mean, yes. I mean, I'm not Slavist," Anya said. "And 'Good Perun' isn't a greeting, anyway."

He scratched his head. "How do you know that if you're not Slavist?"

"My *dyedushka* is. And he doesn't like being called a heathen," Anya said, then pressed her lips together. Dyedka wouldn't have liked her talking to a strange boy. Babulya and Mama wouldn't have liked her talking to a strange anyone.

"Well," Ivan said, reaching his hand out to shake hers again, "thanks for teaching me something new!"

She didn't move to take his hand. "How old are you?"

"Thirteen." He wiggled his fingers, as if trying to get her attention. "How old are you?"

"Eleven."

"Oh. You're just really skinny, huh?"

She let go of the cart so she could cross her arms. "Are you lost?"

Zvezda ambled up behind Anya, chewing on onion stalks.

Ivan forgot about his attempted handshake. He reached over and scratched the goat on top of his head.

"No," Ivan said. "My family moved here from Ingria. Is this your goat?"

"That's Zvezda."

Ivan laughed and traced the star on the goat's face. "Zvezda. I get it!"

Anya shifted on her feet. "You've moved to Zmeyreka?" She wasn't sure how to feel about that. On the one hand, there weren't many children her age to play with. On the other, even if there were, Babulya wouldn't want her to play with them.

Ivan nodded. "Yes. Is it nice here?"

"Yes," Anya said. "What does your father do?" Most of the men in Zmeyreka were fishermen, but Ivan was too well dressed to be the son of a fisherman.

Even though his clothing was fastened all wrong, it was still made of fine cloth, with delicate embroidery in places.

"He's a fool," Ivan said, still petting the goat. "We're all fools. Well, Mama isn't. She's a princess."

Anya furrowed her brow. *A fool? A princess?* "What?"

"A princess." Ivan lifted his eyebrows. "You've never heard of a princess before?"

She stared at him sideways. Of course she'd heard of a princess. She'd heard of a fool, too, but she thought it was probably in a different context from the one he was talking about. "I meant a fool. I've never heard of that as a job."

"Oh," Ivan said. "Well, fool magic runs in my family, and my father used it to defeat a bunch of monsters and marry a princess."

Anya's eyes widened. He mentioned magic like it was no big deal and everyone was allowed to use it. In a hushed voice, she said, "You can't use magic here."

"We can," Ivan said. He pulled at his necklace,

extracting a coin with a seal stamped on it. "We have the tsar's permission."

Anya squinted at the coin, strung on the end of a cord. A curious pronged symbol had been stamped onto the front. "What's that?"

"It's the Kievan bident," Ivan said, returning the coin beneath his shirt. "The tsar gave coins to my whole family, so we're allowed to use magic."

Anya had only ever heard of legal magic use by one group of people. "Are you a *bogatyr*, then?" She studied him, not ready to believe that this boy was a bona fide hero. At festivals, storytellers would recite the epic adventures of the most popular *bogatyri*, the tsar's most trusted and magical knights. Anya's favorite was Ilya Muromets, because he wasn't noble like the others. He was a farmer's son, and Anya liked to imagine that if Ilya could go from being a peasant to a knight, maybe she could too.

Ivan snorted laughter. "A *bogatyr*? I wish! No. We're *fools*. My father heard there are still magical creatures here, so we came to help you out."

"There aren't magical creatures in other places?"

"Not anymore." Ivan shrugged.

Anya frowned. Without magical creatures, what were there? Birds? Squirrels? The thought chilled her. "We don't need any help. You can go back to wherever you came from."

"I'd like to," Ivan said. "But my father is stubborn. It will be fine, though. Our house in Ingria was two stories, and he said our new house is a little small, but we can build." He looked around. "I was trying to get a look at it before my brothers do. Is there a house around here? The magistrate told us it was north over the bridge."

Anya blinked a few times, certain he wasn't talking about her house. But as she thought about it, what other house was there north of the village, over the bridge? Ivan's words opened up a gaping hole inside Anya that nearly sucked the sound out of her ears. She swallowed the hole away as her eyebrows met and she picked up her cart again.

"There's no house around here," Anya said. "Just fields. The magistrate was lying."

Ivan's eyes widened. "Wha— But why would he lie?"

"I don't know," Anya said. "There's not a house. Go away."

She pointed toward the village, and Ivan followed her finger.

"Um . . . all right." His shoulders slumped as he turned, dragging his feet all the way across the field and heading south on the road.

Anya watched him go, heart rattling. She took a deep breath and tugged her cart across the field, glad there were trees to hide her little house from the road. After making sure Ivan was gone, she pulled the cart at a trot across the road and down the slope onto her property.

Anya halted the onion cart in front of the house, and once the crunching of the wheels on dirt faded, she heard her mother's voice from inside the house. Mama sounded loud and frazzled, and Anya looked down at Zvezda.

"I don't feel good about this," she said to the goat.

Zvezda turned his head a little, studying her with a single eye. *"Myah."*

"I know."

Anya hurried up to the door and leaned close to listen.

"I need more time," Mama said. "We were told—"

A man's voice, greasy and exasperated, interrupted her. "Whatever you were told was incorrect. Rybakov was trying to help you, that's all. His offer wasn't valid."

Anya recognized the voice. It was Magistrate Yuriy Bobrov. He rarely came to the house. Usually Mama had to go to his office with her grievances. What was he doing there, and so early? And why was he talking about Demyan Rybakov? Demyan was Papa's best friend and had been the magistrate until this new one had appeared one day, declaring that he was the tsar's new tax authority in the little village, and sent Demyan to the front with Papa.

Mama spoke again: "Other families in the village had the same offer. If we sent a man to the front, we wouldn't have to pay taxes. And we sent . . ." Her voice cracked. Papa hadn't so much been sent as taken. But he was gone all the same.

The magistrate sighed loudly. "Yes. But this offer isn't valid for everyone. It doesn't extend to . . . *you*."

"What do you—" Mama's voice quaked.

"Jews," the magistrate said, and the hairs on Anya's arms stood on end. "It's very complex. You wouldn't understand. And in the meantime, your taxes have been unpaid. There are fines for not paying. You owe five hundred rubles now."

Anya clamped her lips together. Five hundred rubles? That was a fortune! The entire village together didn't have five hundred rubles. Where were they supposed to get that much money?

Mama sputtered. "But that—"

"That's the law, Miriam," the magistrate said, and Anya bristled. What right did he have calling Mama by her given name? He should have called her Gospozha Kozlova, or at least Gospozha by itself, but instead he was calling her Miriam like she was a child. At least he didn't call her Masha. That was only for the family.

Mama wouldn't correct the magistrate, so Anya was determined to do it for her. As she reached for the handle, the door swung in, and the magistrate jerked to a stop when he saw her.

"A little eavesdropper!" the magistrate sneered. "Such bad manners."

Anya searched her brain for something to snap back, but she was too afraid, and nothing came up. The magistrate was skinny under his coat, balding but bearded, and the skin on his face was yellowy and pockmarked. His narrowed eyes were the unremarkable color of wet hay, and even though he was a scrawny, hunched little man, he was still terrifying somehow.

"Get out of my way, little girl," the magistrate snapped. He didn't wait for her to move before shoving past her, almost knocking her into the rosebushes. He paused at the garden gate and turned back to Mama, who joined Anya at the house's door. Mama set her hand on Anya's shoulder, fingers trembling.

"Thirty days, Miriam," the magistrate said.

"Thirty days to bring me at least half of your back taxes, or go to prison. Or"—he splayed one hand out—"you can forfeit your property, and I'll clear your debt."

Mama's fingers tightened on Anya's shoulder.

The magistrate shot Anya a dark look before turning away and heading up the hill to the road. Anya waited for him to disappear around the trees before she spun to Mama and said, "What did he mean? Prison? Forfeit our property?"

Mama shook her head. The puffiness under her eyes was deeper and darker. She didn't say anything.

"Mama, does he want us to leave?" Anya asked. "We can't leave! Papa's side of the family has lived in Zmeyreka for a hundred years! Where would we go?"

"Anya, hush." Mama's voice was so quiet and thin that to Anya it seemed as brittle as the magic from earlier. "I have to go to the market."

"But Mama!" Anya grabbed Mama's hand as she tried to pass by, and Mama came to a slow stop. She gripped Anya's hand.

"We'll be fine," Mama said. "We just need to work hard. I need you to work hard. Can you do that?"

Anya nodded. Her tongue felt too heavy for her mouth.

"Be a good girl, Annushka," Mama said. "Help Babulya with the challah."

"I will, Mama." Challah wouldn't be enough. The magistrate wanted two hundred and fifty rubles in thirty days. How were they supposed to get that much?

Mama smiled, kissed Anya limply on the forehead, and then turned away. She picked up the cart's handles and pulled it up the hill, toward the village. Anya watched her mother disappear around the trees, a hard lump forming in her belly. Then she went into the barn.

CHAPTER THREE

DYEDKA HAD BUILT both the house and the barn in his youth, and though the house was comfortable, it was obvious where his priorities had been. The barn was twice the size of the house, built on top of a natural cave that served as a root cellar and cold storage. Anya was of the opinion they should let the goats sleep in the house, and her family could move into the barn. She was always scolded and sent away when she suggested it.

Anya marched through the goat-free barn—Dyedka had taken them out grazing—past the chickens, and into the old tack room. They didn't have a horse, so they didn't use tack anymore, and she wondered how much money their old junk would get them. She pushed aside an old fishing net to get to a saddle. The saddle's leather was cracked and dry, so probably not a lot there. A bridle fell apart in Anya's hands, so she expected no one would pay for it. A pair of old, rusty horseshoes gave her pause. The blacksmith in town might be interested in them. She dusted them off and dropped one each into the front pockets of her apron.

When another inspection of the tack room didn't reveal a secret box of gold, she left, horseshoes bouncing against her legs. She could stop by the smithy on her way to the mill to get flour for next week's challah — it took that long for their yeast starter to make the dough rise — and maybe somewhere in all that walking, she'd come up with a real solution.

Before she left, she went into the house to check on her grandmother. This particular Kozlov house had stood for fifty years, having replaced the old home when it was damaged in a flood. It was a little different from the other houses in Zmey-reka: instead of building a single room with the stove against the wall, Dyedka had commissioned a special oven that was installed in the center of the house, with a room built on either side. The way the bricks of the oven were laid made a twisty labyrinth inside it, which helped heat the oven better and hold that heat longer. In the winter, the long brick wall on the bedroom side warmed the whole room nicely. The kitchen and sitting area were at the front of the house, separated by cupboards and a tall, precarious bookshelf that was Papa's most prized possession.

The house smelled like loamy earth and sharp, pungent herbs. Long shelves lined the walls, crowded with clay pots in varying sizes. Every pot grew some sort of herb, flower, or other plant Babulya carefully cultivated and tended to. She had been collecting these plants her entire life, and some of them were deliciously exotic: saffron from the high plateaus of Persia, rhubarb-currant from the Caucasus Mountains, and ginger from the Far East. Once, when

Anya had asked Babulya how she had gotten them, she had just smiled and said nothing.

Now Babulya was in the kitchen in front of a boiling pot, her ghostly eyes staring at nothing as she stirred the concoction with short, angry strokes. Perched beside the stove, their family's house spirit examined the mess of chopped herbs and leftover stems that littered the countertop. The *domovoi*'s little kippah sat askew on his curly brown hair. He plucked herbal detritus out of the thick hair on his arms. His long, bushy beard collected more stems as it brushed the countertop, and his shirt and pants were spattered with whatever Babulya was furiously stirring in the pot.

The door thumped shut behind Anya, and Babulya cocked her head.

"That had better be my Annushka and not some horrible bureaucrat!" Babulya yelled in the language she had brought with her from her homeland, those seaside southern mountains that Anya swore she would see someday. Juhuri—a mix of Hebrew and Persian—could be so soft and musical, but not when Babulya spat it out like she was doing at that moment. "I'm not in the mood for bureaucrats!"

"It's me, Babulya." Anya spoke Juhuri as well, although it wasn't as flowery as when Mama or Babulya spoke it. "Were you here when Mama was talking to Magistrate Bobrov?"

"Your mother made me leave," Babulya grumbled, "so I wouldn't offend him. I got some herbs in the meantime. Come here and taste this."

Anya crossed to her grandmother's side. Babulya lifted the steaming spoon to Anya's face. It was stained purplish red. "It's for the little Mihaylov baby. Zinoviya. I heard her coughing last week."

Zinoviya was cute. She was the littlest baby in the village and still couldn't quite figure out how to crawl. Now that Anya thought about it, Zinoviya did have a cough. How had Babulya known?

"How do you know it's Zinoviya with the cough?" Anya asked.

"Magic," Babulya said, wiggling the spoon. "Taste this."

The *domovoi* stood up to his full height, which

was just barely taller than one of the chickens. He shook his head and chopped his hand across his throat.

Anya ignored him and slowly took the spoon from Babulya's wrinkled hands. She blew on the potion. It was thicker than any other potion Anya had seen, and instead of being a soft green, it was a dark, dark red. Anya sniffed it. The *domovoi* stuck his tongue out and rolled his eyes back in his head. He was just being obnoxious—if the potion were actually dangerous, he would slap the spoon out of her hand—but his actions didn't make her feel good about what she was about to put into her mouth.

"Quit stalling and just taste it!" Babulya barked, and even though she couldn't see Anya, her pale eyes glared.

Anya sipped the potion off the spoon and immediately regretted it. It tasted like dirt and grass and a spice that made her eyes water, plus an unwelcome sweetness. One of her eyes popped wide and the other scrunched shut. Her right cheek pulled back into a grimace, and she made a sound like *"Krrrkkk."*

Babulya snatched the spoon back. "It's not that bad."

"Did you put *beets* in it?"

"Sugar beets!" Babulya said. "To make it sweet for the baby!"

The *domovoi* pantomimed vomiting.

"I don't think a baby is going to drink this," Anya said.

Babulya grumbled and dropped the spoon into the potion, then hooked her fingers in the air over the simmering pot. She pulled at threads invisible to Anya, and the smell coming out of the pot changed. Babulya thrust another spoonful of potion at Anya.

The liquid was still thick, and still the color of old blood, but the dirt taste was gone, as was the spicy bitterness. Instead, it was vaguely grassy, but mostly tasted like sugar beet juice.

Anya nodded. "I think a baby would take that."

"Good." Babulya handed a small stoneware vial to the *domovoi*, and he ladled some of the potion into it. "Now maybe she can get rid of that cough. Those can be nasty in the wintertime."

"It's spring."

The *domovoi* handed the vial to Babulya, and she stoppered the top before shoving it at Anya. "And if we're lucky, the cough won't last into the winter!" She handed a long section of twine to Anya with the other hand.

Anya took the vial and the twine. Whenever Babulya was making potions, it always fell to Anya to deliver them. At the last moment, she remembered she needed to go by the miller. She grabbed the empty flour sack from the counter and stuffed it in her pocket behind a horseshoe.

As Anya headed to the door, Babulya said, "Don't let them see you, Annushka."

"I know," Anya mumbled.

The *domovoi* waved at Anya as she left, following the same road Ivan, the magistrate, and her mother had all taken that same morning. Ash and birch trees clustered on either side of the road, and birds flitted on the branches and twittered at Anya as she passed. She crossed the bridge over the Sogozha

River, which separated the Kozlov property from the village of Zmeyreka. She peered into the water as she crossed the bridge, eyeing the dark line on the pylons where the water had once risen. It was a hand's width below now, even when the river was at its fullest. Zmeyreka had been so named because the villagers once believed it was blessed by a river dragon. The stories still persisted—every now and then, someone would swear on whatever god they put faith in that they had seen a dragon in the river —but dragons were extinct. Everyone knew that. The falling water level was proof enough. Dragons didn't let their rivers dry up.

She crossed the bridge, passed through the village, and followed a little dirt road east along the river until she reached the Mihaylov house. Oleg Mihaylov had left with Papa when the conscription officers had come through, leaving his wife, Sveta, alone with their new baby. Sveta and her sister, Zlata, liked to take the baby around the village, and Anya hoped they were gone so she wasn't caught.

Anya hesitated on the road, looking around. When she was sure she wouldn't be seen, she dashed to the home's front door and tied the vial to the handle.

She made sure it would stay tied there, and then she ran away. Babulya mixed potions and salves for people all over the village, but she never wanted anyone to know she was the one making them. "They won't take them," she said. "Because of what I am. What *we* are."

Anya knew what that meant: because they were Jewish, and they were foreigners. Well, Anya liked to think she was only half-foreigner. While Babulya and Mama had been born far to the south where the mountains touched the sea, Papa had been born in Zmeyreka, and his papa, Dyedka, had been born in Zmeyreka, and so on, back to the beginning.

Only half-foreigner, but entirely Jewish. Babulya said only mothers mattered in this case. Anya could trace mothers and grandmothers back all the way to Hadassah in Persia. Or so Babulya said.

Once Anya was out of sight of the Mihaylov

house, she slowed to a walk. The Mihaylov *domovoi* would tell Sveta the potion was safe, and hopefully the baby's cough would get better.

She detoured on a riverside path and threw pebbles into the water. One splash spooked a bird in a nearby tree, and it flew away with a rustle of feathers. She watched the bird startle into the air, and something red flashed in her peripheral vision.

Anya jerked toward the red thing. She swore it had been in the water upriver, but now there wasn't anything there but ripples.

The red thing had been a fish, she decided. And it hadn't really been red. It was a trick of the light.

"Just a fish," she whispered, and she ran the rest of the way to the miller.

CHAPTER FOUR

T HE VILLAGE OF ZMEYREKA sat in the crook where two arms of the Sogozha River met. A wide open space in the middle was ringed with shops, all of which were currently decorated with flower garlands for Semik. The villagers who still practiced the old Slavist rituals would decorate birch trees, string up flowers and branches, and leave extra offerings for the *rusalki*. The ghostly water nymphs were normally confined to their homes in the river, but during Semik, they could come out at night and would dance in the fields under the stars.

Mama liked to set up shop near the docks and

the village center. The miller and the smithy were also in the town center, right next to each other. The mill was on the southernmost end of the town, and the miller, Rostislav Melnik, met Anya outside as she approached. His grandson Sasha lingered in the doorway. Sasha was two years older than Anya — still too young to be conscripted — and one of those fellow village children she didn't play with. He held a bag of flour in his arms.

"You're a little late this morning." Gospodin Melnik tilted his head down at her, arms crossed. "You'd better get this mixed and rising, or you'll have very sad bread next week."

She nodded. "I know, Gospodin."

"Hmph," he said, and then he motioned at Sasha. "Get on with her flour, boy!" He turned back to Anya. "He's got rocks in his shoes today."

Sasha darted forward, handed the heavy flour sack to Anya, and took the empty one from her. It snagged on the horseshoe as she pulled it out of her pocket, and Sasha raised an eyebrow. Anya didn't offer an explanation, and Sasha didn't ask for one.

Anya clung to the heavy flour sack as she made her way toward the blacksmith's soot-stained smithy. It sat beside the river next to the mill, but the coolness of the Sogozha's waters couldn't make a dent in the stifling heat the forges inside breathed out. Anya was sweating before she even opened the door.

Walking into the smithy felt like looking into her oven while challah was baking. Kin the blacksmith had his back to her, hammering out a sheet of glowing red metal on his anvil. As sunlight flooded into the room, he turned toward the door.

Kin frowned at Anya. She didn't know if his frown was directed at her specifically or was the permanent expression on his face. He was always grumping around town, limping here and there. No one could pronounce his full name properly—he was from somewhere far away, and whatever gobbledygook they spoke there was impossible to make sense of—so everyone called him the first syllable of his unmanageable name, which was something like *Kin-edge-or-kwart*. He was shorter than most of the men in the village but easily twice as thick, with a tangle of graying red hair that matched his bushy beard. Above the beard, a fading black ropy tattoo stretched across his cheeks and nose.

"Ye need help?" he said, his strangely accented Russian reaching her ears on a heat wave that smelled of fire and metal.

Anya set the flour sack by the door and shuffled forward. "Um, yes." She fished the horseshoes out of her pocket. "I found these, and we don't have a horse, and I wanted to know . . . if . . ."

Kin turned back around. "No."

"But—"

"I'm busy, little girl," he said. "If ye have something worth buying, bring it. Those are old and brittle. They're worthless."

"You didn't even look at them," Anya said.

He didn't turn around. "I can tell from here. Now get out."

Anya hesitated in the smithy, sweat rolling down her face, and then she dropped the horseshoes back into her pockets. She stiffened her lip to keep it from trembling and took a deep breath to seal the tears inside.

She grabbed her flour and hurried outside, sighing as a cool wind hit her face. With her dress's long sleeve, she wiped the sweat from her forehead, and then she went to find her mother's favorite market spot.

Anya spotted Mama's cart wedged between two fish stalls by the river. Each of the flanking booths had a small pile of onions on it, and two thick packages wrapped in cloth sat on Mama's cart, probably fish she had traded onions for.

The onions were almost all gone, which was a relief but not surprising. Mama used her plant magic to coax delicious, sweet onions out of the earth. Anya was certain everyone in the village knew Mama used magic, and equally certain that none of them cared. She knew the fishermen used water magic to pull the edges of their nets wider as soon as they hit the river's surface. And Gospodin Melnik used it to grind his flour faster, blasting air magic past small stiff sails he had rigged to his mill. She had it on good authority that even Father Drozdov, who openly preached against magic whenever he could, used it to dust the hymnbooks at the church.

The magistrate was the only one who seemed to care at all about magic. He had fined people for open magic use, but only if he could prove it. The villagers were too smart for the most part.

Mama spotted Anya and waved, her mouth hanging in a tired scowl. The sight of her mother's grimace made Anya's heart heavy. Anya was sad that Papa had gone to Rûm, but Mama had changed completely. She hardly smiled anymore. She didn't tell jokes. She didn't laugh. Papa had left just before Purim, which was normally Mama's favorite holiday, but she had barely acknowledged it that year. She certainly hadn't dressed up, and when Babulya recited the story of Esther to them, Mama had barely made a sound.

"Anya," Mama said, wiping the sweat from her forehead with the back of her hand. Strands of black hair peeked from under her kerchief. "You'd better get that flour home now. You're getting a late start."

"I know," Anya said, setting the heavy bag on the ground. "I had to deliver a potion to the Mihaylovs for Babulya."

Mama put her hand atop Anya's kerchief and rubbed it around on her head, tousling her hair. "That's a good girl, Annushka."

Anya ducked away from Mama's hand and smoothed her kerchief. Papa had always been the one to mess up Anya's hair, and Mama had dutifully taken over the role when he had gone. She didn't do it right, though, and it made Anya miss her father even more.

A low murmur rippled through the crowd behind her. Anya turned to see a gray charger clop into the village square. A man sat astride it: the largest person Anya had ever seen. Curly hair as pale as spun straw spilled over his shoulders, and eyes like icicles touched on the crowd of villagers for a heartbeat each. He wore a vest of metal scale armor and a cloak of what appeared to be bear pelt. Atop his head rested a smooth metal helmet with metal wings on either side. A long sword hung from his belt, sharp edges gleaming in the sunlight.

Anya swallowed hard. The man on the horse exuded coldness, bringing with him a wind that gave Anya goosebumps.

Mama slipped her hand to Anya's shoulder and pulled her closer. "Who is that?"

From behind them, a voice said, "A Varangian, I think." One of the older fishermen, Andrei Vasilyevich, stepped carefully away from the river, watching the man on the horse with wide eyes. "I seen them a few years ago up North. They're traders, but some of them are just mean, nasty warriors."

Anya held her breath as she looked back at the alleged Varangian. What was a warrior from the North doing in their little village?

The man on the horse steered the animal along the street, past the miller and the blacksmith, to the announcement board. As he went, townspeople stopped whatever it was they were doing and watched him, eyes wide. A few people hurried away from the square, but most stayed and began to gather. Anya remained next to her mother and watched as the man with the winged helmet dismounted and studied the various postings.

Father Drozdov stepped from the crowd and approached the horseman, who squinted at the announcements with a heavy scowl.

"Welcome to Zmeyreka," the priest said.

The Varangian turned slowly, his movement smooth and calculated. He studied Father Drozdov in his black robe and white collar with a snarl. With a finger as thick as Anya's wrist, he jabbed at the square and rumbled, "Zmeyreka?"

Father Drozdov nodded as he inclined away from the angry warrior. Anya could imagine his round face, scrunched with confusion, blinking slowly as he tried to work out how best to help the mountain hulking before him.

"*Hvor er dragen?*" the warrior bellowed.

Finally, Father Drozdov said, "I'm sorry. I don't underst—*grk!*"

The Varangian snatched Father Drozdov by the

collar, wrenching him forward and up. The priest's feet hardly touched the ground; he pointed his toes in an effort to support himself somehow. The warrior smashed Father Drozdov into the announcement board; Anya could hear the crunch of his face connecting with the wood all the way back where she stood.

She gasped and ran forward, shoving past people. She heard Mama shout her name, but that didn't slow her down.

The warrior pulled Father Drozdov away from the board, yanking him around by the collar like he was a disobedient dog. Half the crowd surged forward, and half of it shrank back. Father Drozdov lifted his arms up to halt the crowd coming forward, blood dripping from his nose down his face.

Anya didn't stop. A bad feeling was crawling its way across her skin, making her feel sick.

"Hvor er dragen?" the warrior demanded, screaming it into the priest's face. He turned to the crowd. *"Hvor er dragen?"*

Father Drozdov shook his head. "I can't understand you!"

The warrior snarled again and lifted the priest up,
bringing his feet completely off the ground. Father
Drozdov kicked feebly, trying to feel for the ground,
and his face turned the color of a sliced beet.

Townspeople screamed for the warrior to release
the priest. Anya waited for someone to do something, but, looking around, she realized no one in
the village *could* do anything. They were all very
young or very old, or they were women, like Mama,
who were small compared to the Varangian. Anya
shoved past them. Up close, he was even bigger than
he had seemed.

Anya hesitated, not sure what she could do
against such a giant bear of a man, when a choking
noise wrung itself out of Father Drozdov's mouth.

She had to do something, or Father Drozdov was
going to die.

CHAPTER FIVE

ANYA REACHED into her apron pocket and touched a horseshoe. She hesitated—Mama and Babulya would have told her not to interfere, and to wait for someone else to step in. She balanced it in one hand. "Hey!" she yelled. Without waiting for the Varangian to look at her, she flung the horseshoe with all her strength.

All that practice throwing onions into the handcart paid off. The horseshoe hit the warrior —*crack!*—on the side of his helmet's bottom brim. He dropped Father Drozdov to the ground. Anya pulled the other horseshoe out of her pocket as the warrior turned to her, face twisted in a furious snarl. The first one had cut him at the top of his cheek, and blood trickled down the side of his face.

The crowd behind Anya had gone silent. Father Drozdov's coughing was the only sound in the village square. Anya brandished the other horseshoe in her hand, planting her feet in the dirt, certain the monster of a man was moments away from literally ripping her head off her shoulders.

Anya heard her mother scream her name, but Anya had to focus on the Varangian before her, or she was going to lose every last bit of her nerve and collapse to the ground. Already her legs were shaking.

She gasped and ejected a quiet, trembling order: "Go away."

The Varangian inhaled hard through his nose and bared his teeth at her. He stepped forward, one giant foot slamming hard on the ground. Anya couldn't move out of his way. She was too scared. She could only watch as he reached down toward her.

"Hello!"

A voice called out from behind her somewhere. She hardly heard it past the blood pounding in her ears. It attracted the Varangian's attention enough to break his stare, and she dared to turn and see who it was.

A tall, thin man with fair hair ambled into the square. Anya was certain she hadn't ever met him, but he looked familiar. He strolled past booths, picking up random items as he dropped coins in their place. As the stack of items in his arms grew, he got closer.

"My goodness," he said, stopping beside Anya. His accent was strange but familiar. His brilliant blue eyes twinkled. "We've got quite an angry Varangian with us, haven't we?"

It seemed to Anya a stupid question to pose while they were both within stabbing distance.

"Hold this." He handed her the items in his stack one by one: a white candle, a pair of sour apples, another white candle, a coil of string, one of her mother's onions, a third candle, and a gutted fish.

The newcomer hesitated, thought for a moment, then picked the fish back up. He spun to the Varangian and extended his non-fish hand for a shake.

"Good day! I'm Ivan Ivanovich! But"—he executed a flamboyant bow—"you may call me Yedsha." He popped back up. "I understand your name is Sigurd!"

Anya stared at him, wide-eyed. *Ivan Ivanovich.* That's why he looked and sounded familiar. This man was the father of the boy she'd met on the road, and the tsar's fool.

The Varangian—apparently named Sigurd—growled at Yedsha.

Yedsha pointed to the Varangian's mount. "That's a beautiful horse!"

With another low growl, Sigurd grabbed the horse's reins in one giant fist.

The fool laughed and turned to Anya, then dropped the fish in her arms again. As he did, his eye caught the horseshoe she held, and he said, "Ooh, horseshoe!"

He grabbed it with the hand he'd been holding

the fish with. The fish slime glistened on his fingers as he raised the horseshoe, and Anya caught the briefest flash of magic spiderwebbing out from it. In the next second, the horseshoe slipped out of Yedsha's slimy hand and rocketed at Sigurd's face. The warrior ducked and avoided the brunt of the projectile, but it clipped his helmet and sent it tumbling off his head. The helmet hit Sigurd's horse on the flank, and the charger whinnied, spooked.

Sigurd released the reins and tried to step away from the horse, but he stopped short. The reins were tangled in the buckles of the metal bracer on his arm.

Yedsha pulled Anya back as the horse reared, tearing Sigurd off balance. The horse brought its enormous front hooves down and galloped south. Sigurd was dragged after it, twisting from one arm, shouting what Anya assumed were the worst swear words he knew.

The crowd stood, silent, watching Sigurd dragged out of town by his own horse. Then, one by one, they turned to Yedsha.

"Thank God!" Father Drozdov yelled. His voice sounded wet and nasally. "You saved my life!"

He stumbled toward Anya and Yedsha, and she smiled uneasily as he shouted his thanks. She had just saved him, but she'd broken her grandmother's cardinal rule: *Don't stand out.*

Father Drozdov shot straight past Anya and went to Yedsha instead, clapping him on the shoulder as he shook his hand energetically.

"A blessing," the priest was saying. "We are truly blessed to have you here. I would be dead if not for you."

"I'm blessed to be here," Yedsha said, extending his hand toward Anya. "But—"

He never finished whatever he was trying to say. The crowd surged forward, pushing Anya aside, patting and congratulating and thanking Yedsha for his bravery.

Anya lingered, wondering if anyone had even seen her throw the first horseshoe, and then Mama shoved past the crowd.

"Anya!" Mama grabbed her in a violent hug. The force of it knocked Anya's armful of miscellany to the ground. "What were you thinking?"

Anya mumbled against Mama's dress, "He was going to die. I had to do something."

"You let a grownup do that kind of thing!"

Anya wanted to point out that none of the grown-ups had done a thing, but she kept it inside. Mama was trembling as she hugged Anya, and Anya's guilt at scaring her mother welled up. She didn't want to upset her even more.

"Sorry, Mama," Anya said.

"It's fine." Mama didn't sound fine. "Go home, Annushka."

There was no way Anya could go home and do her normal chores when clearly *something* was happening in the village. She wouldn't go home right away, but Mama didn't have to know that. She nodded. "I will."

Mama released her. Anya watched Yedsha continue to receive praise for saving the priest, and she followed her mother back to the onion booth with a scowl. She trembled as disappointment wound its way up her arms.

At the booth, Mama gave Anya one more hug, handed her the cloth packages that definitely smelled fishy, and said, "Home."

Anya picked up the flour bag and took the fish from Mama. "I know." She dragged her feet past the crowd toward the northern road. As soon as she was out of eyeshot of her mother, she ducked behind the butcher's store and doubled back, heading south behind the row of shops.

As she neared the smithy, the door opened. She stopped and pressed herself against the wall as Kin burst out of the back of his forge. He paced by the river, rubbing his hands together, then his tattooed face, then running his hands through his hair and beard. Even at the distance she was from him, Anya could see him trembling.

She wanted to leave, but she didn't want Kin to know she'd seen his fear. But before she could decide whether to stay or try to sneak off, a voice from behind her called, "Hello! Hello there!"

Kin's head snapped up, and Anya whirled around. Ivan, the boy from the road, waved at her from around the corner of the butcher shop. He trotted toward her, and she glanced back at Kin. The blacksmith had seen her, and he glared as she stepped away from the wall.

Ivan exclaimed, "That was quite something!"

"I suppose," Anya murmured, still embarrassed she'd been caught spying on Kin.

The blacksmith was only a head taller than Anya, but at that moment he seemed to tower over her.

"Ye've made a huge mistake," he said to them. "Ye both stay away from Sigurd. And I mean it!"

Anya squinted at Kin. Had he been close enough to hear Yedsha say the warrior's name? She couldn't remember seeing him at all, but she'd also been distracted. "The Varangian?"

"He ent just a Varangian," Kin said. "Varangians are good, ye hear? But Sigurd is as dark a man as can walk this earth. He's mad, but a cunning mad. The kind of mad that'll leave nothing but ashes where he goes."

Kin was trembling again, and his fear was contagious.

"Is that what you are?" Anya asked. "A Varangian?"

"No, I—"

Ivan said, "Do you know Sigurd?"

Kin clenched his jaw. "That ent important! Little boy, ye tell yer da not to challenge him. I know enough to know fool magic when I see it, but Sigurd's strong. He won't fall for it again."

Ivan scoffed. "Gospodin, you don't *fall* for fool magic. It just happens."

"Until it *doesn't* happen." Kin's tone was ominous. A cold tickle made goosebumps rise on Anya's arms.

Ivan didn't look worried. "My father has defeated monsters stronger than Sigurd."

Kin glared hard at Ivan, then opened the door to his forge. "Sigurd ent a monster, though. He's a man."

He went inside and shut the door. The thump

punctuated Kin's warning, and Anya stared at the empty spot where he'd been standing until Ivan grabbed her arm.

"Hey!" he said. "My papa wants to talk to you!"

He tried to pull her back the way he'd come, but she yanked her arm away from him.

"About what?"

Ivan hesitated. "I should let him tell you."

"Well, I'm not going." Anya was certain she was going to get into trouble. Yedsha had already embarrassed her in the square, and now he was going to scold her too.

Ivan's shoulders slumped, then perked back up. "It's a good thing. What's your name?"

She realized she hadn't ever told him, so she said, "Anya."

"Anya," Ivan said with a grin on his face, "have you ever hunted a dragon?"

CHAPTER SIX

ANYA EXPECTED YEDSHA to still be in the square, but he wasn't. Which was good, because if Mama saw that Anya hadn't gone home, she'd get mad. Ivan led Anya south out of the village, toward the Widow Medvedeva's home. Her husband had never come back from a past war, and her children were all grown and gone. She had turned her considerable home into a boarding house, which was normally patronized by lost travelers.

It was one of the nicer houses in the village — made of stacked stone with tall chimneys on both ends and polished wood around the windows—and the only building besides the church to have two stories. Anya had seen it only in perfect condition, but today it looked as though a storm had blown through. Many of the windows were open, with various items of laundry hanging out to dry. A wagon was parked askew in the grass of the front lawn, with the horses nowhere to be seen.

The widow herself sat out in the grassy front yard in a rocking chair. She never wore a kerchief, instead preferring to style her graying hair in a braid around the crown of her head.

"Gospozha," Anya murmured as she approached, eyes wide and staring at the house, "did something happen? Were you robbed?"

Widow Medvedeva snorted out of her nose and jabbed a crooked finger toward Ivan. "Not robbed. This fool family!"

Ivan beamed and bowed. "Thank you for your hospitality, Gospozha."

Widow Medvedeva narrowed her eyes at him.

"Your parents are paying me real good, or else I'd kick you all out."

Her gruffness rolled off Ivan like water off a duck. "Is my papa here?"

The widow leaned back in her rocking chair. She nodded.

"Thank you," Ivan said, and off he went toward the home's front door.

The widow sighed in exasperation, and Anya hurried after Ivan. The front door stood open, and Anya poked her head inside, surveying the mess that marred Widow Medvedeva's usually pristine living room.

Ivan was nowhere to be seen.

"Ivan?" Anya called.

The frantic thumping of several pairs of feet sounded from the upper level, along with the trumpeted cry of "A girl!"

Anya tried to back out of the house, but someone blocked her retreat. She turned and beheld two blond boys who bore a strong resemblance to Ivan.

They looked to be the same age as each other—a little older than Anya herself—clearly twins.

The one on the left grinned, tugging at his ill-fitting shirt. "Hi."

The one on the right said nothing as he raised his hand and smiled.

"Hi," Anya said. She hugged her flour sack closer and stepped away, running into yet another boy who looked like Ivan. "Um, I'm looking for Ivan."

Two more heads peered around the door frame, but they were brunets rather than blonds. All the boys had the same startling blue eyes, though, and soon five pairs peered at her.

Anya was about to escape when a new voice from within the house hollered, "I'm Ivan!" A moment later, a sixth brother, another blond—who was not the Ivan Anya wanted—came barreling down the stairs, crashing into the two boys standing inside the door. The three of them stumbled into the fourth, and then those four rolled into Anya and the twins.

The seven of them tumbled away from the front

door, landing in a pile on the front lawn with Anya on the bottom. She coughed and gasped for air, trying to tell them to get off her.

The six boys struggled and flopped around, digging elbows and knees into Anya. A bare foot swept by her head, its big toe catching on her kerchief and pulling it in front of her face. Blind, gasping for air, and unable to speak, Anya was convinced these fools were going to crush her to death.

Then she heard the voice of the correct Ivan: "Get off her!"

One of the brothers hollered, "I found her!"

Four pairs of hands lifted her up off the ground, and four pairs of hands dusted her off. She swayed and sucked in breath after glorious breath, trying to push her kerchief back onto her head, and didn't realize one of them had his arms around her until he leaned his dark, shaggy head on hers and said, "Are we getting married now?"

"No!" Anya shoved him away. She dashed to where her flour sack had fallen and picked it up, examining it for tears. It hadn't broken open, and neither had the packages of fish. She clutched her fish and flour and scrunched her shoulders, trying to erect some sort of wall between herself and the boys surrounding her.

Four of them stood in a line, two sets of twins, distinct mostly because of their hair color. One set was as golden blond as Yedsha, and the other set had hair the same dark brown as Anya's. A third, and what appeared to be the oldest, set of twins was blond, standing apart with hands on hips, and Ivan was face-down on the ground in front of them. He had his tunic up over his head, and his underwear had been pulled up out of his pants.

"Dvoyka!" Ivan's voice was muffled from inside his tunic. "Troyka! Let me go!"

Their names made Anya pause: "Number Two" and "Number Three." Who had names like that?

The younger two sets of twins laughed and pointed at Ivan on the ground. The oldest twins tapped their fists together. They didn't look like they had any intention of letting him go.

"I'm serious!" Ivan yelled. "Let me go, or else—"

"Or else what?" Dvoyka said. "You're going to shoot water at us?"

Troyka wiggled his fingers around in an idiotic imitation of pulling strings. "Ooh noooo! We'll get all wet!"

All Ivan's brothers had a good laugh. Anya ground her teeth together and stomped to Ivan, pulling him free from his tunic. He clambered off the ground as he glared at his brothers.

"That's not funny!" Ivan snapped.

Dvoyka splayed his fingers at Ivan and said, "Splash!"

"Stop it!" Anya said, shoving his hands away. "What does that even mean?"

"Oh, he didn't tell you?" Dvoyka said.

Troyka said, "He has water magic!"

He hadn't told her, and a pang of jealousy hit her. It was a glancing blow, though, because of what Ivan's brothers said next:

"Like a girl!"

"A girl!"

"That must be why he thought that boy in Ingria was cute!"

"Where's your dress, Ivanna?"

They all made kissy noises at Ivan. His hands were clamped into shaking fists at his sides, and his face was twisted with anger. Ivan shoved past his brothers. Troyka said, "Don't pout, Vosya!"

Anya dashed after Ivan. Vosya meant "Eight," like the number, and she opened her mouth to ask Ivan why they were all calling each other by numbers. He stomped up a flight of stairs, muttering to himself.

"Bunch of jerks, pulling my underwear out, making me look stupid. *They're* the stupid ones. I said *one time* I thought a boy was handsome. One time! They just do it because I don't have a twin. Someday they're not going to be able to, and I'm gonna . . ." He stopped talking as he stopped climbing the stairs, and he turned back to Anya, still shaking with anger. "It's not like I *use* the water magic."

"What's wrong with water magic?" Anya asked.

"Nothing," Ivan said. "Except in this family . . . Only Mama uses water magic. Papa doesn't have it, and none of my brothers have it." He took a deep breath. "But I don't use it. It will go away, and then my fool magic will get better."

"Right." Anya didn't know much about magic, and she wasn't sure if ignoring an inborn gift meant another type would get stronger. She wasn't going to bring that up, though. He was upset enough already. She shifted on the step, trying to think of some way to change the subject. "So is your name really Ivan?"

"Yes."

"But they called you Vosya."

"Yes."

Anya took a deep breath, waiting for him to expound. He did not. "Why?"

"Oh," he said. "It's short for Vosmyorka."

"'Number Eight'?" When he nodded, she said, "Why Number Eight?"

"Because I'm the seventh son."

She reminded herself she was dealing with fools. "Wouldn't that make you Semyorka?"

He snorted a laugh. "What? No! Why would —oh." He bonked the heel of his palm against his forehead. "My papa is Ivan Yedinitsa, Number One! And my oldest brother is Ivan Number Two. I'm the seventh son, the eighth Ivan, so I'm Ivan Vosmyorka. Number Eight."

Anya blinked. "Are you all called Ivan?"

"Yes." He grinned, then continued up the stairs.

Anya followed him to a room at the end of the hall, where Yedsha bent over a washbasin and scrubbed at his face.

"Papa," Ivan said from the door, "I found Anya."

Yedsha turned toward them, water dripping off his face. "Oh! Good!" He crossed to Anya without drying his face off, wet hand out and dripping on the wood floor. "Yedsha, my dear!"

Anya set her flour sack and fish down before she shook his dripping hand, wondering what Ivan felt with the water right there. When Yedsha released her, she wiped the wetness off on her dress. "Anya Miroslavovna." She didn't include her surname, Kozlova.

She had only just met Yedsha, and she wasn't sure he needed to know who her family was just yet.

"What a beautiful name," Yedsha said. "Did Vosya tell you why I wanted to speak to you?"

She thought of Ivan's question: *Have you ever hunted a dragon?* "Some. Not really."

Yedsha rubbed his hands together, his still-wet face brightening with excitement. "What do you know about dragons?"

Anya knew only what the village rumor mill had churned out. "They're extinct."

"Yes. Extinct in Kievan Rus', in the Northlands, in Ingria and the land of the Karelians, even all the way to the islands of Alba." Yedsha waggled his eyebrows. "Or so we thought." He stuck his finger into the air. "Anya, I'm going to tell you something, and I hope it doesn't alarm you."

She shifted, worried. "What is it?"

Yedsha leaned closer, and in a conspiratorial whisper, he said, "This river valley has more magical creatures in it than anywhere else I've been."

Anya's brow wrinkled. They didn't have that

many. Did they? She'd never been outside the river valley. "Why?"

"That's what we came here to figure out," he said. "Your magistrate sent a letter to the tsar asking for help. And then the tsar sent a message to me. And then I started my journey to your village. And then I got *another* message from the tsar." He puffed his chest out. "A warning."

Her skin crawled. What would the tsar need to warn one of his heroes about?

Yedsha continued: "The tsar heard of a Varangian here. The one you threw your horseshoe at. Sigurd Dragedreper is a famous dragon slayer in the North. A seer told him of a very dangerous, very powerful dragon in Kievan Rus'. Do you know how the seer told Sigurd to find the dragon?"

He waited expectantly, like Anya would actually know. After a few breaths of silence, Anya said, "No."

"The seer told Sigurd to seek the village of the river dragon!" Yedsha lifted a hand in the air and ticked off two fingers. "Zmey. Reka."

"But there's no dragon here," Anya said. "That's

just old stories. I've lived here my whole life, and I've never seen a dragon."

"It could be very small," Yedsha said.

The red thing in the water. But it was just a fish, wasn't it?

"But if it's powerful, wouldn't it be big?" Anya asked.

He waved his finger at her. "Now, power doesn't always mean size. Look at you! You're very small, and you were still powerful enough to stand up to Sigurd!"

Anya felt her cheeks getting hot as her embarrassment rose. She couldn't think of anything to say, but that hardly mattered. Yedsha yammered on.

"You were very brave. You saved Father Drozdov's life."

She shuffled her feet and mumbled, "Thank you."

"You're welcome!" Yedsha rubbed his whiskery chin. "The tsar asked me to come here, because if there's a dragon here, it's very dangerous. And a dragon might be why there are so many more magical creatures here than other places. They're attracted to the dragon's magic. They'll try to defend it."

"I don't see why you need me, though," Anya said.

Yedsha grinned. "You know all the local terrain, and you're clearly brave enough. What do you say?"

Before Anya could say no, Yedsha added, "I'll pay you ten rubles a day."

She tried not to let her eyes get wide. *Ten rubles a day?* If he really meant that, and really paid her, that would make a nice dent in the money her family had to pay the magistrate. It would take only twenty-five days, and she'd earn enough to postpone their eviction.

She blurted, "I want five hundred rubles if we catch it."

Yedsha grinned. "Of course!"

He extended his hand for another wet shake, and this time she was happy to take it.

CHAPTER SEVEN

THERE WERE SOME THINGS more important than dragon hunting, and baking challah
was one of them. Yedsha wanted to get started on
dragon hunting right away, but Anya shook her head.

"I have chores, Gospodin," she said.

Yedsha frowned. "What are they? Cleaning something? I'll send some of Ivan's brothers. Shestka and
Semya have been restless lately."

Anya grimaced at the thought of Ivan's brothers
running wild in her house. "It's not something anyone else can do," Anya said.

Yedsha stroked his chin. "Well, Vosya can educate

you, then. While you chore, he can teach you about dragons. Right, Vosya?"

"Um," Anya said, about to decline, but Ivan cut off any response she could make.

"Yes!" Ivan ran out of the room, then ran back in. "I'll get my books!" he said, and ran out again.

Anya's eyes grew wide. She didn't want Ivan to know where her house was. Then he'd know she lied to him. He would know her family was about to lose their home.

"Gospodin Yedinitsa, I can't learn about dragons today," Anya said, edging out the door. "I, uh . . ." She bent and grabbed her package of fish. "I have to cook my fish before it spoils!"

"What?" Yedsha said. "But it's important!"

"I know," Anya said, hurrying down the stairs. "I'll come back later."

"Today?"

"Tomorrow!" Anya dashed out the front and up to the road, ignoring Ivan's voice calling after her.

Anya didn't stop running until she got to her property.

Then she panted as she trudged into the barn and pulled open the cellar door. Down the stairs, the natural cavern beneath the barn welcomed her with a cool breeze. It came from the well that accessed an underground arm of the Sogozha River. The well itself was twice as wide as Anya's shoulders and shallow, reaching only about a foot before it hit the fresh, clear water of the river. The water bubbled past the stones that Dyedka had built around the well's mouth, creating a low wall. She set the fish package down on the wall, where it would stay chilled until she was ready to cook it.

On the opposite side of the cellar, a wooden crate shielded a bowl full of challah dough from the brunt of the river's chill. During the summer, they kept the dough and yeast culture in the cellar so it didn't get too hot. In the winter, they kept it inside the house so it didn't get too cold. Yeast was very fussy about temperature.

Anya hoisted the bowl, careful not to knock down too much of the dough's rise. She walked up the cellar steps with it, heading to the kitchen, inside the house. The oven was probably already heating—that was something the house spirit took care of—so all Anya had to do was break off a piece of the dough to save a yeast culture for next week.

She stopped dead in the middle of the yard, groaning. She had left the bag of flour at Widow Medvedeva's home, with Ivan's foolish family.

"Great," she muttered as she started walking again. She'd save the culture and put it back in the cellar, then get the bread baking and go pick up the flour. Easy.

The doors and windows of the house were all open to vent the oven's heat. The *domovoi* sat on the top step leading up to the door, fanning himself with a leaf.

Anya paused to glance down at the house spirit. "Do you want to help me knead?"

He sighed and flopped back against the floor.

Anya laughed at him and continued inside. The *domovoi* appeared on the countertop, which had been cleaned since Babulya's potion-making adventure that morning. He centered the kippah on his head, patted it once it was settled, then stretched out his arms toward the bowl. Anya gave the counter a cursory brush before she let the dough glomp out into a sticky heap.

The *domovoi* rolled up his sleeves and then dug his hands into the dough, kneading it with the might of his entire body. Anya plucked a fistful of dough and returned it to the bowl. While the *domovoi* kneaded, Anya went back outside and returned the bowl to its cool spot in the barn cellar.

Inside, the *domovoi* continued his energetic kneading. The dough was starting to form up more, be less sticky, and roll easily. Anya let him rest for a moment and poked the ball with one finger. Some of the dough stuck to her skin, so she shook her head. "Not yet. Almost."

With a sigh, the *domovoi* leaned back into the kneading, and then someone knocked on the open door.

The *domovoi* looked up and bared his teeth. Anya didn't turn around right away. The only knocks on that door recently were bad ones. The last knock

that Anya had heard had been the conscription offi-
cer coming to take Papa away four months ago. Her
stomach knotted at the memory.

But she couldn't just stand there while someone waited on the steps. Slowly, she turned, and her
stomach knotted further at Ivan's silhouette in the
doorway.

"Hi, Anya," he said.

Anya approached him. "Ivan, what are you . . . ?"
She got closer, and the bundle of books under one
arm and her flour sack under the other became
clearer. "Oh."

He lingered on the stoop, eyebrows pulled into
a concerned W. "I asked some people in the village
where you lived."

Anya shifted on her feet. She crossed her arms.
"Here."

"You said there weren't houses north of the
river."

"I lied." Anya scratched her nose. "I didn't want
you to know."

"Why?"

She pointed to the bag under his arm. "Can I just have my flour?"

Ivan looked down at the sack, then up at her. "I brought my dragon books. So I could teach you."

"I'm making bread," Anya said.

He perked and peeked past her. "Really? Can I help?"

"Do you even know how to make bread?" Anya asked.

"Yeah!" He hurried in and set the flour sack on the floor, and slid the books onto a clear spot on the counter. Too late, Anya realized that Ivan might be able to see the *domovoi*. Usually, only family members could. But he was a fool, and magical, and—

The *domovoi* glared at Ivan's books, then shot a particularly hateful look at Ivan. But Ivan didn't react. If the *domovoi* did something like push Ivan's books off the counter or throw something at him, Ivan might get mad. He said his family was there to get rid of magical creatures. Did that include *domoviye?* But Ivan just stood over the smoothing lump of dough, stared at it, and said, "Do we put it in the oven now?" Anya let out her held breath. He couldn't see her *domovoi* after all. The house spirit turned his glare to Anya, and she shook her head. He vanished without further fuss.

Anya joined Ivan. "You have no idea how to make bread."

"Fine, I don't, but you lied to me first."

She glanced at him, guilty about lying. Was he mad? He was . . . smiling at her? She risked a smile in return. "Fair." She grabbed the dough and began kneading it. "I'm almost done with this part. The kneading. If you don't knead it, your bread will be flat and tough."

"Flat and tough," Ivan said. "Got it."

"It's done if you can do this." She pulled a ball off one side and stretched it out into a thin sheet. "If the dough breaks when you stretch it thin, you need to keep kneading." Her dough held, though. "This is ready. It didn't break."

"Do you have bread magic?" Ivan asked.

Her mouth dried up at the memory of him almost catching her using magic. "I don't think that's a thing," Anya said. "But no. I don't have any magic." She cleared her throat and added, "No one here uses magic."

"Oh," Ivan said. "I guess that's true. So if the dough is ready, do we bake it now?"

"It has to rise now," Anya said. She shaped the dough into a ball and set it in the middle of the counter. "When it's twice as big as it is now, we can braid it."

"*Braid* it? Like hair?"

Anya laughed. "Kinda."

"How long does that take?" Ivan said.

Anya shrugged. "It takes as long as it takes."

Ivan brightened. "While we're waiting, we can read my books!" He snatched the books from the counter and slid into a seat at their little table. "You've got a lot to learn."

Anya wiped her hands off on her apron as she joined him. When she sat, he said, "Oh, here." He reached into a pocket and pulled out a handful of rubles.

"For what?" Anya asked, almost breathless.

"Because Papa said he'd give you ten rubles a day to help," Ivan said. When she didn't take the money right away, he wiggled his hand side to side.

Anya took the rubles and slipped them into her pocket, the weight there somehow even heavier than the horseshoes from earlier.

"These all have information about dragons in them," Ivan said, pulling a book from the stack and thumbing through it. "My brothers mess them up. Like here." He showed Anya a beautifully rendered drawing of a fairy of some kind. Someone had inked a pair of crude breasts onto the fairy's chest, and Ivan frowned as he looked at the graffiti on his book. "I can't believe Pyatsha did this," he muttered.

Pyatsha. If Ivan's father was also Yedinitsa, and Ivan was also Vosmyorka, then Pyatsha must have been short for Pyatyorka: "Number Five." Which was strange. Pyatsha didn't mean "Five" or anything even close. It meant . . . "Fuzziness." "Should I call you Vosya?"

He shrugged. "You can. They all call me Vosya or Ivanushka."

Anya was absolutely not going to call him Ivanushka; it was much too familiar. She wouldn't have allowed him to call her Annushka. "I think just Ivan is good for me. Which book has the most about dragons in it?"

Ivan managed to tear his eyes away from the defaced fairy. "Oh, this one." He put away the fairy book and pulled out an impressive tome, then opened it on the table between them. A two-page spread of an illustrated dragon practically clawed its way off the page. It was enormous, wrapping its serpentine body around the outer wall of a cavern, wings spread wide across the ceiling. Three heads with three faces snarled. All six eyes blazed ferociously, and one head seemed to snap teeth at them. Another head breathed a column of fire, and the third head dripped what looked like greenish poison from between its fangs.

Ivan drew his fingers over the page. "Dobrynya Nikitich defeated this dragon and saved a princess."

"Dobrynya Nikitich?" Anya asked. The name was

familiar, but she didn't know much about him. She knew just Ilya Muromets, the farmer-turned-knight.

"The *bogatyr*." Ivan's eyes shone with reverence. "He worked with my papa once, a long time ago. He's not like the other knights. Ilya Muromets uses holy magic to smite his enemies, and Alyosha Popovich uses strength magic to crush them. But Dobrynya's magic is . . ." He tapped his temple with a finger. "He outsmarted Zmey Gorynich." Then he tapped the picture of the dragon. "He's the smartest man alive."

Ivan smiled wide, and Anya looked back down at the drawing of the dragon. She gulped. How exactly was she supposed to help capture something like that? It had taken the smartest man alive to defeat it, and she was surrounded by the not-smartest people alive. She hoped the dragon in Zmeyreka was much smaller.

Ivan flipped to the next page, where writing was stacked in neat lines along the paper. Anya squinted at the words. She couldn't make any of it out. When Ivan mumbled the words on the page as he followed along with his finger, Anya realized he wasn't speaking Russian, or Hebrew, or any language she had ever heard of.

He tapped at one part of a paragraph. "Here. I remembered reading something about dragons and water. *Primaevitas*. They live in rivers when they're small." He cleared his throat. "There are actually a few schools of thought on dragons. Some of the old taxonomists thought they were all one species that just developed through different life stages, starting out in water, then moving to land, and eventually taking to the air."

He flipped past more pages stacked with strange letters until he found a drawing of one of these life stages. The first step was an egg, then beside it coiled a smallish, snaky-looking creature with tiny wings. Next to it, the winged snake had legs and breathed fire, and the next step in dragon development had three heads.

Ivan kept flipping pages. "But others—and I think this is the better theory—they thought there were different subtypes of dragons, like how there are different types of magic." The page he stopped on now had multiple types of dragons illustrated. A blue water dragon twisted through waves that splashed across the page, all fins and no wings. A red fire dragon bellowed hot flames over the water dragon's head, its ruby eyes glittering madly. A brownish-green earth dragon roared from within a dark cave, and a white air dragon cut graceful spirals above its earthbound cousin.

Ivan ran his fingers through his hair. "Whatever their real nature is, they're unique among magical creatures because they aren't limited to one kind of magic. You can find them anywhere, adapting to anything."

Anya lifted an eyebrow. "Does that help us catch this one?"

"Well, kind of," Ivan said. "We haven't seen one flying around, and there aren't swaths of scorched forest. So unless either of those things happens, we can assume we're dealing with one that's either still young enough to be confined to water, or a water dragon."

"What about living in a cave?" Anya asked.

Ivan shrugged. "Are there caves around here?"

Anya turned her face north. In her mind's eye, she could see in the distance, off toward the west, the grayish smear of cliffs cutting through the forest.

"There are cliffs. There are plenty of caves and crevices. Plus water. One of the Sogozha's tributaries comes from up there."

"Water and caves?" Ivan said, rubbing his chin. "That sounds like a perfect dragon lair."

Anya smiled to herself. She was already earning the rubles in her pocket. "So what's the best way to catch a dragon?"

Ivan concentrated on the drawing. "I'm not sure. My father will know. He's been doing this his whole life."

She wished her own father were there to answer questions about dragons. He'd probably know something. Papa always knew something about everything.

Then a realization hit her. It was the first of the Jewish month of Sivan. In exactly one month, she would be twelve years old, and for the first time in her life, Papa wouldn't be there to celebrate with her. What if she became a bat mitzvah and got her magic then and he missed that, too? That wasn't something that would ever happen again.

"Anya?" Ivan asked.

She blinked away the burning in her eyes. "Huh?"

"You got really quiet." He had that worried *W* on his forehead again.

"I was just thinking." Anya got up from the table and checked on the dough. It had risen but not enough. She wiped at her eyes with her back to Ivan.

He didn't say anything until she returned to the table, and then he opened another book. "In this one, it theorizes that dragons aren't magical at all but are just normal animals that ancient people *thought* were magical. And the legends persist to this day."

He yammered about the evidence that dragons had no magic, and Anya listened, her pain about Papa's absence draining away as the afternoon wore on.

CHAPTER EIGHT

THE DOUGH WAS done rising. Ivan stood beside Anya with his sleeves rolled up past his elbows, wrestling with the dough she had given him.

"Why won't it . . . ?" he grumbled, trying to roll a piece of his dough into a long strand. "How did you finish so fast?"

She had already braided and set aside one loaf. "Practice," Anya said.

"Are you sure you're not using magic?" Ivan muttered.

She laughed. "I'm sure."

"I don't believe you."

Anya picked up her last piece of dough, rounded it into a ball between her palms, and then rolled her hands back and forth. The dough ball elongated some, and then Anya put it down on the countertop. She rolled her hands over the dough, working it out toward both its ends, until eventually it was long and snakelike.

Ivan tried to keep up with what she was doing. His dough snake looked like it had been trampled by a horse.

"It's . . ." Anya paused. "Better."

Ivan sighed and added his lumpy strand to Anya's row of five smooth ones. She lined them up next to one another and pinched the tops together, then started braiding the six strands together.

Ivan watched, silent, and then he said, "Have you ever heard of Baba Yaga?"

"Yes." Since she was talking to a fool, she added, "But she's just a story. She's not real."

"I dunno," Ivan said. "Mama told us stories, but I think they were real. Like how Baba Yaga's as strong as a hundred men, and she gets her strength from her braids. So even if you cut her head off, she can still walk around on her braids, like a spider."

Anya frowned. "That's disgusting."

"And she drinks blood, and eats children," Ivan continued. "She doesn't live in a normal house. She pulled the legs off a chicken and put them on her house, so it can stand up and walk around. If a *bogatyr* finds her house, she can just tell it to run away, and it will!"

Anya finished braiding the challah, tucking the ends under and arranging them longer than she normally would. The idea of a blood-drinking, spider-braid-legged witch's head walking around was making her stomach flop. "Well, your papa is practically a *bogatyr*, right? So no witch would come here."

Ivan brought his hands up, fingers curled like claws. "No! She loves to destroy *bogatyri*! She once enslaved a *bogatyr* who came to defeat her, and put his soul in a heartwood box she keeps over her hearth! And to make sure he wouldn't ever try to kill her, she cut off his hands!"

Ivan wiggled his fingers, and Anya pushed his shoulder. "She did not! That's disgusting!"

With a laugh, Ivan set his elbows on the counter and balanced his chin in his hands. "Do you know any stories about witches?"

"Not witches," Anya said. "But my *babulya* told me stories about spirits that possess people. There's one, an *ibbur*. The *ibbur* will get inside someone's body and help them do a difficult task."

Ivan huffed. "I give you a witch with hair like spider legs, and you give me a kindly spirit that helps you do hard things?"

Anya scrunched her mouth. "Babulya *also* told me about an evil possessing spirit! She called it *ru'ach tezazit*. It's a bad spirit that gets inside someone and makes them say or do things they would never do." She hesitated, wanting to make the story more frightening. "It could make you kill someone, and you couldn't do anything to stop it!"

Ivan made a very big show of yawning wide and loud, and Anya was about to tell him to knock it off when a voice from the door said, "Do you like scary stories, little boy?"

Ivan choked on the yawn and whirled. Babulya stood in the doorway, a basket full of gathered plants hanging from her arm. The *domovoi* perched on her shoulder, still glowering at Ivan. Not that his dirty looks mattered, since Ivan couldn't see him.

"I . . . Yes, I do, Gospozha," Ivan said, his voice cracking.

Babulya shuffled into the kitchen and set the basket down beside the braided challah dough. "Well, I've got a very scary story for you. Would you like to hear it?"

"Is it about Baba Yaga?" Ivan sounded hopeful and very nervous.

Babulya shook her head. "No, boy. It's about a very bad, bad man."

Ivan fidgeted with his tunic's hem. "Of course, Gospozha."

Anya held her breath. She knew what story Babulya was going to tell.

"A long time ago," Babulya said, "a girl named

Channah lived on a mountain, and she longed to travel to faraway places and have adventures. One day, a caravan of traders came through and camped for a few days. One of these traders was Channah's age, and his name was Ötemish. Channah thought he was very handsome, and he thought Channah was very pretty. When the traders packed up to leave, Channah went with them to their land, Khazaria. To the beautiful city of Sarkel, all made out of white stone. And Channah and Ötemish fell in love and got married, and they had two little girls."

Babulya patted each of the challah loaves softly and said nothing. Ivan looked between Anya and Babulya, clearly trying to figure out if that was the end of the story. Anya caught his eye and shook her head.

Babulya sighed. "Channah thought she would be happy forever. But one day, a very bad man rode with an army into Sarkel . . . and destroyed it. And while the bad man was destroying the city, and the homes, and the synagogues, Ötemish told Channah to take their daughters and the Torah they saved from the burning synagogue, and to run. He would meet her later, he said, up the river."

Babulya tipped her sightless eyes in Ivan's direction, as if she were staring at him. "Channah went, and waited, and Ötemish never came. When Channah saw the army on the move, she knew Ötemish was dead."

She kept her blind eyes drilled on Ivan for several breaths, neither of them moving or making a sound.

Finally, Ivan broke the silence: "Who was the bad man? Was it Koschei the Deathless?"

Babulya said nothing.

"Is that the end of the story?" Ivan said.

Anya winced. He couldn't just shut up, could he?

Anya expected Babulya to walk away then and leave Ivan to be puzzled. But to Anya's surprise, Babulya said, "It's not. Channah ran and ran and ran, until one day during a terrible blizzard, she found a little boy in the snow. She wrapped him up and put him in the sled with her daughters, and when Channah found the little boy's father, Boris, he was so grateful she had brought him home, he offered her a room to stay in. When Channah learned the little boy's mother had died, she couldn't leave him. So she stayed, even though Boris kept too many goats, and many years later, Channah's daughter Miriam married the little boy, Miroslav. They had a little daughter they named Channah but whom everyone called Anya, and one day Anya brought home a stupid boy who made their *domovoi* angry."

She trundled past Ivan, and the *domovoi* snarled soundlessly at the fool as they passed. To underscore Babulya's words, the house spirit stood up tall on Babulya's shoulder and flicked his wrist at Ivan. A stray wooden spoon sitting on the counter flew up and hit the back of Ivan's head.

"Ow!" Ivan grabbed at where the spoon had struck him and looked back at the kitchen, searching for who had thrown the spoon.

Babulya cackled on her way to the bedroom. "And *that* is the end of the story." Babulya shut the bedroom door, the thump of the latch driving the story into Anya's chest.

Ivan stared at the shut door, rubbing the back of his head, and then mumbled, "That wasn't scary."

Anya sighed. "You really are a fool, you know that?"

◆ ✳ ◆

Anya tore a tiny piece of dough from each of the challah loaves, rolled them together into an olive-size ball, and set it aside. Ivan watched, quiet, his eyes darting to the bedroom door every few seconds.

"They have to rise again," Anya said.

"Is that all bread does?" Ivan asked. "Rise?"

"It's all flat and hard if you don't let it rise."

Ivan fiddled with the ends of his sleeves. "That story was about her, wasn't it?"

"Yes." Anya had heard the story countless times, usually when Anya wondered why they couldn't live in the village proper, or why they didn't go to more festivals, or have more friends. "The man who destroyed Sarkel was the old tsar of Kievan Rus'. Tsar Kazimir's father."

Babulya could have taken Mama and Aunt Tzivyah to a bigger city where there were other Jews,

◆ 100 ◆

but she hadn't. She had stayed in a little tiny village for a reason. If the old tsar had so mercilessly killed the people of Khazaria in Sarkel, what would the new tsar do to the large communities of Jews living within his borders?

"He was a heathen," Ivan said softly, as if that explained it. "Tsar Kazimir isn't."

"That same thing has happened to us in other places," Anya said. "Places without Slavists."

"To your family?"

Anya shrugged. "Kind of. Not my family specifically. But anything that happens to other Jews happens to us. So when the old tsar killed everyone in Sarkel and Atil and everywhere else in Khazaria, everyone felt it."

Ivan's eyes widened, and she knew what he was going to ask before he did: "*Literally* felt it?"

"No, not—"

"Because my mama's people can do that," he said quietly. He scrunched his mouth up, his concerned forehead *W* deepened, and he said "Hmm" a few times to himself. Then he stuck one finger up in the air and said, "What kind of greeting do Jews use to one another?"

She remembered his "Good Perun" attempt at a greeting earlier when he had thought she was Slav- ist. "Just 'hello,' I guess," she said. "On Shabbat, we say 'Shabbat shalom,' but you don't—"

"What's Shabbat?"

"The Sabbath," Anya said. "It starts tonight and ends tomorrow night."

Ivan nodded. "Can I say it today?"

"I guess," Anya said. "It can be a hello or a goodbye."

Ivan pointed to his stack of books on the table. "Can you read?"

A little offended, Anya said, "Of course I can read, in Russian *and* Hebrew."

He collected two of the books but left the others. "These are in Latin," he said on his way past Anya toward the door. "I should get home, but I'll leave those books for you to read more about dragons. You can bring them tomorrow when you come over."

She should have been glad he was leaving, but

she wasn't. It was nice to talk to someone who wasn't her immediate family, or a goat. "Okay."

At the door, Ivan stopped and raised a hand in goodbye. "Shabbat shalom," he said with a grin, and then he trotted up to the road and disappeared.

CHAPTER NINE

ANYA READ ONE of her borrowed dragon books until the challah had risen enough, and then she stuck both loaves plus the little extra piece in the oven. The loaves would bake and the little piece would char. Babulya said a long, long time ago, everyone had given some of their food and harvest to the high priests in the temple. And now, even though there was no more temple and no more high priests, they still left a little piece. To remember.

The *domovoi* appeared on top of the oven, still looking sour. Anya shut the oven door and put her hands on her hips. "He's gone now. You can stop being upset."

He stuck his tongue out at her.

"Or don't," she said, walking back to the kitchen. "Fine." She picked up the flour sack and took it to the barn cellar outside. She returned to the kitchen again so she could get some sugar, an egg, and water that wasn't the freezing stuff from the cellar well, and returned to the barn. She added flour and sugar to the reserved dough in its bowl, then mixed in water until it was the right consistency. She'd do the same tomorrow, and the next day, until all the flour was gone and they had enough dough for next week.

She finally returned to the house and checked the challah in the oven, pulling out a loaf and knocking on it. It sounded hollow and the crust wasn't too soft, plus the tiny piece was burned. She used towels to pull out the loaves and left them to cool on the table. When she turned back, the *domovoi* was on top of the oven again, peering down at the leftover little piece burning inside.

He pointed at the little piece, bushy eyebrows raised.

"It's not for you," Anya said. "You know that."

He pinched his fingers together.

"Not even a little bit." She shut the oven door. The little piece would burn up before the oven cooled. "You can have some later. But not *that* piece."

The *domovoi* screeched in protest and vanished. Anya could hear him banging on the walls as he retreated to wherever he went when he disappeared. He was crankier that day than normal. Usually when she told him he couldn't eat the challah sacrifice, he just shrugged and let it go.

Anya checked on Babulya, pausing by the bedroom door and listening for the old woman's snores. Once she heard a few, Anya returned to read the dragon books. The big one with the terrifying two-page spread had been in Latin, so she didn't have it. The three Ivan had left were much smaller than that one, but still incredible.

Papa had only three books total, leather bound and heavy, which Babulya had gifted to him when he had converted to Judaism. All three had been in the pack Babulya had fled Sarkel with, along with the Torah scroll: two different copies of the Talmud, and a geography book.

Anya flipped open the first book Ivan had given her. On the very center of the first page, it read:

A Compendium of Dangerous Creatures
Written and Illustrated by
Ivan Vosmyorka Ivanovich Ivanov

Eager to see what he knew, Anya flipped deeper into the text. Ivan's book read very matter-of-factly, with diagrams and illustrations of various magical creatures:

Rusalki, which Ivan said were the fishtail-having souls of women who had drowned, and the only way to put them to rest was to christen them. A note had been scribbled next to the illustration: Rusalka *seen today didn't have a fishtail—investigate*. Anya had never seen one with a fishtail, and everyone knew the only way to put them to rest was to either bury their bodies or avenge whoever had caused them to drown in the first place.

The *leshy*, a forest spirit that looked like a man crossed with a tree, who would lead travelers astray until they died. She wrinkled her nose. Zmeyreka's resident *leshy* would get people lost as a prank, but he always returned them to the road eventually.

Vodyaniye, the sinister river-grass spirits who lived in bodies of water and would regularly capsize fishing boats and drown the fishermen. That entry, at least, was mostly correct. The fishermen in Zmeyreka affixed little knives to the bottoms of their boats to keep the *vodyaniye* away.

Anya flipped a page and saw an illustration of a *domovoi*. The one in the book—a small ape with a beard—looked nothing like her own house spirit. It didn't even have clothing on. According to Ivan's description, a *domovoi* was a ghostly entity that would destroy the home unless appeased with sacrifices, and could shape-shift into a wolf or rat if it wanted.

She studied the illustration, puzzled. The Kozlov *domovoi* protected their home, and would destroy things only if he felt insulted somehow. They didn't sacrifice anything to him; he mostly got leftovers. Sometimes Dyedka would give him something special, like tobacco. He could change into a small dog or a cat, and sometimes he would make himself look like a very tiny version of Papa. He hadn't done that since Papa had been gone, though.

She made a mental note to educate Ivan about the true nature of some of his entries, and also to ask about the emotional state of his house spirit. Or whether his family had a house spirit at all.

A ruckus of hooves and bleating outside alerted Anya to Dyedka's return. She shut the book and peeked out the door. The herd hurried past, heading to the barn, and her grandfather followed behind them in a little cart. Two of the billy goats pulled it like draft ponies.

Dyedka waved at Anya. "Come help me put the goats up, Annushka!"

Anya followed the herd into the barn. Zvezda

limped up to her, bleating loudly, with his tongue lolling out of his mouth. She scratched his long nose.

"Did you behave?" Anya asked.

"*Myah,*" Zvezda said.

"I didn't think so."

Dyedka heaved himself up, and Anya ran to help him step out of the cart. Once he was steady, she unhooked the goats that pulled Dyedka around.

"Thank you," Dyedka said, rubbing at one leg absently. "Did you have a good day?"

She thought of the *zmeyok*, the magistrate, Sigurd, Ivan and his family, and Babulya's story.

"It was busy," she said.

"Good." He pointed at the back of the cart, where stoneware bottles rested in hay that a few of the goats nibbled on. "I milked more in the field. Put it in the cellar, will you?"

Anya grabbed the bottles and lifted the barn's cellar door up. She balanced the milk bottles in her arms and stepped carefully down the stairs into the cave-cellar. A cold, damp breeze blew the hair out of Anya's face as she reached the bottom of the stairs.

She arranged the milk bottles around the well's edge, picked up the fish, then checked on the bread in its bowl at the other end of the cellar.

She retreated into the warmth of the main barn, and she lowered the cellar door as Dyedka said, "Zvezda did well out there, even with his leg. Good for you, Anya. Maybe you got some of your papa's magic after all."

Anya picked up the single milk bottle she had left in the main barn and said, "If I did it, it was by accident. Can people use magic by accident, Dyedka?"

He shrugged as he hobbled to the door. "Not real magic."

It had taken every ounce of concentration she had to spray a little dirt in a *zmeyok*'s face that morning. The idea that someone could do that without meaning to was something Anya had a hard time imagining.

Once in the house, Dyedka went straight to the bread cooling on the table and sniffed it. "Smells good."

"You can't have any yet." She pulled the white

cloth out of its cupboard and ran to the table, drap-
ing it over the loaves before Dyedka could pick
pieces out of them. "Wait for dinner."

He grumbled and went to the bedroom.

When the door shut and she heard his bed creak
as he sat on it, Anya went about cooking the fish.
Mama fried it when she cooked, but Anya wasn't as
confident. She boiled it into a stew instead, tossing
in various vegetables and herbs she found around
the house. Today she stewed the fish with potatoes,
onions, and leeks, plus a handful of random herbs
from Babulya's collection.

As the fish stew boiled away, Anya opened the
special cupboard in the kitchen, where she had gotten the challah's white cloth. She pulled out the long,
white candles they would light, noting they had only
one set left. There were six of them, mandated by
Babulya: two that every family lit, plus one each for
Mama, Aunt Tzivyah, Papa, and Anya. Babulya had
started out lighting two extra candles for Mama and
Aunt Tzivyah, and then added Papa, and then Anya

last. Even though Aunt Tzivyah and Papa were gone, she still lit their candles.

Anya lined the candles up on the counter. She read Ivan's books more while the stew cooked. Ivan had talked about conflicting schools of thought when it came to dragon development, but there were some points common to both schools. Dragons loved treasure, gold, and precious jewels. They were master linguists and could understand any language. They brought rain, but depending on the dragon's temperament, it could be good rain or bad rain. And they attracted birds.

"Why birds?" Anya wondered aloud as Mama walked through the door, a large sack in her hands. Behind her, the long, orange sunlight heralded the approach of evening.

Anya shut the book and took the sack from Mama. Inside were several items she had traded onions or rubles for, and among them, new candles. *Good.*

Mama tasted the fish stew and aimed a tired smile at Anya. "This is good."

Anya smiled as she went to wake up Babulya and Dyedka. A few minutes later, they were all gathered around the counter, where the candles were lined up. Dyedka stood at the end, even though, as a Slavist, he could have just sat at the table and ignored their prayers. Mama held a long, thin stick she had lit from the oven. Anya held on to Babulya's arm to steady her as Mama lit all six candles one after another. She made it to the last one just as the stick had almost burned down to her fingers, and she let it drop on the counter to burn itself out. Mama waved her open hands over the candles three times, as if sweeping the candlelight toward herself. Then she covered her face with her hands, took a deep breath, and said, *"Baruch atah Adonai Eloheinu . . ."*

She trailed off. Anya could see her swallowing hard, time after time after time. That was something Mama did when she was trying not to cry. Babulya shifted against Anya's arm, cocking her head, probably wondering if she had suddenly gone deaf, too.

Mama took a sharp breath and continued, *"Melech ha-olam, asher kidishanu b'mitzvotav vitzivanu l'hadlik ner shel Shabbat.*" She dropped her hands, tears shining on her cheeks in the candlelight. She wiped them away with her sleeve before turning around and saying, "Shabbat shalom."

"Shabbat shalom," Babulya said reverently.

"Shabbat shalom," Anya mumbled.

"Shabbat shalom," Dyedka grumped. "Can we eat now?"

◆ ✖ ◆

They had been eating quietly for several minutes before Dyedka said, "Annushka, have you seen the *domovoi?*"

Anya paused, mouth full of soup.

Babulya interpreted Anya's silence as an invitation to say, "He'll probably be hiding somewhere all night because of that boy."

Anya choked on her soup a little as Dyedka roared, "*Boy?* There was a boy here? Which boy? That Sasha Melnik? I'll poke his eyes out!"

"Not Sasha!" Anya interrupted. "The *domovoi* got mad because I wouldn't give him the challah that I separated and burnt."

But Dyedka was stuck on the boy topic. "If not Sasha, then it must have been Kolya Lagounov!"

Anya scrunched her face. The Lagounovs were the village chandlers. They made candles, which was fine, but Kolya was way older than she was. "Dyedka, Kolya isn't—"

"If you marry him, your great-grandmother-in-law will be Bogdana, and she's terrible!" He pointed his spoon at Anya. "You're too young to get married."

Anya groaned and threw her head back. "I'm not going to marry him! I'm never going to get married!"

Mama shook her head. "Oh, Anya, of course you will."

"I won't," Anya said. "Babulya says marriage is for fools."

Babulya cackled. "What a smart girl. Don't you settle for anything, Annushka!"

Mama rubbed her eyes wearily and muttered, "I wish you wouldn't, Mother."

"You married a good man, Masha," Babulya said. "But not everyone does. That awful what's-his-name who wanted to marry your sister . . . Wouldn't take no for an answer. It's his fault she left!"

Mama's lips tightened. "Tzivyah was always impulsive and hotheaded. She would have left regardless."

Dyedka, having finished his stew, slammed his spoon on the table. "Well, there you have it! Now we know Anya gets her attitude from your side of the family! Miro was as even-tempered as they come. Not an ounce of strife in the boy, not ever." He looked down at his empty bowl and sighed heaviness into it. "Ah, Masha. I'm sorry."

Mama's expression didn't change, save for a subtle blink that was longer than usual. "You miss him as much as I do, Borya."

Anya hadn't finished her stew, but her appetite evaporated as she thought about her father sitting in a ditch with a sword. She pushed her chair back, standing abruptly, and said, "I'm going to sleep in the barn."

"Anya . . ." Mama said.

Tears burned the corners of her eyes, and Anya hurried out of the kitchen before she lost her composure altogether. She let herself cry about Papa only in front of the goats, because they didn't try to comfort her or tell her it was okay or offer her false hope about his safe return.

She walked across the garden, but then broke into a run the rest of the way to the barn. When she slipped inside and pulled the door shut, she shuffled to the nearest pile of straw and plopped onto it as the first tears forced their way out of her eyes.

Anya put her hands over her face and cried, pausing only when she felt light pressure on her thigh. Zvezda lay next to her with his head on her leg, and when he saw her look at him, he offered a gentle bleat.

CHAPTER TEN

ANYA STARTLED AWAKE. The barn was still dark, but the faint glow of sunrise lit the window in the hayloft. She moved to sit up, not entirely sure what had caused her to stir from sleep in the first place.

As she turned her head, she noticed something was amiss. Her scalp felt different: tight and itchy. She reached up to feel her head and groaned when her fingers touched a hundred hay straws tied into her hair.

Anya moaned. "Oh, come on!"

Further evidence of nighttime mischief became apparent as she looked out of the hayloft and into the main part of the barn. Lined up along the hayloft railing were the bottles of milk she had put into the cellar the night before. All the tools that normally hung along the walls had been knocked off and scattered around the floor. That must have been what woke her up.

The source of the mischief materialized on the other end of the hayloft on the railing. The *domovoi* tugged on his long beard with one hand, and with the other he pointed a stiff finger at Anya as he bared his teeth.

"Are you still mad about Ivan?" Anya asked him.

At the mention of Ivan's name, the *domovoi* narrowed his eyes and growled.

Anya pointed down to the mess on the barn floor. "You didn't have to go and do that! How long have these bottles been here? The milk's going to spoil."

The *domovoi* arranged his fingers into a very rude gesture.

Anya made the rude gesture back. "You can't tell

me who to spend time with. Ivan's my friend. Deal with it!"

The *domovoi* pointed his finger at her again, then scooted the finger to her right. At a milk bottle.

She realized what he was going to do a second before he did it.

"Don't you dare!"

Too late. The bottle, moved by the *domovoi*'s magic, flew off the railing and smashed into pieces on the floor below. The one next to it followed, and the next.

"Stop!" Anya lunged for the remaining bottles, but each one flew away from her fingers as she grabbed at them. "It's almost Shavuot!" Mama would make thin, yeasty bliny and then stuff them with cheese, fold them up, and fry them. They needed the goat milk to make the cheese and to add to the bliny batter itself. Without milk and cheese, the bliny would just be sad pancakes.

The dull tinkling of broken pottery echoed around the barn over and over, until the last milk bottle remained.

She nearly got it. Her fingers brushed the cool, sweating side, but the *domovoi* was faster than she was. He snatched up the bottle with one of his hairy little hands and leaped away from her, dancing along the railing to where she had been standing a moment ago.

As she whirled to look at him, he uncorked the top of the milk bottle. He held the bottle out, tipped it over, and let the milk spill.

"You worthless spirit!" Anya yelled, running for him.

He threw the empty bottle to the barn floor, where it smashed with the others. Then—*poof!*— he vanished, and the barn was quiet except for the clucking chickens below.

Anya seethed for a few minutes. The house spirit wouldn't ever have pulled a stunt like that if Papa were home. Who did the *domovoi* think he was?

The house protector, she reminded herself. Before he had gone, Papa had told the *domovoi* to mind the family. Maybe this was his way of doing so, even if his opinion of Ivan was wrong.

She climbed down the ladder and surveyed the damage from ground level before picking a shovel off the floor. She used it to push the broken ceramic of the milk bottles into a mound by the wall, and then she picked up the tools and returned them to their spots. Once that was done, she took one last look at the bottle mound and sighed. Hopefully, Dyedka would be able to replace the milk before Shavuot.

Anya patted the goats on her way out of the barn, and she made her way to the house as she untied hay from her hair.

Babulya was awake and tracing her withered fingers along the plants in the kitchen when Anya opened the door and walked in. Babulya perked up, turning her milky eyes toward Anya, and said, "Shabbat shalom, Annushka."

"Shabbat shalom."

"How did you sleep?"

"The *domovoi* tied hay in my hair," Anya said.

Babulya cackled. "That fool made him upset."

Anya added, "And he broke all the milk bottles."

She didn't cackle that time, instead pinching her

lips together and blowing air out of her nose. "Is that right?"

"I guess he was really mad." Anya tore two pieces of bread off the leftover loaf and handed one to Babulya. "Ivan's nice. I don't know why the *domovoi* is so upset."

Babulya made her way to the table, bobbing as she took tiny steps and swept her hand in front of her. Anya darted to the table and pulled a chair out for Babulya, helping her ease into it.

"That boy might be nice to you," Babulya said. "But fools aren't kind to everything."

Anya slid into the chair beside Babulya and chewed thoughtfully on her bread. "He wouldn't hurt anyone."

Babulya picked at her slice with gnarled fingers. "He wouldn't hurt a person, my dear. But what if you were something else?"

"Like what?"

"A *rusalka*, let's say," Babulya said. "Do you think Ivan and his family leave offerings for the *rusalki*?"

Anya pressed her lips into a thin line. Ivan's book

wasn't entirely correct about the *rusalki*, and if that was his only source of information . . . "No."

Babulya nodded. "Does your friend know what a *domovoi* is?"

Anya nearly answered in the affirmative—that was like asking if Ivan knew what the moon was —but then she stopped. His book, again, had been entirely wrong. She didn't know if his family had their own *domovoi*, and if they did, how did they bring it with them from house to house every time they moved? Where was it staying while they were at Widow Medvedeva's home? How did they keep their *domovoi* from fighting with the Medvedev *domovoi*?

Anya's silence was enough for Babulya. She nodded and said, "I'm old and blind, but I still hear things. A fool never prospers in peace. Do you know what their magic is?"

"No," Anya said.

"Chaos!" Babulya waved her challah in the air. "Disruptive, destructive, and it serves only them. And the *domovoi* knows that. He hears things too."

Anya sat, uneaten bread in her hand, eyes wide.

Disruptive magic, indeed. She would count uprooting her family as disruptive. But once Yedsha paid her the money, she'd pay the magistrate, save her farm, and life could go back to normal.

"Babulya, do you know a lot about magical creatures?" Anya said.

"Oh, my fair share," Babulya said. "Did I upset you, Annushka?"

"No." Anya stuffed the rest of her bread into her mouth and mumbled around it, "What do you know about dragons?"

Babulya smiled. "Ah, dragons. We used to see them in the river sometimes, when your mama and papa were just little babies. Borya would tell everyone that the dragons ate goats, but they never did. They liked fish better, if I remember. And when we saw dragons, there was always good rainfall, and the chickens laid better. They're good luck, dragons."

Anya said, "The tsar thinks there's a dragon here. He sent Ivan's papa here to find it. If dragons are good luck, why does the tsar want to hunt them?"

Babulya's smile dropped into a deep frown. "The tsar has done many bad things. You shouldn't speak ill of the tsar because you're still young, but I'm old, and if he arrests me for treason, I won't live long enough to make it to prison. Ha!" She leaned back in the chair as she hooted with laughter. "Anyway, he's done bad things. He made magic use illegal, and he called for the extermination of dragons."

"But he wants this one alive. Not exterminated."

Babulya nodded. "That's how it always was. They were to be delivered alive to him. Thousands went into that palace in Kiev, but none ever came out. Of course he killed them. What else did he do? He used his *bogatyri* to do it. They used to be so noble, but now they're hired killers." She snorted. "He lets them use magic to kill, but I can't use mine to grow plants?"

"Ivan said his family's allowed to use magic," Anya said.

"Fools," Babulya said. "They do the tsar's work. I hope that poor dragon escapes them all."

A heavy feeling of shame twisted inside Anya, and she got up from the table. "Do you need anything else, Babulya? I'm going out."

"Don't break the Sabbath, Annushka."

"I won't," Anya said. "I'm just going to walk around."

"Hmm." Babulya waggled her unfinished bread in the air. "I'll finish this challah and then talk to my roses." She winked when she said *talk to*.

Anya grinned and put her hand on her grandmother's shoulder. "I love you, Babulya."

"And I you, Annushka," Babulya said. "Be safe."

CHAPTER ELEVEN

WIDOW MEDVEDEVA was snoring in her rocking chair on the front lawn as Anya walked up to her house. She had a blanket tucked around her, and her head was thrown back. Little snores issued from her wide-open mouth. Anya was certain a bird would poop in it, so she used a single careful finger to tap the widow's mouth shut.

Several Ivanov sons were asleep around the fireplace, resting on one another at various angles. The smell of hot breakfast filled the air, and she followed the sounds of cooking to the kitchen.

A woman flitted from the stove to several bowls on the counter, stirring and kneading and folding as she went. The pan on the stovetop popped and sizzled with whatever she was cooking there, and Anya's mouth watered.

The woman herself was barely taller than Anya, and much rounder, with black hair like Mama's braided all the way down her back. Her skin was dark like Ivan's, and the dress she wore looked luxurious even from the kitchen door. It was actually fastened properly. She was a princess, not a fool.

Ivan's mother reached one hand out and pulled an invisible thread of magic. A stream of water flowed upward from a bucket near the door, crossed the room, and cascaded into a large pot on the stove. The water started to steam almost immediately, and she slid a dozen eggs into it carefully.

Anya lingered at the doorway, watching with wide eyes.

Then someone grabbed her wrist.

"Ah!" Anya spun and yelped, coming face-to-face with one of Ivan's brothers.

"Ah!" he yelled back.

"Who—"

"AAAHHHH!"

"Semya!" Ivan's mother hollered from the kitchen.

"MAMA!" Ivan's brother screamed.

"Come sit down and be quiet," she said, pointing at the chairs lined up at the kitchen table.

Semya released Anya and slid into a seat. His mother handed him a piece of bread. He crammed it into his mouth and smacked it around loudly.

"Goodness." Ivan's mother sighed. She smiled at Anya. "Well, come in. Get some food for yourself."

Anya shuffled into the kitchen, not wanting to stand by Semya and get screamed at again. Ivan's mother handed her a shiny apple.

"You must be Anya," Ivan's mother said.

Anya nodded and took the apple. "Are you Ivan's mama?"

"Yes, I am," she said, scooting the pot with the eggs away from the stove's heat. She set her finger on its edge, and lacy frost spirals coated the pot. It stopped steaming. "You can call me Marina."

Anya chewed on a bite of apple, nearly hypnotized by Marina's casual magic. "Ivan said you're a princess."

Marina nodded.

"Of where?" Anya asked.

"Oh, very far away," Marina said. "Far to the east. Would you like a boiled egg?"

Anya nodded, and Marina spooned an egg out of the water. When she placed it in Anya's hand, it was cold. Anya knocked the egg against the counter and said, "I've come to talk to Gospodin Yedinitsa about hunting the dragon. I figured he'd be up by now."

"No," Marina chirped. "The boys all sleep in. Except Vosya, and this one, apparently." She jerked her head toward Semya. "Why are you awake so early, my little dummy?" She said "dummy" so nicely, like she was calling him "sweetheart" instead.

"There was that little man again," Semya said. "And I wanted to catch him, but he was very fast and ran away. Then I saw her." He pointed to Anya. "Hello!"

"Hello." She paused in knocking her egg against the counter to break it and waved at him.

To his mother, Semya whispered loudly, *"That girl and I are getting married someday."*

Anya grimaced. They certainly were *not*.

"Let's get your older brothers married before we worry about you," Marina said idly as she spooned more boiled eggs out of the cold water. "And Semya, the little man is Widow Medvedeva's *domovoi*. I told you not to bother him, didn't I?"

"Yes, but listen to this." He took a deep breath in and blew it out. "He's a *demon*."

Anya stared at Semya. He could see the widow's *domovoi*? How?

Marina ticked a finger at Semya. "He's a spirit, and this is his home. You leave him alone."

Semya tented his fingers under his chin, eyes narrowed in thought. "If he's a cat, can I pet him?"

"Only if you ask first," Marina said.

Semya slid off the stool, fingers still tented under his chin. Without looking at Anya, he said, "Goodbye, future wife," and hurried out of the kitchen.

Anya watched Semya go, and then she turned back to Marina. "Can all of them see the *domovoi*?"

Marina shook her head. "No. Just that one."

Anya made a mental note to never invite Semya to her house. "You said Ivan—er, Vosya gets up early. Where is he?"

"Probably by the river," Marina said, motioning vaguely in the direction of the water. "Would you mind finding him? It's breakfast time."

Anya nodded and took her egg out the back door into Widow Medvedeva's vegetable garden. It was a very nice, well-tended garden, but the widow clearly didn't have plant magic. Anya dropped the eggshell into the garden as she passed.

She rounded a stand of trees, looking for Ivan by the river while she took bites out of the egg. She stopped near the shore and watched the river for a few minutes. She thought of the red thing—the red thing that hadn't actually been red and was clearly just a jumping fish—and then she heard a peculiar, rhythmic thumping. She stuck the rest of the egg in her mouth and crept quietly toward the sound, soon coming to a flat spot on the riverbank.

Ivan leaped into the air, tapping his heels together off to the side, and landed on his feet as lightly as fall leaves. He leaped again instantly, bringing both legs up to either side in a split, touching his fingers to his toes before landing again. Another jump, this one with a spin attached, but it was clear he was getting tired. He didn't go quite as high as he had before, and he spun around only halfway before thumping to the ground.

He knelt, breathing hard, and Anya decided now was as good a time as any to make her presence known. She said, "Ivan!"

He looked up, eyes wide, and then stood quickly. His hands went behind his back first, and then he tugged at his earlobe. "Uh . . . hey."

"What were you doing?"

Ivan scratched the back of his head, eyes darting from place to place on the ground. "Um, dancing. I learned it when we lived in Kiev." He cleared his throat. "It's harder than it looks."

It had looked hard. Anya said, "You lived in Kiev?"

"When I was little. Then we moved to Ingria, and now we live here."

The farthest from Zmeyreka Anya had ever gone was Mologa, which was only a few hours away. There was a harvest festival there every year at the end of the summer, and Mama sold a lot of onions.

"Why does your family move so much?" Anya asked.

Ivan shrugged. "We go where the tsar says we need to go. Or Papa hears about a demon that needs exorcising."

Whenever Anya complained about something, Babulya would inevitably swoop in with the story of her journey to Zmeyreka so many years ago. The way she told it, moving from one village to another was horrible, humiliating, and something she would never do again. And now Ivan said his family moved all the time. Fools were strange.

"Your mama said she's from the east," Anya said.

Ivan shrugged. "Yeah, but we've never been there. She doesn't want to go back."

That seemed strange to Anya, but maybe it was just much too far. As Anya understood it, someone could spend several lifetimes wandering the lands to the east.

"Your mama wanted me to tell you it's time for breakfast," Anya said.

Ivan's eyes widened. "Are my brothers up yet?"

"No, except—"

Ivan ran toward the house, and Anya followed. He was practically frantic, jumping over obstacles and huffing hard by the time he reached the back door. He flung it open and charged inside.

Anya, gasping for breath, stumbled into the kitchen after Ivan. It was still empty for the most part, except for Marina and Yedsha sitting at the table beside each other.

Ivan didn't say anything to them as he dove for the food, cramming meat patties, boiled eggs, and fried, flat cakes into his mouth.

"Good morning, Vosya," Marina trilled.

"Mmurmg mmah," Ivan mumbled through his full mouth.

Yedsha stood up from the table. "Anya! Are you ready to hunt the dragon?"

◆ ✹ ◆

Anya, Yedsha, and Ivan took the road north through the village. Yedsha wanted to explore the ravines and cliffs Anya had mentioned to Ivan the night before, and Anya was happy to oblige. It was Shabbat, so she declined the rubles Yedsha offered her.

As they crossed the bridge out of the village, Anya tensed up. Would Yedsha want to see the house he was supposedly buying? Would Ivan tell him the house was Anya's, and if he did, would Yedsha figure out what Anya needed those rubles for?

"Yedsha," Anya said, skipping to the fool's right side. He looked down at her and away from her home's little turnoff. "I'd never heard of fool magic until I met Ivan. And then what you did to Sigurd was amazing. How does your magic work?"

"Oh, it's very simple!" Yedsha said. "Do you know how regular magic works?"

Anya had an idea, but she shook her head. "No one uses magic here, so no."

"Well," Yedsha said, "everything in the world is connected in some way to a thread of magic. It could be earth magic for stones or dirt, or water magic for water or ice, or even metal magic or fire magic." He whispered, "Or light magic. Dark magic. Those who use emotional magic can calm a foe, or incite a gentle creature to rage. Magical animals can interact with magic threads with special append-ages on their bodies." Yedsha motioned at the sky. "A dragon doesn't fly in the same way a bird does, for example. Their wings have magic hooks all over them, and they naturally snag threads of air magic and use those to propel themselves through the air."

Anya had meant to get him talking as a distrac-tion, but now she listened, completely enthralled.

"The great *bogatyri* are humans who are imbued with magic power," Yedsha said. "With strength or wisdom. And then me." He smiled and bowed his head. "Simple fool magic. All it requires is its wielder not attempt to use it."

Anya furrowed her brow. "You can use fool magic only by *not* using it?"

Yedsha nodded. "Correct!"

They had reached the fork in the road: the western fork led to Ingria, and the other road to the frozen expanses of the eastern kingdoms. Anya steered them west.

"But how do you do it, then?" Anya asked. "You used it to fight Sigurd. I saw you!"

"I didn't try, though," Yedsha said. "As I walked to him, the magic told me to pick up those objects. It told me to hold on to the fish. It told me to take the horseshoe. So I did. I didn't know what was going to happen, but I had trust in the magic. Fools must obey the magic of fate, and never try to control it."

"Fate magic?" Anya shivered. Hadn't Babulya said *chaos*?

"All magic is connected to the magic of fate," Yedsha said. "Manipulation of the right magic in the right way could alter the trajectory of fate magic ever so slightly, and cause far-reaching changes. Only fools can interact with fate magic directly, and only by accident." He grinned at Anya. "Fate is proud. It doesn't like being told what to do."

Anya didn't quite know how to respond. The revelation of the true nature of fool magic chilled her. The fools themselves seemed uncommonly lucky, but how far did that luck extend? If they found the dragon up in the cliffs and it attacked, would fool magic protect Anya, or only the fools wielding it?

They reached another bridge, and Anya stopped them. She pointed off to the right side of the road, northward to the gray cliffs, and said, "This is the place I told Ivan about."

Yedsha rubbed his chin as he looked toward the cliffs, barely visible over the trees. "Is there a road?"

"Of a sort," Anya said, pointing again. A narrow but well-worn path branched from the main road, following the river's shore into the forest. Anya had never taken the trail farther than a few yards off the road, so she hoped it was passable farther north.

"Well, off we go!" Yedsha declared, and he set off into the trees.

CHAPTER TWELVE

YEDSHA LED THE WAY, followed by Anya, and Ivan brought up the rear. Once they were deep beneath the canopy, the temperature dropped several degrees. After half an hour of stepping carefully along the sometimes-mushy, sometimes-crumbly path, they found that it thinned and disappeared as sharp rocks replaced the dirt. The trees thinned as well, getting smaller and more sparse; only the most dedicated among them could get a roothold in the rocky soil between the shaded cliffs.

Ahead of them, the scarce path crossed a wooden bridge over the water, and a little house sat on the other side. Yedsha halted. Anya halted. Ivan ran into the back of Anya and nearly made them both fall into the water.

"Ivan!" Anya hissed.

"Sorry!" Ivan said.

Yedsha turned back to Anya. "Whose house is that?"

"I don't know," Anya said. "I don't ever come up here." She shouldn't have been up there even now. The woods weren't safe, especially so far from the village.

"Well." Yedsha's voice was quiet. "Let's see who lives here."

He advanced up the path. Anya stood still for a few breaths and then followed. Ivan shuffled behind her.

The bridge was narrow but sturdy over the river. On the other side, a tall, thin stone stood in front of the water. Anya paused to look at it. It was as tall as her chest, thinner at the top and thicker at the bottom, carved with a border of knots and loops. A name was etched in the center: *Yelena*. A carved dragon beneath the name seemed to hold it up, supporting it on the stone. The top was worn smooth, the way some stones get after years of foot travel over them.

Anya touched the smooth top with two soft fingers. She hadn't ever seen a stone like it before, with the intricate carvings, but she immediately knew what kind of marker it was.

Yedsha was closer to the house, peering here and there, and Ivan came up behind Anya. "What is it?" Ivan asked.

"A grave," Anya said. "Or maybe a memorial. I don't think you can dig a grave in this earth."

He leaned around her. "'Yelena.' Who is Yelena?"

"I don't know," Anya said. She didn't know of anyone in the village named Yelena. She drew her fingers along the carved dragon, unable to believe the presence of a dragon on the stone was a coincidence.

Yedsha rapped on the front door. The three of them waited and listened for footsteps from within the house. Nothing. Yedsha tried the handle, and the door swung in.

Yedsha poked his head in, then stepped forward slowly. Anya and Ivan watched from their spot by the stone, and then Anya whispered, "Should we follow him?"

Ivan trembled. "We could."

Anya moved first. She stopped at the open door and peered in as Yedsha had done. After a few moments, her eyes adjusted to the dimness. Yedsha stood in the center of the room, surrounded by sturdy wooden furniture, thick animal-hide rugs, and more weapons than Anya could believe existed. Swords, daggers, spears, sickles, axes, and some weapons Anya couldn't even name were mounted on the walls, covering every inch of space. A huge, round wooden shield dominated the chimney over the fireplace. Painted across the front of the chipped, marred shield was an intricate red dragon.

"Another dragon," Anya murmured.

Yedsha stood near a sword, inspecting the handle so closely that his nose nearly touched it. He looked back at Ivan and Anya. "We should go."

She followed Ivan out of the house, and Yedsha

shut the door behind him. On the way back down the path toward the road, he said, "I don't want either of you coming up here again."

Anya nodded, and Ivan said, "Yes, sir."

Babulya was taking her tiny steps across the road with a company of chickens when Yedsha, Ivan, and Anya walked back past the farm. It was hard to avoid going past, since it was off the only road going north of the village, but it was set back too far from the road for the fools to see. But Babulya was heading right for the path down to their house, and Anya didn't want the fools to wonder where the old lady was going. She called out, "Babulya!"

Babulya stopped short of the path. So did all the chickens. Babulya waved in Anya's direction as they approached.

"Annushka!" Babulya cocked her head, listening. "Who are your friends?"

Anya hesitated, fear bubbling up inside her. Would Yedsha realize what house they were near? Would Babulya realize Anya was helping fools hunt a dragon? Would the *domovoi* sense Ivan and destroy more food?

She realized she'd been quiet for too long, so she pointed to the boy beside her.

"This is Ivan, Babulya," Anya said. "And his papa, Ivan Yedsha."

Yedsha bowed low. "It's very nice to meet you, Gospozha."

Ivan mimicked his father. "Very good to see you again."

Babulya nodded, her face puckering. "Ah. Well. Likewise. Come with me, little Anya. You have chores."

Anya offered Ivan a small wave as she went with Babulya. Ivan and Yedsha continued south to the village.

Babulya snaked her arm through Anya's and said, "Walk me home, Annushka."

Anya did, leading Babulya down the sloping drive. As soon as Ivan and Yedsha were gone around the trees, Anya expected Babulya to scold her about doing the exact thing she had warned Anya away from that morning. But instead of asking about the fools, Babulya said, "That boy made the *rusalki* restless."

Anya held in a frustrated groan. She had a feeling any bad fortune would be blamed on Ivan from now on. "How?"

Babulya didn't answer her. "Go hang an offering for them."

"I did that a few days ago."

Babulya shrugged. "They're restless. Hang another piece. It can't hurt."

Anya sighed. "Yes, Babulya."

Inside, Anya rummaged through the cupboard with the linen in it. She dug around for a small piece, found one, and then trudged out the door, south toward the river.

A large willow tree hung over the water, dipping the tips of its branches in the current. Too many of the willow's branches didn't touch the water anymore.

Anya paused a decent distance from the tree,

watchful for the water spirits. She didn't see any, and she'd just started toward the tree when a loud splash from the river nearly made her jump out of her skin. She backed away from the water, out of reach of anything lurking there. Her mind went immediately to a *vodyanoi*, its scaly face and froggy eyes and impossibly wide, hungry mouth. A *rusalka* might not do anything to her, but a *vodyanoi*? She'd be drowned before she realized it.

She searched the river's surface for a full minute, but no splash came again. When nothing sinister leaped out at her, she hurried to the willow and spotted a branch she could tie her linen to.

Movement across the water drew Anya's attention. A *rusalka* sat in the shallows near the other shore, combing her fingers through her copper hair. She watched Anya with empty sockets, somehow still beautiful even without eyes. The spirit smiled, and a chill ran up Anya's spine. Had that *rusalka* made the splash? Anya looped the linen around the branch and went to tie the knot.

The water in front of the *rusalka* rippled, and a second redhead emerged. The *rusalki* exchanged glances, then both turned their empty eyes to Anya.

Anya's fingers trembled as she struggled to tie the knot. The linen's ends kept slipping out, refusing to be tied. She was trying to do it with half of her attention turned to the *rusalki* on the other bank, and that wasn't working.

The *rusalka* in the shallows joined the one in the deeper water, and both water spirits began to swim toward Anya.

With ragged breaths and shaking hands, Anya watched the *rusalki* approach.

Then both of them disappeared beneath the river's surface.

Now she really couldn't take her eyes off the water.

"Tie it, Anya," she muttered to herself. "Just tie it. Tie it! Go!"

One more loop was attempted, and this time the linen slipped from her fingers and fluttered to the ground beside the bank.

Anya spat out an obscenity that would have gotten her a scolding if Mama had heard it. She darted
forward to grab the linen from the bank, and she
saw the pale arm of a *rusalka* half a second before it
emerged from the water.

Anya couldn't stop her forward momentum; her
brain had been numbed too much by fear to make
an intelligent decision anyway. Her hand landed on
the linen as the *rusalka*'s hand did the same, and
the water spirit's cold fingers touched Anya's as they
both grasped the cloth.

Anya inhaled sharply, meaning to yelp or scream
or something, but her voice froze in her throat as she
looked into the *rusalka*'s face. Those empty sockets
were less lovely up close, dripping river water down
her cheeks like never-ending tears. Her stringy, wet
hair hung down her shoulders and arms, spreading
in the water like ruddy tentacles. Her white smock
clung to her like a partly shed husk. The feel of her
skin was like a dead fish beneath Anya's fingers . . .
Anya's own skin crawled.

A second cold, wet hand touched Anya's other

arm, and this time she nearly choked on her own tongue, still unable to make any appreciable sound. The other *rusalka* had arrived and was reaching for Anya, no doubt attempting to drag her into the river to her watery death. People said *rusalki* drowned only men, but Anya wasn't willing to take the villagers' word for it. She lurched away from the water spirits.

Lurching got her only so far. They were waiflike but stronger than they looked. The second *rusalka*'s hand was like clammy steel on her arm.

Anya let go of the linen. "Don't," she muttered, breath hitching with every inhalation. "Please."

The *rusalka* with the linen held it up, examining it, and then she rubbed it on her face, snuggling it like a baby with a blankie. The *rusalka* holding Anya stroked Anya's hair; Anya was torn between trying to be pleasant so she didn't offend the spirits and screaming until she lost her voice.

Linen in hand, the *rusalka* smiled at Anya, fluttering her long eyelashes as she did. Without eyes to offer contrast, the eyelashes looked like insects moving against the hollow sockets.

Another splash from the river. Anya barely heard it over the rush of blood in her ears, but the *rusalki* both turned toward it. They let go of Anya so suddenly that she fell backwards onto the riverbed, and in a matter of seconds, the *rusalki* were both gone into the inky river.

As they swam away, something else moved just beneath the water's surface. It was bigger than any fish Anya had ever seen come out of the Sogozha. Whatever it was rippled just under the water, moving like a gigantic snake rather than a fish.

She watched it, frozen with fear, and then it breached the surface.

This snake—or fish, or whatever monstrosity it was—was red, and it had a row of spines along its back.

She ran. The long grass of the pasture whipped her legs as she fled from the water. When she reached her house, she crashed past Babulya and Mama, and slammed the door to the sleeping room shut.

She dove under the blankets on her bed, peeking only her face out of them, and she could hear Babulya tutting in the kitchen: "Slamming doors like they'll last forever. Children these days."

It took Anya a minute to notice the *domovoi* on the bed beside her, likewise under the blankets and poking only his bearded face out. He looked up at her, reached out a little hairy hand, and patted Anya's softly.

There, there, the pat seemed to say. *I've seen the dragon too.*

CHAPTER THIRTEEN

ANYA COULDN'T STAY HIDING under her blankets all day. Eventually, Babulya opened the sleeping room door and said, "Come study, Annushka."

Babulya shuffled to one of the dining room chairs by the stove. Anya made sure the table was clean, and then she crossed to their bookshelf. Their Torah scroll occupied its own shelf, wrapped in the nicest cloth Babulya had been able to purchase in Zmeyreka. It wasn't as nice as the original cover had been, Babulya said, but the original cover had been singed before she pulled it from the burning synagogue, and stained as she escaped Sarkel and fled across Kievan Rus', and she couldn't leave the Torah in a dirty cover.

Anya slid the Torah off the high shelf and carried it to the table. She removed the cover, spread it on the tabletop in front of Babulya, and set the scroll on top of the smoothed cloth. She went back to the bookshelf to retrieve the wooden pointer Papa had carved after the one Babulya had brought from Sarkel broke.

Babulya ran her wrinkled fingers over the scroll's handles as Anya sat back down at the table. She bent forward to kiss the scroll, then pointed for Anya to do the same.

"When I was your age, I had to read out loud to the women of my synagogue," Babulya said. "But you're lucky. You just have to read to your mama and me. Do you know what you want to read for your bat mitzvah yet?"

Anya didn't. She knew it had to be good. Poignant. "No."

Babulya sighed. "You'd better figure it out! Where did we leave off?"

Anya rolled the Torah open, using the end of the pointer to find her spot. "Moshe on the mountain."

"Ah yes," Babulya said. "This part is very important. These are the Commandments. You must know them by heart."

Anya nodded and began reading, tracing along the words with the pointer so her fingers wouldn't smudge the aging ink. She stumbled over some of the Hebrew; in places the text was so old, the letters were worn away, and in others she couldn't remember where the vowels were supposed to go. It was tough enough to read it just to Babulya, and she couldn't imagine reading it aloud to a larger group of people.

"You shall not . . ." She squinted at the degraded word on the paper. *"Tir . . . Ra . . . Rets—"*

"Tirtzach," Babulya said. "Kill."

"You shall not kill," Anya said.

Babulya shook her head emphatically. "That's an

unforgivable sin, Annushka. Murder, idolatry, and adultery. Never. Never, ever."

"But what if you have to kill someone?" Anya asked.

Babulya snorted. "Why would you have to?"

Anya shrugged. "What if they were going to kill you first?"

"Does it say in there, 'You shall not kill, unless the other person was going to kill you first'?"

Anya turned her eyes back to the parchment. She hadn't been through the Torah as much as Babulya had. Twice by now, but she didn't know every single word of every single verse. "I don't know."

"Well, I know," Babulya said. "And it doesn't." She lifted a wrinkled finger. "In the Talmud, it says, 'Whoever destroys a single life has destroyed the entire world.' Do you want to destroy the entire world?"

"No." Anya held in a groan. Now she was bringing the Talmud into it. Something else she needed to read more of.

"There you have it, then," Babulya said.

Anya mulled over what Babulya had said, not sure if she completely bought into it. It didn't seem right that it was forbidden for her to protect herself. She was pretty sure she remembered some passage somewhere saying it was okay to kill someone for specific reasons. She didn't argue with Babulya because she didn't remember the passage well enough, and coming at her grandmother half-informed was a terrible mistake. Babulya was knowledgeable because she was so old, but Papa had gone through the Torah and both their copies of the Talmud back and forth probably a hundred times in the twenty years since he converted. He and Babulya had heated discussions about every individual letter, it seemed. Anya wished he were there so they could discuss killing, but he wasn't. Maybe that could be what she read for her bat mitzvah: all the reasons killing was acceptable.

That seemed like a strange thing to focus on as she entered womanhood, though.

With a sigh, she went back to reading as before, and made it to the end of the Commandments before Babulya stopped her.

"That was very good," Babulya said. "You're getting better."

"Thanks, Babulya."

"Yes," Mama's sad voice said from the kitchen. "Very good, Anya."

Her mother's voice startled Anya. She hadn't realized Mama had come inside.

"It's almost time for Havdalah," Babulya said. "Go watch for the stars."

Anya looked out the window at the dimming day, wondering once again how Babulya knew some of the things she knew — like that it was almost sunset, even though she was blind. Anya put the Torah back on its high shelf and then shuffled outside, lingering near the house as she watched the eastern sky for the first three stars that would mark the end of Shabbat and the start of the new week.

Three stars twinkled in the purpling sky over the treetops. Back inside, Dyedka waited impatiently for dinner as Mama set out the spice box, a cup of wine, and the braided candle Papa had made. Havdalah was short: four simple blessings, a sip of wine, smelling the spices, and extinguishing the candle. The candle flame hissed out in the leftover wine, and Mama said, *"Shavua tov."*

Have a good week. Anya planned to.

Anya hunched over her dress that Zvezda had torn the day before, drawing a needle and thread through the cloth to repair the tear. She didn't want to patch it, and she was trying to make her stitches as invisible as possible so no one would be able to tell it had been torn in the first place.

Babulya sat across the table, knitting the lumpiest scarf Anya had ever seen. She suspected it would probably be for her. Mama had gone to bed, and Dyedka carved at the end of his walking stick with a knife, forming a goat's head out of the knobby top.

Anya's stitching wasn't going like she'd planned. She was distracted. She couldn't get the red spiny fish *thing* out of her head. She kept telling herself it was a dragon but then telling herself there was no way it was a dragon, and back and forth. If it was a dragon, she could tell Yedsha about it, and hopefully it wouldn't take him long to figure out how to trap it. Then she'd get the money and she could pay the magistrate and save her home.

She wondered if Yedsha would give her the money immediately, or if he would pay her once he took the monster to Kiev. How far away was Kiev? Days? Weeks?

How far away from Kiev was Rûm? Could Yedsha drop off the dragon and then pick up Papa? The old geography book had maps in it. She set her dress down and retrieved the book from the shelf, flipping pages until she found a map. Kiev was up at the top, and down below, on the southern shores of the Black Sea, was Rûm.

On the opposing page, a portrait of the old sultan of Rûm gazed out at her. The caption beneath said, "Sultan Osman the Merciful." He was young, smiling slightly, and looked pretty merciful to Anya. Too bad he wasn't the sultan anymore. The new one was Sultan Osman's son, Suleiman the Unsmiling. There was no portrait of him, but Anya imagined his title was "the Unsmiling" for a reason.

Dyedka leaned over toward her. "Maybe your papa will kill the sultan, and he can come back home."

"Maybe."

"What are you looking in there for?" Dyedka asked.

"I want to know how far away Kiev is," Anya said.

Dyedka snorted. "Are you planning a trip?"

"No," Anya said. "Just curious."

"It's a long way," Dyedka said. "Depends on how you get there. On foot? I don't recommend it. On horseback or in a carriage, twelve, thirteen days, if you travel all day."

Anya drummed her fingers on the book as Dyedka went back to carving his stick. That didn't seem so far. Hauling a dragon would probably slow them down by a day or two, but still. Two weeks and this would all be over.

Her mind went again to the spiny red thing in

the river. She decided that if she slept in the barn, she ran the risk of being eaten by a dragon.

But then, so did the goats and chickens. They didn't have a choice but to sleep in the barn. She should make sure the barn was closed up tight against any dragon invasion. Plus, she could protect them if anything did come in.

Anya kissed Babulya on the cheek before heading for the door.

"Sleeping in the barn tonight?" Babulya asked.

"Yes," Anya said.

"Take something for the *domovoi*," Babulya said. "He's still upset."

Anya said good night to Dyedka before grabbing half of the remaining bread from the counter and a lantern from the floor. She lit the lantern before she let herself out of the house and into the night.

As soon as she crossed the garden, Anya could hear the chickens raising a huge ruckus inside the barn. The goats were bellyaching as well, bleating loud enough to compete with the chickens.

Anya's stomach knotted as she hurried to the

barn. It was most likely the chickens and the goats getting into a turf war again.

Or so she hoped.

She threw open the barn door and stepped inside, lifting the lantern up to get a better look at the situation.

Anya's hands went numb from shock. She dropped the loaf of bread at her feet and barely managed to keep a hold on the lantern.

Most of the chickens were up in the rafters of the barn, screeching at the scene on the floor below. The goats stood around the walls, bleating as they watched the *domovoi* in the shape of a cat run around on the floor, hissing and spitting, dodging the claws and teeth of the red dragon that lunged at him.

CHAPTER FOURTEEN

THE DRAGON WAS at least twice as long as Anya was tall, and a deep red that reflected the lantern's light like a vest of rubies. It had two legs near the front of its long, snakelike body, and it used them to propel itself around the barn in pursuit of the feline house spirit. Its long tail whipped behind it as it ran; a row of spines stretched from its head to the tip of its tail, colored gold and reddish gold. As it snapped at the *domovoi*, its teeth flashed in the lantern light.

It had only one head, and it didn't seem to be interested in the goats at all.

Anya stood by the door, incredulous, convinced she must be having a hallucination of some kind, when the *domovoi* spotted her.

He meowed loudly and ran to Anya, leaping to her shoulders and digging his claws into her. He yowled and spat at the dragon.

The dragon coiled, motionless. Its eyes met Anya's, slit pupils slicing a black scar through each bright blue eye. Its mouth gaped open, teeth shining, tongue lolling. Two straight horns jutted from above its eyes, pointing backward. Anya could envision herself impaled on those horns.

She wouldn't die like that in her own barn with the chickens watching. Anya snatched a pitchfork from its place on the wall, pointing the pronged end at the dragon. She hoped it couldn't see her shaking.

Atop her shoulders, the *domovoi* quaked and hissed. She winced as his claws dug deeper, stabbing through her dress and poking holes in her skin.

The dragon watched the pitchfork, eyeing it with what Anya could swear was something close to scrutiny. The face-off lasted for seconds that stretched into eternity, and then, with the scrabbling of claws, the dragon fled to the darkness at the rear of the barn. Anya flinched at the sound of wood splintering and then . . . silence.

She remained still, trembling as the chickens and goats recovered from their fright and began to gobble up the bread on the ground. The *domovoi* growled deep in his throat, claws still in Anya's shoulders.

She shrugged until the *domovoi* slid off her back. He stayed by her feet, staring at where the dragon had vanished. All the hair on his back stood straight up.

After a few minutes, Anya advanced to the rear of the barn, ready to stab the dragon in the face if it came for her. Her legs trembled as she willed them to hold her weight. The pitchfork's wood felt slick in her sweaty hands, and she hoped she wouldn't drop it at the moment of truth.

There was nothing there. Besides the goats and chickens and growling *domovoi*, the barn was still and empty.

Anya's breath hitched in her chest. She couldn't have imagined the dragon, could she? Maybe she had eaten some bad food. Perhaps dinner had been spoiled or had some sort of toxin in it. Maybe she was going mad.

She looked down. The *domovoi* paced, stiff-legged, back and forth. If she had imagined the dragon, then so had the *domovoi*, and that wasn't likely.

She pressed on, to be sure. In the corner behind Dyedka's goat cart, a large hole had been made in the side of the barn. Something glittered in the lantern light, and when Anya inspected further, she saw a broad red scale stuck to a piece of wood.

CHAPTER FIFTEEN

ANYA DIDN'T SLEEP.

She lay in the hayloft with the chickens gathered around her until morning. Dyedka's goat cart sat in front of the hole in the barn. Anya had pushed it there, then reinforced it with whatever she could move on her own. Every tiny noise made her startle, pitchfork in hand. The dragon didn't come back. She might have chalked it up to an extremely vivid nightmare in the light of day, if it hadn't been for the glittering ruby scale in her pocket and the *domovoi*'s refusal to come out from the cellar.

The barn door opened, and Dyedka hobbled in.

He grunted with every step, heading for his cart, and hollered, "Get up, lazybones!"

Anya peered over the side of the hayloft. "I'm already up, Dyedka."

"Liar." Dyedka chuckled. "You sound half-asleep."

She would have liked to be fully asleep. She expected the dragon wouldn't return during the day, and this knowledge turned off whatever inside her had been keeping her awake. Her eyelids drooped.

"I'm fine," Anya said.

Dyedka laughed from below. "Well, that's what you—what the . . . ?"

He trailed off, and only then did Anya remember the gaping hole behind his cart, and her attempts to barricade it. She was awake then and slid down the ladder as fast as she could. Dyedka stood by the pile of stuff in front of the hole, scratching his head, eyebrows furrowed with bewilderment.

He gestured to the pile. "What happened here?"

Anya shrugged. "I don't know, Dyedka." She searched her exhausted brain for some explanation. "Maybe the *domovoi* did it."

"Why would he . . . ?" Dyedka leaned closer to the pile.

"He was angry," Anya said. "He broke the milk bottles. Maybe this is his way of still being mad."

Dyedka turned to fix her with a raised eyebrow. "Maybe."

Anya hoped the *domovoi* wouldn't appear and blow her story somehow. He didn't, and then one of the goats bleated. They were hungry and ready to go graze. Pulling away, Dyedka mumbled, "Bizarre."

Anya nodded and helped Dyedka dig out the cart. She was careful to keep the hole itself blocked so he wouldn't notice it as she hooked his billy goats into their traces. She waved as he rode away with the goats following, and as soon as he was out of sight, she slammed the barn doors shut.

Anya got dressed without seeing Mama or Babulya and made sure to transfer the dragon scale from her old dress to the new one. She half ran, half walked toward the village, nearly frantic to see Ivan.

She crossed the bridge into the village. The square was mostly empty, except for an enormous gray horse that swished its tail in front of the smithy.

Anya slowed and stared at the horse. It was Sigurd's.

Urgency to see Ivan forgotten, she backtracked to the miller's shop and went behind the row, running to the smithy's back door. She pulled the door open slowly, and as soon as the forge's heat blasted into her face, so did angry, heated words.

Sigurd. She'd never forget the sound of his voice.

He was speaking harshly, presumably to Kin. Anya pulled the door open a little more, enough to put one side of her face through and see the back of the smithy. Piles of metal scrap sat here and there, with three anvils positioned around the forge itself. On the other side were two figures.

Anya watched as the taller figure, Sigurd, spat furiously at the shorter figure. Kin didn't flinch, at least as far as Anya could tell, and when he spoke, it was measured and calm.

It was also in Sigurd's tongue.

Sigurd shoved something long at Kin, and Kin shook his head as he tried to hand it back.

Slam! The noise made Anya jump. She wasn't sure what exactly had caused it, but she knew Sigurd had done something to Kin's forge. Sigurd shoved Kin's chest, said one more thing in a threatening hiss, and then stormed out the front of the smithy.

Kin remained where he was. As Anya watched, his shoulders slumped. He looked down at the long object in his hands and sighed.

Anya was ready to back away from the door when Kin's voice pierced the heat: "Ye don't have to spy from the door, girl. Come in if yer gonna be nosy."

Her heart thudded hard in her chest. She pulled the door open more and slid into the sweltering smithy. Kin set the long object down on top of an anvil and crossed his arms as she approached.

"Well," he said.

"Well," Anya mumbled. They stood in silence for a breath, and then Anya blurted, "So you *are* a Varangian, huh?"

"I am *not* a Varangian." Kin's jaw tightened.

"But how do you—"

"I was stolen by them," Kin said. "All right? When I was as old as ye, maybe a mite older. They came to my village and took me from my family, sailed me over a great sea back to their land, and kept me as a slave until I ran away. There. Now ye know, and now ye can stop being so blasted curious about it."

Anya listened, lips pressed shut and eyes open wide. His revelation made her even more curious. How had he escaped? Why had they kidnapped him? What had brought him to Zmeyreka?

She pointed to her own cheeks, mirroring where his tattoo spread. "Did they do that to you?"

He touched it, frowning. "No. I had that before."

"What did—"

"Girl, yer trying my patience."

"—Sigurd want?" she finished.

He snorted a sigh out of his nose. "He wants me to sharpen his sword."

"That's all?"

"That's all."

"How did he know you speak his tongue?"

"Lucky guess," Kin said.

The way his shoulders caved in just slightly, and the way he looked at the sword, and the way his voice sped up when he said it . . .

Anya knew he was lying.

He knew Sigurd, somehow.

She decided to move on. Instead, she asked, "Are you from Kievan Rus'?"

"No," he said.

"What brought you to Zmeyreka?"

He swallowed hard. "A . . . friend. I needed somewhere to go, and she brought me here."

"She?"

"Listen, little girl—"

"My name is Anya."

"Fine. Anya." He bunched his shoulders. "It doesn't matter. She's gone now." He motioned to the front door. "And you can go too. Try minding yer own business for once."

Anya dragged her feet on the way out, and Kin

pushed the door shut against her backside as she exited. Sigurd and his horse were gone, so Anya hurried through the golden morning light to the boarding house.

CHAPTER SIXTEEN

T HE GREAT HOUSE was still and dark, even though it was already an hour past sunrise. Anya knocked on the front door; when there was no answer, she opened it and peered inside.

There was a pile of Ivans sleeping in front of the fireplace as there had been the other morning, resting on one another at various angles. Anya tiptoed past them and up the stairs. One stair creaked under her foot, and she froze as the Ivans stirred. She watched them with wide eyes, frightened they'd awaken, but then they all settled back into sleep.

Anya hurried as quietly as she could up the stairs.

She wasn't sure which room was Ivan's, so she started easing doors open and peeking in. She found him in the second room, along with two of his brothers, all piled on the bed with feet and heads sticking out at odd places. Ivan's head hung off the foot of the bed, and he drooled in his sleep.

With hushed shuffling, Anya crept close to Ivan and poked his face. "Ivan," she whispered.

He didn't stir, but one of his brothers did. Anya ducked to the floor, not wanting to be seen, and stayed there until the bed stopped creaking.

She stayed low to the floor and poked Ivan again. She didn't whisper that time, just rammed her finger into his cheek. When that accomplished nothing, she grabbed a few strands of his hair and yanked.

"Ow!" Ivan groaned, and Anya put her hand over his mouth as his eyes opened.

"Be quiet," Anya whispered. "Don't wake them up."

From under her hand, Ivan said, "Anya? What are you doing here?"

"I saw it."

He yawned under her hand. "Saw what?"

"The dragon."

Ivan's sleepy eyes widened. He slid off the bed, thumping unceremoniously to the floor with a tremendous *whump!*

"Ivan!" Anya hissed between her teeth. "They're going to hear you!"

He stood and brushed his pajamas off. "You saw the dragon?" He practically shouted it.

"You're going to wake everyone up!" Anya whispered.

He looked at his closest brother. "No, I won't. Watch." He turned back to the bed, and before Anya could stop him, he tugged on the foot closest to him. "Dvoyka. Dvoyka! Wake up!"

The foot Ivan tugged on kicked out at him and then withdrew. A sleepy grumble issued from near the head of the bed: "Go away, Vosya."

Ivan turned to Anya, eyebrows raised, and shrugged. "See?"

Anya was partly impressed with his brothers' dedication to staying in bed. She stepped out of the room to give Ivan a chance to get dressed, and then they ran down the stairs. She was still wary of waking his brothers, but the rest of them were just as asleep as the ones upstairs were.

Outside, Ivan tugged on her sleeve as they walked toward the road. "So you saw the dragon?"

Anya nodded. She reached into her pocket and, after a furtive glance around, pulled the scale out for Ivan to see.

Ivan's mouth dropped open. He reached for the scale, then pulled his hand back. "Can I touch it?"

"Sure." Anya proffered it to him, and he took it with trembling fingers.

The scale flashed in the sunlight, catching the sunshine and staining it crimson. It reflected red bursts onto the packed road. Ivan marveled over it and whispered, "It's beautiful."

"Don't let anyone see it," Anya said, searching their surroundings for one of Ivan's brothers. Ivan cupped the scale in his hands, also checking for intruders. When he determined no one was around, he peeked at the scale again.

"So the dragon is really here," Ivan said.

Anya nodded. "It was in my barn, chasing the chickens! And when it ran away, it went straight through the wall." She was a valuable member of this dragon-hunting team now. She could probably ask for more rubles. "I have to patch the hole in the barn."

"I'll help," Ivan said. "Wait until my papa finds out."

"Where is he, anyway?"

Ivan shrugged. "Probably checking for the best places for a dragon to hide."

The front door of the house opened, and Anya snatched the scale from Ivan. She returned it to the safety of her pocket just as Marina came out, a mixing bowl full of some kind of batter under one arm.

"Vosya!" Marina called. "Oh, hello, Anya! Breakfast is almost ready, if you're hungry."

Anya was, but she didn't want to waste time eating. She wanted to go patch the hole in her barn and do some chores quickly so that by the time Ivan's papa came back, she'd be free for the day.

"Thank you, Gospozha," Anya said. "But I have chores to do."

"Oh dear." Marina's lovely face creased with disappointment, but it brightened a moment later. "Well, get something to go, then! And have Vosya help you with your chores."

Ivan grimaced. Anya said, "Thank you!"

At Anya's barn, Ivan measured the hole with his hands. He said "Hmm" a lot. Anya sat on the pile of hay behind him and watched his assessment of the hole.

Finally, he turned back and said, "How big was this dragon?"

Anya stood. She took two long strides, turned back, judged the distance, and took half a step forward. "This long."

"How big around?"

She made a loop with her arms, fingertips barely touching. "Not terribly huge. Kind of like a giant snake, but with legs."

"How many legs?"

"Two," Anya said. "At the very front."

"No wings?"

Anya shook her head.

Ivan turned back to the hole. "Hmm."

"What does that mean?" Anya asked.

"It's a *lindwurm*," Ivan said.

Anya blinked. "A what?"

"A *lindwurm*," Ivan repeated. "They look like giant snakes with two legs."

"Do they have horns?"

Ivan shrugged. "I don't know. I guess they could."

Anya motioned toward the door. "Come on. I'll show you the spot on the river where I saw the dragon."

They started through the field of tall grass. The sun was bright in the sky, and little birds clung to tall grass stems and chirped at Anya and Ivan's passing. The willow tree's branches shifted in the soft breeze coming off the river.

Someone stood beneath the tree: a huge man wearing a winged helmet.

Anya grabbed Ivan's arm and pulled him to a stop

as Sigurd turned. His icy eyes seemed to glow from the willow's shadow. He pointed a giant fist at Anya, and his voice rolled like thunder across the field:

"You. Come here. Now."

The Russian out of his mouth was thick with an accent, but it was still intelligible. He hadn't spoken any Russian when he'd tried to kill Father Drozdov and Anya in the square the other day.

Anya took a step back. There was no way she was going to approach him. Ivan retreated with her, hand trembling as he gripped her forearm.

A bird hanging on a grass stem released a happy trill, and Sigurd whipped around completely, bear cloak flapping behind him, as he strode toward them.

"Run!" Anya yelled, and she took off across the field. Ivan was a step behind her, and then abreast, and then ahead, long legs pushing him faster.

The dense crashes of Sigurd's enormous boots in the field grew closer behind her, getting louder, and she pumped her arms and legs faster.

Ivan rounded the corner of the barn, gone from view.

The kerchief on her head was gone. Sigurd had grabbed it. She put everything she had into one last burst of speed. If she could escape around the side of the barn, if she could hide somewhere, then maybe Sigurd would go—

Anya's dress tightened as she reached the barn. She slowed, stopped, and skidded backwards.

Sigurd had caught her.

CHAPTER SEVENTEEN

NYA COULDN'T EVEN SCREAM. She just made a small choking sound as Sigurd yanked her to him. She tried to grasp at the barn wall, but her fingers only grazed against it. Then she was spun around roughly, and her shoulders were enveloped in enormous, hard fists, and Sigurd was squatting before her, glaring.

"Tell me where it went," he rumbled. "Where did it go?"

The dragon. Somehow he knew it had been there.

"I—I—I don't kn-now," Anya stammered. She

hoped Ivan stayed away. Maybe he'd get Yedsha. The fool had gotten rid of Sigurd last time.

"Don't lie to me!" Sigurd bellowed, and he slammed his fist against the side of the barn. The wood splintered. "Tell me!"

Anya shook, unable to stop herself. She wondered if Sigurd recognized her as the same child who had thrown the horseshoe at his face. She hoped not.

Sigurd's frown grew even deeper, if that was possible. "Maybe a swim in the river will refresh your memory." He stood, grabbing her by the back of her dress as he did.

"I don't know!" Anya screamed. "Let go of me!"

Sigurd turned and dragged her away from the barn. He crashed through the tall grass. Anya dangled from his fist. Her dress tightened around her neck. Her heels gouged ditches in the soil as she struggled to stand, to push up, to run away.

She reached up and grabbed his wrist with her hands. Metal bracers covered his skin, leaving no vulnerable spots. She moved her fingers up and down, searching for the end of the bracers, and finally found where they stopped and left his fingers exposed.

Anya grabbed one of his fingers with both of her hands and tried yanking it back. It didn't move. His grip was stone.

Sigurd dragged her under the shade of the willow tree and said, "Hope the dragon's hungry."

She yelped as he grabbed her under one arm, then moved his other hand to her knee. Sigurd picked her up and, with a grunt, threw her into the river.

Anya put her hands out and squeezed her eyes shut, holding her breath in preparation. She knew how to swim, and she was a strong enough swimmer to make it to the other side of the river. The Sogozha had undercurrents in places, though. The village wasn't unaccustomed to deaths by drowning.

Arms stretched out before her, eyes shut, breath held, Anya was wholly unprepared for what she hit when she landed.

She slammed hard into dry sandy dirt, coming down on arms that hadn't been braced hard enough for connection with solid earth. Her face hit the dirt; she was lucky her eyes were shut.

Anya shoved up, gasping in surprise. Had he thrown her all the way across the river?

When she opened her eyes, she saw that no, he had not. She stared at a wall of water that shimmered and lapped at the air before her. Above her, the water wall extended to twice her height. She spun and saw a path back to shore, lined on both sides with water, like a canyon lined with rock.

Movement to her left drew her eye. A large fish swam by on the other side of the water wall. It watched her with one eye, then flipped its tail to dart away. The water from the fish's tail flip splashed on her and startled her out of her daze.

This was magic, and she needed to get out of the river before the magic ran out.

Sigurd stood at the entrance of the water ravine, his back to her. Beyond him stood another giant man who rivaled Sigurd in sheer mass. His face was obscured almost entirely by a huge beard and mustache, and a domed helmet with a point on top came down to his eyebrows. His armor looked like hundreds of small metal rectangles attached to somehow make them flexible; every time he moved, his armor flowed and clicked.

He had a sheathed sword on his belt that caught the sunlight and shone. His hands were in the air, artfully manipulating strings. Watching him really was like watching a *gusli* player. He made motions like tying strings into bundles, then tacked them to the firmament above him in the same way garlands were hung at the festivals in Mologa.

He brought his gauntleted hands down, and Anya prepared herself for the walls of water to crash down on her. But they stayed up, just as solid as when he had held the strings himself. He put his hand on his sword's pommel but didn't draw it.

Sigurd had no sword to draw, but he did have a pair of hand axes on either side of his belt. He pulled them off and balanced one in each hand. "This is none of your business," Sigurd said to the man.

"I disagree." The man took a step forward. "I am Dobrynya Nikitich, a *bogatyr* of the empire, and

I have sworn to protect the citizens of this land. Now . . . you will leave this village."

Anya's eyes widened. *Dobrynya Nikitich?* Hadn't Ivan told her Dobrynya was his favorite *bogatyr* because the hero defeated foes with his intelligence? Ivan hadn't mentioned Dobrynya having water magic.

A chuckle dripped out of Sigurd's snarly mouth. "Are you going to fight me?"

Dobrynya advanced another step. "I hope I don't have to." He looked past Sigurd, and his eyes met Anya's. "Little girl, are you hurt?"

She shook her head and said nothing, afraid a loud sound would rupture the magic.

"Your friend is out on the road," Dobrynya said. "Come out and join him when you can." His voice was like thunder, but the warm rolling of a welcomed summer storm. Sigurd's was the rumble of a winter squall.

Dobrynya turned his attention back to Sigurd. "We were discussing your evacuation from this village."

"Never," Sigurd said. "Not without the dragon."

"Tsar Kazimir has an outstanding bounty for any dragon brought to him alive," Dobrynya said. "If you'd like the entire reward, we could—"

"Ha!" Sigurd spat out a laugh like it tasted foul. "I don't want your tsar's reward, and I leave no dragon alive."

Dobrynya frowned. "I cannot allow you to take this dragon. It is my sacred duty."

"I don't care." Sigurd tilted his head to the side, and his neck popped. "Fight me, and I'll show you what dragon blood can do."

Sigurd spun and descended into the magical dry spot in the river, coming at Anya. He put each of his axes up and dragged them along the water walls, cutting long gouges that poured water in.

Anya backed up until she had nowhere to go. She judged the space on either side of Sigurd, ready to time a run at escape, when a column of water blasted sideways from the wall and hammered Sigurd in the face.

Sigurd slammed to the side, and Anya took her

opportunity. She ran, feet slipping on the now-wet river bottom. Sigurd swung his axe at the water column, cleaving a piece off, and he grabbed at Anya as she scrambled by.

His fingers grazed her muddy leg, but she slipped away.

She waded as fast as she could out of the river. Dobrynya walked toward the shore, sword in one hand and the other pulling threads.

Before Anya could clear Dobrynya, one of Sigurd's axes whooshed past her, somersaulting toward the *bogatyr*. Dobrynya artfully yanked a magic thread with only his thumb, and a ball of water intercepted the axe, knocking it off its path. It went wide, sinking into the trunk of the willow tree with a *thump* and a *splash*.

Sigurd tore out of the river as Dobrynya pulled his handful of water threads and the canyon collapsed. The water crashed as it came together, and a moment later, Sigurd's remaining axe crashed against Dobrynya's sword.

Anya hid behind the willow tree and watched

the two giants hack and swing at each other. She was mesmerized but terrified. What if Sigurd won?

Dobrynya fought with practiced movements and the ease of a man who spent years learning his art. Sigurd's attacks were wilder, though still practiced. Dobrynya fought like a man. Sigurd fought like a beast.

I'll show you what dragon blood can do.

Anya shuddered. He didn't actually mean he drank dragon's blood, did he?

Sigurd turned and ran at the tree. Anya ducked behind it, terrified he was coming for her again.

Water tore out of the river in balls, splashing as they slammed into Sigurd on the other side of the tree. Some of the water sprinkled Anya's arms.

Sigurd grunted, and then his axe came out of the tree's trunk with a wet rip. Metal clanged against metal, and a battle between the two warriors erupted around the tree. An axe swing missed Anya's head by a finger's width.

Anya threw herself away from the fight and turned to run when the willow tree moaned. The branches above her shuddered and whipped from side to side, as though the tree were angry for the damage that had been done to it.

Sigurd and Dobrynya realized at the same time that the tree was moving. They each hesitated, looking up, and then Sigurd swung his axe at Dobrynya.

Before the axe could make contact, a whiplike willow branch smacked the weapon out of Sigurd's hand.

"Augh!" he grunted, and swung his remaining axe at the nearest branch. That one dodged his blow, then wrapped around his wrist and shook the axe loose while four other branches wrapped around his ankles, other wrist, and waist.

Dobrynya was suffering a similar fate. The willow pulled his sword from him and knocked him back, picking him up by his ankles a moment later and hanging him upside down. Both warriors struggled in the air, but the willow reinforced their leafy bonds as they squirmed. Sigurd was almost entirely wrapped in branches.

Anya gaped up at the tree, and a branch snaked

toward her. She stumbled away from it, and it wrapped around her wrist. Before she could try to dislodge it, the branch pulled her up, and another pushed her from behind. She was on her feet again, and the branches dusted her off.

"Annushka!"

Babulya's voice made Anya spin. The old woman advanced through the field, hands up and strumming the threads of magic in the air. Yedsha and Ivan trailed after her. Ivan's eyes were huge, and he watched Dobrynya with awe.

"Babulya!" Anya ran to her grandmother, wanting to hug her but not wanting to disturb her magic.

"Are you hurt?" Babulya asked as Anya approached.

"I don't think so," Anya said.

Babulya sighed with relief. "Good." She turned an angry face toward the men suspended in the tree and said loudly, "No thanks to these hooligans!"

"Unhand me, old wench!" Sigurd bucked against the branches around him.

"My apologies," Dobrynya called, loud enough to drown out Sigurd's curses. "For myself, and for him!"

Babulya halted at the edge of the willow's branches and said, "Who's that one? At least he's polite."

Yedsha strode up behind Babulya. "He's a *bogatyr*!" he said, then waved at Dobrynya. "Good to see you, Dobrynya!"

"Hello, Yedinitsa," Dobrynya called. "How's Marina?"

They called back and forth as Ivan sidled up beside Anya, still staring at Dobrynya. She elbowed his arm. "You didn't tell me he used water magic."

Ivan blanched. "He does?"

Anya nodded. "Really well."

"I didn't know," Ivan mumbled.

Babulya wove her fingers through the air, and the branches holding Dobrynya descended to the ground. They dropped him gently on his head, then helped pull him up as they had Anya. They even brushed him off.

"Thank you," Dobrynya said, eyeing the branches. He turned to where Sigurd dangled in the air. "I'll ask you one last time. Leave this village."

Sigurd stared hard at Dobrynya, then clenched his teeth. Anya could see the muscles in his neck flex and the areas around his arms buck.

"Oh no, you don't," Babulya growled, and she directed another branch to wrap around Sigurd's chest.

The branch had almost reached him when he shoved one arm through those around him. He grabbed the new branch and yanked hard on it with a grunt. The branch snapped and went limp.

Sigurd punched his other arm out the side, grabbed handfuls of willow branches, and ripped them away from his chest.

Dobrynya dashed to where his sword lay in the loam beneath the tree. He seized it just as Sigurd dropped down, tearing greenery from him as he fell. The Varangian landed on his feet. Pieces of the destroyed willow branches rained down around him.

The *bogatyr* circled back to Sigurd's front, and Yedsha moved forward to stand by his side. Babulya remained where she was, pulling more threads. The willow's unharmed branches snaked toward Sigurd, keeping a distance from him but ready to whip at him if needed.

"One last time," Dobrynya said. "Leave this village."

Sigurd's icy eyes ticked over each of the people facing him. He lingered on Anya for longer than the others. By the time he looked away, she felt cold inside.

"This isn't over," Sigurd hissed, and he turned. He shoved past the willow branches and left, stomping in the field along the riverbank until he was out of sight.

Babulya let the willow branches drop. She pointed at Dobrynya and Yedsha. "What are heroes for if they can't defeat a monster like that?"

Dobrynya's jaw tightened, but he smiled through it. "What's the need for heroes if every citizen uses magic as well as you do?"

Babulya shrugged. "I have no idea what you're talking about. Come on, Annushka." The old woman shuffled back to the barn, and after a quick glance at the fools and the knight, Anya followed.

CHAPTER EIGHTEEN

BABULYA SAID NOTHING to Anya as they walked back to the house, but Anya could practically feel the heat of Babulya's anger wafting off her. They went into the kitchen, and Anya shut the door.

Babulya rounded on Anya so fast, it frightened her. "Explain that!" the old woman snapped.

"It was just—"

"It was just you and a *bogatyr* and a fool and a monster having a battle by the river!" Babulya clenched her fists, and all the plants in the kitchen turned, like they were looking at Anya.

"We didn't want to!" Anya said. "Sigurd started it."

"Why are they even here?" Babulya extended a crooked finger at Anya. "You're about to do what your auntie Tzivyah used to do and talk your way around a straight answer. I can tell."

Anya scoffed. "No, I was not."

"Then why were they here?"

"Because . . ." Anya sighed and let her head drop. "There's a dragon in the river. I saw it in our barn. They want to catch it."

Babulya's wrinkly little face grew redder, until she looked like she'd been out in the sun too long. "And you were helping them?"

"You don't understand."

"I understand that dragons are almost extinct!" Babulya hollered. "That could be the last dragon in Kievan Rus'! Or even the last dragon in the world! And you're helping them kill it!"

"The magistrate is going to take our house!" Anya yelled over Babulya, and her grandmother went silent. "He told Mama we owe too many taxes, and she has thirty days to bring him two hundred and fifty rubles, or else she'll go to prison! Or we can give up the house, and she won't go to prison, but we'll be homeless!"

Tears stung her eyes, and her nose tickled as it ran. She wiped the back of her sleeve across her face. "Gospodin Yedsha is paying me, and if I help him catch this dragon, we'll have enough money to stay here. I care more about us than I do about a stupid dragon!"

Babulya said nothing. The plants around the room swayed gently from side to side.

Anya took a deep breath. "You told me when you had to leave your town that it was the worst part of your life. And I'm not going to let that happen to you again. I'm not going to let it happen to Mama." She couldn't say out loud what she feared most if her mother was thrown out of their home: Mama wouldn't survive it.

Babulya's lips tightened as they pressed together. "There's an exemption. Since your papa went to the war—"

"No," Anya said. "The magistrate told us that exemption didn't apply to us." She swallowed hard. "To Jews."

"No." Babulya's voice was much softer. "I thought living out here would protect us. I thought we could hide."

Anya shook her head. "We can't."

"Annushka, that burden isn't yours to bear."

"It's got to be someone's." Anya fisted her hands, puffed out her chest, and marched to the door.

"Wait," Babulya said.

Anya shook her head. "No." She pulled the door open and ran out before Babulya could say anything to stop her.

CHAPTER NINETEEN

ANYA RAN TO THE BRIDGE she had taken Yedsha and Ivan to, where they'd found the house along the river. She couldn't believe that a shield with a red dragon on it was a coincidence, seeing as the dragon in Anya's barn had been red. Whoever lived in that house knew something, and she was going to find out what.

She went as fast as she could along the riverside path but eventually had to slow to keep from sliding into the water. As she slowed, something crunched on leaves behind her.

Anya's heart ricocheted upward until it lodged

itself in her throat. She bent, grabbed a rock off the ground, and spun, screaming as she brandished the stone.

Ivan screamed with her as he recoiled back, arms up to shield himself.

"Ivan!" Anya's chest heaved. "What are you doing?"

"I was trying to catch up to you," he said.

"You could have said my name!"

"I . . ." He paused. "Yes, I could have. I didn't think of that."

She dropped the rock. "Where are your papa and Dobrynya?"

"They went to church," Ivan said.

"And they didn't make you go?" Anya asked, surprised.

Ivan shrugged. "I bet they'll notice me gone sometime. Maybe not."

"But you could be in church with your hero," Anya said. "Dobrynya Nikitich."

"I could," Ivan said. "I wanted to make sure you

were okay, though. And then I saw you running on the road, so I followed."

Anya smiled. She hated to admit she was a little glad he'd showed up. More than a little glad. *Very* glad.

"Well, you can come with me," she said. "But you have to be quiet and listen to what I say."

"Deal," he said.

They went north on the path again while Anya explained her thoughts on the little house in the ravine. Ivan agreed that the shield was too much of a coincidence. He pulled ahead of Anya, excited and gesticulating as he spoke, so he got caught in the trap first.

His foot sank into the leaves, and he stumbled. Anya had time to yell, "Ivan, look out!" before a tarp snapped up, the corners fixed to ropes that pulled it into the trees, Ivan screaming within.

Anya skidded to a stop and gaped upward, watching the tarp swing. Her shock lasted seconds, forced out of her by rapid, heavy footfalls approaching.

She spun and ran toward the village, but not quickly enough. Her scalp burned as someone grabbed a handful of her hair and wrenched her backwards. Her feet skidded ahead of her body and she lost her footing, plummeting to the ground and slamming into it hard enough to knock her breath out.

Sigurd appeared over her, snarling. He picked her up with a fist snared in the front of her dress and held her in the air, feet kicking, trying to find purchase. His icy eyes blazed with anger, and with triumph.

"That trap *was* for the dragon," he spat. "But good for little brats, too!"

His Russian was getting better and better. He almost didn't have an accent anymore. How was he doing that? She struggled against his hold. "Let me go!"

"Oh." His frown deepened. "I intend to."

He readjusted his hold on her, throwing her over one shoulder like a sack of wheat. She kicked and screamed, but it made no difference. Sigurd went about his business as though he didn't have a flailing child attached to him.

The Varangian walked to a tree and removed a rope that had been tied to a branch. Its other end was attached to the tarp Ivan had been caught in, and Sigurd let the tarp down without an ounce of consideration for the boy within it.

Ivan yelped as he hit the ground. He thrashed within the tarp, trying to find the exit, and Sigurd pulled it open. Ivan froze, staring up at the furious warrior, and Anya screamed, "Ivan, run!"

Ivan's eyes darted to the side, panning for an escape route, but Sigurd was faster. He shoved Ivan down into the folds of the tarp before he tossed Anya on top of him. Tangled in each other, they couldn't escape from the tarp's canvas hold fast enough, and Sigurd wrapped them back up in it like a picnic lunch, forming a bag around them.

"Stop!" Anya yelled. The bag stank, like he had kept old cabbages in it, and the loamy scent of the leaves trapped inside did nothing to improve the smell.

Sigurd did not stop. Anya and Ivan clashed together again, leaves jumbling around them, as the Varangian picked up the sack and threw it over a shoulder. The swaying of his walk alerted them to movement, and a moment later, Sigurd dropped the bag on the ground.

"Ow!" Ivan yelled. He kicked against the bag. "Let us out of here! We won't bother you anymore, we swear!"

Before he could say anything else, something heavy landed on top of them. It was long and ropy and . . . sharp. Barbs poked through the canvas. It was a rope with barbs attached, something Anya had sometimes seen fishermen use to catch fish. He was wrapping the bag with it.

"What is he doing?" Ivan wondered aloud.

Sigurd tied another barbed rope on the outside of the tarp before Anya realized what he was doing.

"Ivan!" Anya kicked at the sack, trying desperately to find the opening. "Ivan, he's weighting it!"

"He's what?" Ivan yelled as Sigurd pushed the bag.

Both the children fell into each other, and Anya's search for the opening was halted.

"He's weighting the bag!" Anya screamed. "He's going to—"

The bag dropped, the weightlessness lasting half a second, and then a splash, and cold water rushed through the canvas.

"NO!" Anya screamed, clawing again at the canvas sides. "He threw us in the river! Help!"

"HELP!" Ivan joined in, but no one could hear them. The weighted bag disappeared beneath the water of the Sogozha, taking Anya and Ivan with it.

CHAPTER TWENTY

THE BAG FILLED rapidly with icy water, and in the wet darkness that stank of rotten cabbages and leaves, Anya and Ivan struggled to find a way out.

"No, no, no," Anya muttered as she searched for an opening in the canvas. If she could only open it enough to let them through, they'd be able to hold their breath long enough to get to the surface. The river wasn't that deep.

Ivan grunted, and a moment later, Anya felt warmth fill the bag.

"Ivan!" she shrieked, appalled. "I know you're

scared, but really, peeing while we're trapped in here?"

"I'm not peeing!" Ivan snapped. Anya could hear the exertion in his voice. "I'm pushing the water away."

"What?" Anya said. "But how could you . . . ?" She trailed off, remembering Marina cooking, pulling water up through the air in a stream. "Your water magic."

Ivan grunted. "This is going to undo all my work I did *not* using it." He breathed hard. "I can't keep this up for long."

Anya's eyes were adjusting to the near pitch-darkness of the bag. She noticed they were still sinking, but it was slower than their initial descent. With the bag weighted, she didn't think they'd float, but at least they weren't on the bottom yet.

"Okay, good," Anya said. "Can you hold the water back while I try to find a seam in the bag?"

"Maybe." Ivan sounded strained. "I don't know . . . for how long . . ."

Anya hoped she didn't need long. She ran her

fingers along the bag's inside, and Ivan sucked in a breath.

"Careful!" he said. "You're going to disrupt the magic!"

Anya snapped her fingers back. "If I touch it, that messes it up?"

"Apparently!"

"Well, that's stupid!" Anya yelled. "We can't stay in here until you run out of magic! I've got to find a hole!"

"Well, if you touch it, the magic will pop!" Ivan said through clenched teeth.

Anya searched her brain for a solution, and she found a weak one quickly. "If I disrupt the magic, can you get it back?"

"Maybe," Ivan said. "It's hard."

"It's hard," Anya said, "but you can do it, right?"

Ivan sighed. "I did it once. I guess I can do it again."

"Okay." Anya reached her fingers out slowly, carefully caressing the inside of the magic bubble they were in. "I'll try to feel through the magic."

"Okay," Ivan whispered, the strain in his voice apparent.

Anya tenderly ran her fingertips over the magic bubble, pressing on it enough to feel the bag past it. Finally, Anya's searching fingers located a seam, and she said, "I found a seam. I'm going for it. If the magic pops—"

Ivan cleared his throat. "I'll bring it back. If I can."

"You can do enough just to cover our heads," Anya said.

Ivan said nothing, just grunted agreement. She took a deep breath and wriggled her hand out of the seam. The warmth dissipated, and water flooded in.

Anya's breath hitched as she gasped, desperately trying to keep her panic at bay. "Ivan!" she said. "Bubble our heads!"

"I'm trying!" he said.

She couldn't see Ivan to know how he was doing, so she concentrated on tearing a hole in the side of the bag. But the barbed wrapping wasn't only for weight; Sigurd had knotted and arranged it so it made a net around the outside, to prevent exactly what Anya was attempting.

The bag filled with water. She could feel it advancing rapidly up her back and belly, moving for her head. She had yet to feel the magic warmth of another bubble there.

"Ivan?" she said.

"Trying!" he grunted.

With fingers weakening in the cold, Anya tugged futilely at the barbed rope on the outside. The water continued to fill the bag; she could feel it on her chest now, and her neck, and over her chin.

"Ivan!" She hated the sound of panic in her voice.

"I'm trying!" Ivan yelled back at her.

She couldn't respond to him. The water crept up her face, and she took a huge breath before it filled the bag entirely.

Anya clawed at the barbed rope, then tore at the bag to widen the opening. She was skinny. Maybe she'd be able to fit through. Then she could drag the bag to the surface and let Ivan out. She wondered if she was strong enough to drag the bag up, but she pushed the thought out of her mind. She *had* to be strong enough.

Her lungs were beginning to burn, her brain screaming for a breath of air. This couldn't be how her life ended. She refused to believe it.

Ivan's arms wrapped around Anya, and at first she thought maybe he'd been able to get the magic back. But when nothing happened, she realized it was a hug of goodbye, and she gritted her teeth. She waved her arm around in the water, searching for something to grab onto, but there was nothing there except cold water.

The bag stopped descending. Anya's legs pressed into the fabric, and she thought they had finally reached the bottom. But then her legs pressed in harder, and in her stomach she felt the distinct sickness of rising rapidly. Someone was pulling them back up.

Ivan's hold around her was getting weaker, and she grasped him, praying he hadn't given up and taken a breath. She was close—her head felt like it was about to erupt from the lack of oxygen—but she could hold out for a few more seconds. Hopefully, that was all it would take.

The bag sagged around them, and light rushed in as the water rushed out. A hole had been cut in the side and the barbed rope torn away. Anya tumbled out, gasping for air. She caught some water with her first breath and coughed violently as she collapsed to the ground. The day's brightness blinded her, as did the spots in her vision.

The first thing she saw was Ivan, lying on the ground. She grabbed his shoulders and shook him, unable to yell his name like she wanted to, and his eyes popped open. He coughed and screamed at the same time, the look of terror on his face mirroring what she felt.

Finally, she choked out, "Ivan!"

He pushed himself to his knees, and they hugged, both hysterical with happiness that they were alive.

Suddenly, Ivan went rigid. He gulped and trembled in Anya's arms, and she pulled back from him. He stared at something behind her, mouth pulled into a frightened grimace. Anya turned, expecting to see Sigurd looming behind them.

It wasn't Sigurd.

The dragon coiled before them, ruby scales shiny with water. It didn't move at all, just stared at them with its blue eyes, nostrils flaring as it breathed. Anya watched its snout, noting that within the nostrils a little flap of skin smacked shut periodically.

She found herself wondering why, in her last minutes of life before the dragon ate her, she was staring up its nose.

She heard Ivan's ragged breathing from behind her, but she didn't want to look back and take her eyes off the dragon.

No one moved for several minutes. Anya's heart still hammered and her belly twisted with fear, and the first coherent thought she could dredge up was why the dragon hadn't tried to eat her yet. It could have. It wasn't enormous, but it was twice as big as any wolf in the area and more than twice Anya's size. Plus, it had those teeth and claws that would easily turn Anya's flesh into ribbons.

Anya inched a hand up and watched as the dragon's eyes flicked toward the movement. She froze, it froze, and then she moved her hand again.

Ivan began to wheeze behind Anya.

She licked her lips and brought her hand closer to its face. Her fingers itched to know what a dragon felt like.

Not *a* dragon. Maybe the *last* dragon. The thought made her pause. The last dragon in Kievan Rus' had saved her life, and what was she planning to do to it?

The dragon's eyes darted from her hand to her face and back to her hand again, and it shifted its body as it reached a clawed foot toward her outstretched hand.

"Anya!" Ivan jumped forward and grabbed Anya's arm, yanking her away from the dragon. He pulled her off balance, and she flailed her arms. One of them caught the dragon's claws across the back of her forearm. Anya yelped as the claws split her flesh in three gouges. Blood gushed out.

Ivan pulled Anya a few steps, and then he let go.

Her feet tangled in each other and she fell onto the ground, clutching her bleeding arm. She could hear Ivan's rapid footsteps retreating down the river. Did he not realize she wasn't running with him?

The dragon disappeared into the river with a splash, and Anya huddled on the ground, cold and wet and alone.

CHAPTER TWENTY-ONE

ANYA PEEKED under her hand to look at the wound on her arm. As soon as she moved her hand, blood flowed, so she clenched her fingers down on her arm again. She gritted her teeth against the pain, her heart beating so hard and fast, she could feel it in her toes.

She was certain Ivan was going to get his father. They'd be back soon, and the dragon would be gone, and it probably wouldn't come near her again.

Something red peeked up over the river's bank.

Anya managed to catch a glimpse of the dragon's

wide blue eyes for a second before the beast vanished under the water.

"Wait!" Anya struggled to her feet and stumbled to her knees a step later. She rested on the ground, gasping for air. Her head swam. The forest spun around her. She knew her wet dress should have been making her cold, but she felt hot.

Anya squeezed her eyes shut to try to stop the spinning. It didn't work. She huffed, her frustration manifesting as a quiet sob, and then nearby splashing and rustling made her open her eyes.

The dragon was half out of the river, peering around a tree at her.

It hadn't fled, and it hadn't attacked. It could have killed her ten times by now. Why hadn't it?

Anya tried again to stand up, but her legs were too weak. Blood ran down her arm. She squeezed tighter, and the pain made her gasp a breath into lungs that felt too small. Pinpricks of black crowded the edges of her vision.

A shadow fell over her. When she looked up, the

dragon was there, its surprisingly expressive blue eyes passing back and forth between Anya's face and her arm. She panted, and the pinpricks turned into the outer edges of a tunnel.

This was what it felt like to die. She supposed it wasn't too bad. It could have been worse.

Everything went gray, and she hardly felt herself fall onto the ground.

Being dead was unexpectedly warm and soft.

Anya left her eyes shut for a moment. Babulya said when people died, the next time they woke up was when the Messiah came. She was about to see the Messiah, and while she was eager to do so, she was also nervous, and sad. Mama would be heart-broken that Anya had died.

When she opened her eyes, she realized being dead was dim, too. She sat up, and a wave of dizziness made her lie back down. Pushing up had made her arm throb, and she felt it carefully with her other hand. Her fingers touched a soft bandage that had been clumsily applied to her slashes.

From the ground, Anya saw something glittering red. She didn't remember Babulya talking about a glittering red Messiah, but she supposed Babulya couldn't be right about everything all the time.

But when a serpentlike head emerged from the darkness, Anya's peace with death vanished and was replaced with cold fear. The dragon coiled in front of a fireplace, the flames lighting its ruby scales.

"You're not the Messiah," Anya mumbled.

The dragon said nothing and stayed in a neat coil by the fire. Anya pushed herself up slowly, never taking her eyes off the serpent. As she pushed up, the thick blanket that had been covering her slid down her shoulder, and she realized she wasn't wearing her dress but an enormous tunic instead. Her dress, to her dismay, hung on a chair near the fire, behind the dragon.

A shield with a red dragon painted on it hung above the mantel. Dozens of weapons hung all over the walls.

She was in the house in the ravine.

The dragon crept forward until she looked back

at it, and then it stopped. It blinked once, then said in a quiet, nervous voice, "I'm sorry I hurt you."

Anya's mouth dropped open. Nowhere in the stories and myths did anyone ever say dragons could speak. But this one could, apparently, and she gaped at it. At *him*, she supposed. He had sounded like a boy. A regular human boy. *The dragon could talk.*

She managed to squeak, "You didn't mean to."

The dragon crept closer. He used his two legs to walk across the floor and undulated his long body like a snake, helping to push himself along. The spines on his back caught the firelight and blazed.

As he approached, she held up her arm and pointed to the haphazard bandage. "Thank you for bandaging the cuts."

"You're welcome." The dragon scooted closer. "Are you afraid of me?"

She didn't answer right away. Was she? Yes, but no. She thought of what the stories said—fearsome, violent, monstrous—and then what Babulya said. Gentle. Benevolent. Good luck. The dragon coiled before her had pulled her out of the river and had brought her to his home to have her wounds bound. That was benevolent, wasn't it? "Should I be?"

"No." When he spoke, his words rushed out like water bursting through a weakened dam. "Does that mean you're not? Really? That's so great! Because my father always said I should stay away from the villagers because you'd all be afraid of me, and I thought you were afraid when you saw me in your barn, but you're not anymore, right? What's your name?"

Her mouth felt like she'd eaten a handful of sand. She tried to swallow away the dryness, but her tongue stuck to the roof of her mouth and made it impossible. A dragon wanted to know her name.

Anya managed to wet her mouth and say, "Channah Miroslavovna Kozlova." She cleared her throat. "But everyone calls me Anya."

"I'm Håkon." The dragon cocked his head and looked at the ceiling, like he was pondering something. "My father is called Jernhånd. So I suppose I'm Håkon Jernhåndssen." He laughed. "I've never thought about it before!"

At his laugh, the tension in Anya's body began

to relax away. If she closed her eyes, she could have been speaking with a normal boy her age. She held the blanket against her chest and said, "It's nice to meet you, Håkon Jernhåndssen."

"You too!" Håkon said. "Do you want to play with me?"

Anya stared. "Play with you?"

"Yeah." The dragon shifted from foot to foot. "I've watched villagers playing with one another. We could pretend you're a princess and I'm a *bogatyr* and I have to rescue you!" He spun in a tight circle. "Oh! Or we could be on a quest to find a treasure!"

She had no idea what to say. This was the most bizarre thing that had ever happened to her. She started to think maybe she was dead after all.

"How old are you?" Anya asked.

Håkon bobbed his head from side to side. "I don't know exactly. My father brought me here when I was very tiny. I don't remember it. That was nearly thirteen years ago."

A dragon her age, or close enough. She'd always thought of dragons as being ancient somehow, but a child dragon made sense. Those ancient dragons had to start somewhere. "Brought you here?" Anya said. "From where?"

"South," Håkon said. "I think my father has marbles around here somewhere. Do you know how to play marbles?"

"No," Anya said.

"It's hard for me." Håkon brought one clawed foot up and flexed his toes. "But I can usually get some if I concentrate, or if I'm allowed to use magic."

"Magic?" Anya perked up. "What kind?"

"A bunch." Håkon turned his nose toward the fire and inhaled sharply. A stream of flame jutted from the rest of the fire and toward his mouth, but he blew it back in before it went anywhere. "I can't play with flames in here. I'll catch something on fire and then I'll be in *big* trouble. Let's go outside!"

Anya opened her mouth to say that wasn't a good idea; Ivan and his father would be searching the woods for her by now, and going outside put Håkon at risk of being seen. But the dragon zipped out of the house, slither-crawling through the door before

Anya could say anything. She pulled the blanket away from herself enough to see if what she was wearing was appropriate for walking around in. The tunic was enormous on her, but it covered everything clothing needed to cover, so she tossed the blanket away and ran after the dragon.

CHAPTER TWENTY-TWO

ANYA SQUINTED against the brightness of the late afternoon as Håkon sprinted around the outside of the house. He went toward the back, where Anya hadn't been yet. She followed carefully, hugging the oversize tunic to herself as she stepped gingerly around rocks and sticks.

Behind the house, Håkon had gone to the river's edge. As soon as Anya appeared, he said, "Behold! Tremble before my power!" A column of water blasted up from the river behind him, and two watery tentacles peeled off the sides, whipping back and forth.

Anya watched the tentacled column with wide eyes, and then she examined Håkon. He didn't move like he was pulling threads—the most he had done was whip his tail around a bit—and she wondered how he was creating the column. But then she remembered Yedsha talking about magical creatures. He'd described the way dragons flew, with special appendages on their wings. Anya's eyes fell to Håkon's twitching tail. Did he have magical appendages there that allowed him to control water? Did that mean he was a water dragon and not an air dragon?

The dragon brought his tail up, then down, and six more tentacles appeared. The column looked like a giant liquid spider.

"How are you doing that?" Anya asked.

Håkon peered back at her. "What do you mean?"

"I mean, how are you making the water do that?"

He looked back at the water spider, then at Anya again. "The same way *you* would, I guess."

Anya shook her head. "I can't do that."

"Oh," Håkon said. "You don't use water magic.

What kind do you use? Earth? Air?" He perked. "Fire?"

"None of those."

"Not elemental, then?" His tail swished, and the water spider swayed back and forth. "Oh, wow! What is it? I've heard of emotional magics. Is it one of those? Or sense magic? Or natural?"

Anya vaguely remembered Yedsha talking about emotional magic in the woods, but she definitely didn't have that. She shook her head. "No. Nothing. I can't use magic."

Håkon let his tail drop, and the water spider collapsed back into the river with a dull crash.

"No magic at all?" He sounded incredulous.

She shook her head.

"That's impossible."

"I swear," Anya said. "I tried to use some earth magic, and all I did was throw dirt in a *zmeyok*'s face. I can't even see threads most of the time."

Håkon stared at her, his dragony face pulled into an expression of skepticism. Finally, he said, "So you *can* use magic."

"Not very well," Anya said. "Not well enough to be useful."

"You just need to practice more," Håkon said. He jerked his head toward the ground. "You used earth magic, right? Use it again right now."

Anya sighed and searched the air for threads. None appeared. "I don't see any threads."

"Any what?"

"Threads," Anya said. "There are no magic threads anywhere."

Håkon pursed his lips. "I don't see any threads either."

"How do you do magic, then?"

"I just feel it!" Håkon arched his back, and a mound of earth rose up, then split apart. A little cave formed in the hard ground, and Håkon dove into it. The cave opening vanished and the mound flattened again.

"Håkon!" Anya ran to where the dragon had disappeared. The soil was softer, but there was no other sign that anything had happened. She spun in a circle, trying to discern some way to find the dragon in his cave, but there was nothing.

A laugh came from the river, and Anya looked over to see Håkon's red head peeking over the river-bank. He climbed out of the water and shook water off his scales.

"How did you do that?" Anya was so jealous, she could hardly stand it. "That's incredible."

Håkon arched his back again. "There's magic all around, and I can catch it." He wiggled from side to side. "Like there, earth magic." He stopped wiggling, and another mound rose up. A cave mouth appeared, but this time it didn't collapse right away. A stream of water poured up from the river and into the little cave, forming a rudimentary table and chairs. Anya wondered how she would sit on the chair, and then the water crunched as it turned to ice.

"What?" Anya ran to the ice furniture, clasp-ing the oversize tunic around herself. "How?" She rapped on the ice tabletop with her knuckles. They came away pink and cold.

"Sit," Håkon said. "It's strong enough."

Anya did. The chair made the same groan beneath her as an icy pond made in the wintertime when she walked on its frozen surface, but it didn't break.

"I wish I could do magic," Anya whispered.

Håkon crawled into the little cave and carved on the icy table with a claw. "I wish I could do human stuff."

"Like what?" Anya asked. "Humans are boring."

"No way," Håkon said. "Humans can do all kinds of things. Your hands are . . ." He trailed off, lifting up his clawed feet.

Anya brought her hands beside his feet. She flexed her fingers, and he flexed his claws. He had three toes facing forward and one facing back, like a bird. When he flexed his toes, the rear one bent only at one knuckle.

"You can pick things up," Håkon said. "I can, sometimes. If it's big enough. If the surface is just right. And do you know what I heard about human hands?"

"What?" Anya said.

"You can feel things," he said. "Textures. The table feels different from your tunic."

"Of course it does," Anya said, feeling both. "You can't feel the difference?"

"I can feel the table is colder," Håkon said, patting the table with his foot and then patting the tunic's shoulder. "But other than that, they're the same."

Anya hadn't ever thought her hands could be as magical to a dragon as his . . . well, his actual magic was to her. "I guess we're each magical to each other, huh?"

Håkon laughed. "I guess! Hey. Are you hungry?"

Anya's day had been such a mess that she hadn't had anything since Marina's breakfast, which had been hours and hours ago. The sun was so low, she couldn't see it past the cliffs anymore. "I am, actually," she said.

They got up from the ice chairs in the cavern, and Håkon slithered toward the house. Anya followed him a few steps, then stopped. The dragon's magic had been so astonishing, she had forgotten all about the danger in the forest. Yedsha and Dobrynya were still hunting Håkon, and so was Sigurd. Ivan had certainly told Yedsha by now about the dragon, and they'd be by the river searching for him, and for Anya.

If Anya told Yedsha where Håkon was, she'd have all the money she needed to save her farm. But what would happen to Håkon if they found him?

Babulya's story flashed in her mind. *The tsar killed them. He used his* bogatyri *to do it.*

"Anya?"

She looked up. Håkon peered around the house's corner, head cocked. She didn't realize she had stopped following him. "Huh?"

"Are you coming?"

"Yes," she said, then shook her head. "Well, I want to. I should change first, but then go back to the village."

Some of the light left Håkon's eyes. "Oh."

"I'll come back tomorrow." Anya trotted to him, holding the tunic tight around herself. "I just want to make sure they all know I'm not dead."

"Oh," Håkon said again, but sounded less sad. "Of course. Yes! I'd want to know you weren't dead, for sure. I'll wait for you here, then. Tomorrow."

Anya smiled, excited to come back and learn more about her new friend. But as he turned away, her smile dropped, and she followed him with a guilty heart.

CHAPTER TWENTY-THREE

HER DRESS was barely damp, but even that small amount of wetness chilled Anya as she jogged along the dimming river path back toward the village. Her mind whirled as she ran.

First, she took account of things she knew for certain. Dragons were real, and still alive. Well, at least two were still alive. One was named Håkon, and he had a father named Jernhånd. She hadn't met Jernhånd, so she couldn't speak to his temperament, but Håkon was absolutely kind. He had saved her and Ivan from drowning and had bandaged Anya's arm when she was bleeding. She owed Håkon her life.

Something else she knew for certain: The tsar had done something to the rest of the dragons in Kievan Rus'. Babulya said he killed them, but Anya didn't know that was what had actually happened. She did know that if the tsar got his hands on either of the dragons in Zmeyreka, she'd never see them again.

She knew Yedsha and Dobrynya worked for the tsar, and they were hunting the dragons in Zmey-reka. They thought there was only one dragon.

Sigurd was also hunting only one dragon in Zmeyreka, but for what purpose, Anya didn't know.

That was what she knew for certain. She couldn't make any decisions based on that information, though. There were too many unknowns. Would Dobrynya and Yedsha still take Håkon and Jern-hånd to the tsar if they knew Håkon wasn't danger-ous? Was Babulya right about what the tsar did to dragons? What was Sigurd's plan? What would hap-pen to Anya's family if they had to leave Zmeyreka? What would Papa do if he were here?

This last thought made her slow until she

stopped. She breathed heavy, panting in the shade as she imagined her father's face, his smile, his voice.

"What should I do?" Anya whispered.

What would he say? *Do what you know is right, Annushka.*

Nothing was right, though. If she protected Håkon, she wouldn't ever get the money she needed, and her family would be homeless. Mama would go to prison.

But if she turned the dragons over to Yedsha and Dobrynya, she could be sending them to their death. She'd get money to save her farm, sure, but it would be blood money. She'd never feel clean again.

She thought on what Babulya had said when they had read the Torah together, about destroying one life and destroying the entire world. Did that logic extend to dragons?

She had to find out what happened to the dragons when they went to Kiev. If Dobrynya didn't know, then no one would.

Over the sound of her own rushing breath, Anya

heard a distant voice echoing through the forest: "Anya!"

The voice belonged to a boy, and only one boy would be foolish enough to call her name in the same woods that held a dragon and a murderous Varangian.

The echoing bounced the voice around trees and rocks, and there was no way for Anya to tell where it had come from.

"Anya!" There Ivan was again. She followed her best guess at the direction of his voice.

She saw Ivan before he saw her, and as she was about to call to him, she heard a voice from behind her: "There you are!"

Anya whirled, terrified that Sigurd was back, but the man behind her was smiling wide. Yedsha grabbed Anya in a hug and called, "Vosya! Dobrynya! Here she is!"

Yedsha's hug was suffocating, and when he released Anya, she gasped for air.

Ivan and Dobrynya ran out of the trees. Somehow,

Ivan made more noise than Dobrynya did. Ivan patted her shoulders. "I was so worried! After Sigurd chased us . . ."

His tone carried with it a heavy dose of suggestion, and she realized he hadn't told either of the adults the actual story of what had happened.

"Yes," she said. "He chased us. I got turned around and lost. I was scared."

"You're safe now," Dobrynya said, smiling down at her. "Let's get you home, huh?"

He turned down the path, and Anya and Ivan followed. They had gone only a few steps before Anya blurted, "Why did the tsar kill all the dragons?"

Yedsha and Dobrynya exchanged a quick look, and then Dobrynya said, "Oh, little girls shouldn't worry about that kind of thing."

"But there must be a reason," Anya pressed. "Right? Someone doesn't kill off an entire species for no reason."

Dobrynya slowed and tucked his chin, thinking. He looked down at Anya. "It's a scary and sad story."

"That's okay," Anya said.

"Hmm." Dobrynya glanced at Yedsha, then back at Anya. "Many years ago, the tsar got married, and not long after that, the tsarina was expecting twins. She was out for a walk one day, and a dragon attacked her. She lived, but one of her babies didn't. Isn't that sad?"

"Yes," Anya said quietly, and Ivan nodded to himself.

"After that, the tsar was very angry at dragons," Dobrynya said. "He didn't want anyone else in the kingdom to suffer as he had. So he ordered the destruction of all dragons."

Anya pressed her lips together. The tsar's vengeance made sense emotionally, but it wasn't logical. Some people were murderers, like Sigurd, but that didn't mean *all* people should be judged as such. "But what about dragons that wouldn't attack someone? Do they get destroyed too?"

"They're wild creatures," Yedsha said. "They don't think and feel, like people do. They're like dogs. Any dog could bite, and any dragon could kill."

Anya absently picked at her fingernail, trying

to hide her ire. There was no way Håkon would ever hurt anyone. "So the tsar killed all the dragons because one of them did something terrible?"

"He didn't want the same thing to happen to anyone else," Dobrynya repeated.

Anya didn't say anything. She wanted to ask why the tsar sent men to fight, then, if he was so concerned with people dying. Maybe he was concerned only with babies dying. It didn't seem right that Håkon should have to suffer for the actions of another creature.

"What if the dragon in our woods is a nice dragon?" Anya asked.

"A nice dragon?" Dobrynya asked.

Anya nodded. "It hasn't attacked anyone here, right?"

"Not *yet*," Yedsha said.

"Maybe not ever," Anya argued. "One dragon hurt the tsarina, but what have dragons done otherwise? Who else did they hurt?"

Dobrynya chuckled, a sound that made Anya

grit her teeth with anger. The chuckle said what he didn't: She was just a little girl who didn't understand the world or the creatures in it. She couldn't possibly know how bad dragons were.

Anya braced herself, then asked the question she needed answered most. The question that, depending on its answer, would decide Håkon's fate. "What does the tsar do with the dragons?"

Dobrynya and Yedsha didn't look at her for a long time. When Dobrynya finally did, his mouth twitched and his eyes looked past her, through her, like he was seeing something far away.

"That's not something little girls need to trouble themselves with," he said. "Just know this, Anya. The tsar protects us. He keeps us safe. And he does the hard things others can't."

With that, Dobrynya looked back at the path, and he didn't say anything else until they reached Anya's farm.

✦ ✖ ✦

Anya sat at the table, poking at her stew with a spoon but not eating any. Babulya sipped her soup quietly. Anya watched her grandmother carefully. She was sure Babulya hadn't mentioned the dragon to Mama, because Mama hadn't said a word about it since Dobrynya had dropped Anya off. She knew what Ivan had told everyone: that they had been playing in the woods, and Sigurd had come stomping at them, and Anya had gotten lost in the woods running away from him. Mama had spied the gash on Anya's arm, but Anya said she had tripped and hurt herself on a rock. Everyone was quiet, except Dyedka.

"We've got a *bogatyr* and an imperial fool in this village," he hooted, "and it took them hours to find my granddaughter being chased by a maniac in the woods!"

Mama's lip trembled. "Borya, can we just be glad they found her?"

"Absolutely not!" Dyedka yelled. "What are they good for, if not helping the people? We're the people! Anya is the people!"

"I know," Mama said. "But they went out as soon

as little Ivan came and told them. They did what they could."

"*I* could have gone!" Dyedka hollered.

"Your cart is no good in the woods," Mama said. "And I looked all afternoon. I didn't find her either. Can we just be grateful she's back?"

Babulya kicked Anya under the table and then stood up. "I'm going to bed."

Dyedka waved his hand at her and continued talking to Mama. "Did they even use their magic to find her? I thought that Dobrynya was supposed to be the cleverest man alive!"

Babulya made her way to the sleeping room, and Anya got up after her. "I'm tired too. I'm going to bed."

"Good night, Annushka," Mama said. "I'm glad you're safe."

Anya shuffled to the sleeping room and slipped inside. Babulya was in bed, but she wasn't snoring.

"Annushka, come here."

Anya obeyed. She perched on the edge of

Babulya's bed. Babulya picked up Anya's injured arm and patted it with tender fingers. She had applied a salve and rewrapped it, and now she inspected the dressing's condition.

"I didn't tell your mama about the dragon," Babulya said as she felt Anya's wound. "Or what you're doing with those fools."

"I figured," Anya said. "Thank you."

Babulya nodded. The two of them were quiet until Anya said, "If I killed the dragon, would it be murder?"

Babulya said softly, "That's a difficult question. To answer it, we have to answer another question. Is a dragon an animal?"

"No," Anya answered quickly. No matter what Dobrynya said, there was no way Håkon was on the same level as a dog, or one of the goats, or a fish.

"So a dragon is a person?"

Slower, Anya said, "No."

"Then what is it?"

"I don't know," Anya said. "Something different altogether. But not a regular animal."

"Do you believe dragons are intelligent?" Babulya asked.

"Yes, but so are some animals," Anya said. "Zvezda is intelligent."

Babulya laughed. "He is, isn't he? Well, how about this, then: Can dragons understand death?"

Anya pictured Håkon in her mind. He had saved her from death. Twice. He understood it enough to pull another back from it.

"Yes," Anya said.

"Well." Babulya pulled her blankets up to her chin and snuggled her head against her pillow. "If you kill something that understands death, do you believe you have murdered?"

Anya didn't answer. Soon, Babulya's snores wound up from her bed, and Anya plopped onto her own as the snores got louder. She dreamed of death and dragons.

CHAPTER TWENTY-FOUR

ANYA WOKE UP when Dyedka shut the bedroom door too hard. The scant dawn glowed through the tiny window. Anya rolled over and reached under her mattress, where she had stashed the dragon scale. She couldn't turn Håkon in for money, she'd decided last night, so she needed to do something else.

She started wondering how much dragon body parts could sell for.

Body parts, of course, that would grow back. Nothing that would hurt him too much to remove. She figured he lost scales all the time, and if she could sell them for a decent amount of money, she'd be able to pay the taxes. If she stayed on as Yedsha's assistant dragon hunter, she could take them to places far away from Håkon, and then they wouldn't find him. She'd still earn ten rubles per day as she "helped," and if she could drag that out long enough, she could make enough money to save her farm.

She was feeling awfully smart when she grasped the scale and sat up, but she stopped when she saw her mother.

Mama was on her bed, curled into a ball on her side, clutching a piece of cloth to her chest. Anya didn't need to get a good look at the cloth to know what it was: one of Papa's shirts. In sleep, Mama's face was peaceful. Anya didn't see that side of her mother anymore. She stayed longer than she should have, then crept out when Babulya started to stir.

Anya opened the kitchen door and stopped short. All the chickens sat in front of the door, and all of them had their faces turned up to Anya.

"Uh," she mumbled. "Are you hungry?"

One chicken clucked, which got them all to

clucking. They turned around and waddled back to the barn.

"Strange," Anya mumbled. She thought about following them but didn't want to get sidetracked. She trotted to the road with the scale a gentle weight in her pocket, heading toward the village. Kin knew Sigurd, so he probably knew about dragons, too, and maybe he'd have a use for a dragon scale.

The smithy was barely warming up when Anya got there. She crept in the front door and peered over the counter. Kin moved in the ember-lit dimness in the back of the forge area.

"Kin?" she called, and he stopped shuffling about.

"Eh?" he said. "Who's there?"

"Anya," she said. "I have something to sell you."

He laughed. "More moldy horseshoes?"

"No. Better than that."

Kin groaned as he walked around the forge to her and leaned over the tall counter, a condescending smile on his face. "Yes?"

Anya pulled the scale from her dress pocket and said, "Do you want to buy this?"

Kin's smile remained as he looked at the scale, before he really took in what it was. Then his smile dropped from his face and he limped around the counter. He shut the door and locked it, then rounded on Anya and demanded, "Where on God's earth did ye find that thing?"

She suddenly wasn't sure coming to Kin had been a good idea. She stammered, "Well, I . . . I found it in my barn. Um . . . I was looking for things to sell, and I found it, and—"

"Do ye know what that is?" Kin hissed.

Anya found herself afraid to admit that she did, so she said, "A jewel or something?"

"It's a dragon scale," Kin said. He held his hand out, palm up, and Anya realized he wanted her to give it to him. She hesitated, and Kin heaved a sigh and said, "I'm not gonna steal it."

With trepidation, Anya set the scale onto Kin's palm. He pulled it toward his face, squinting as he examined it. With a frown, he said, "This was in yer barn, ye say?"

Anya nodded. "Maybe Dyedka had it from before, when there were dragons, back when I was a baby. He talks about them sometimes."

"Maybe." Kin didn't sound convinced.

Anya said, "So do you want to buy it?"

Kin redirected his scrutiny from the scale to Anya. "Buy it?"

"Yes."

"No."

Her hopes of saving her family drained away. "Well, do you know anyone who would?"

Kin shook his head. "This is a very dangerous item to have." He held the scale out to Anya.

She slid it into her dress pocket while she swallowed hard. "Dangerous? Will the dragon come back for it?"

"No," Kin said. "But if certain people find out ye have it, they'll wanna know how ye came across it. How yer *dyedushka* came across it. It could attract the wrong kind of attention to this place."

Her heart sank with every word he spoke. "So you don't know anyone I could sell this to?"

Kin shook his head. "Yer best option is to throw that thing in the river and pretend ye never saw it."

✦ ✹ ✦

On the road back to Anya's barn, she kicked every little stone she saw. Her genius plan to get money wasn't so genius after all. Of course she wouldn't be able to sell the scale in Kievan Rus'. Dragons were outlawed here, and if she sold too many scales, people would begin to wonder where she was getting them.

The tsar would find out.

The idea of Håkon being hurt made Anya's skin prickle with cold. She wasn't sure how much good she'd do against the tsar and his *bogatyri*, or Sigurd, or whoever else came for Håkon, but she was sure she'd do her best to protect him.

"Anya!" The voice from behind her was becoming more and more familiar. Ivan trotted up the road, waving a hand. "Hey, wait!"

She did. As he came abreast of her, she started walking again.

A few steps of silence passed, and then Ivan said, "Nice day, right?"

"Why didn't you tell anyone about the dragon?" Anya asked.

Ivan's eyes darted around. "How do you know I didn't?"

"Your papa didn't mention the dragon at all," Anya said. "And I think that's something he would have asked me about."

"True." Ivan scratched the back of his head. "I dunno. I guess . . . I mean, I was going to. Completely. But then I got to the road and I realized you weren't behind me. So I went back some, and you weren't there. And then I started wondering why the dragon had saved us in the first place." He sighed. "Then you showed up and you weren't hurt. I thought maybe I shouldn't talk about the dragon just yet. I wanted to know what happened."

They reached the drive to Anya's house, and they

walked down it together. "What if he's nice?" Anya challenged. "What are you going to do?"

"I don't kn—wait, *he?*"

"He or she or whatever," Anya said.

Ivan pulled at his collar. "I don't know. I can ask Papa for advice. So—"

"If your papa and Dobrynya find out about the dragon, they'll take him to the tsar," Anya said. "And if they take him to the tsar, he's going to die."

Ivan's face went slack as they neared the barn. "Die?"

"Yes," Anya said, stopping outside the barn doors. "So this is very serious. If I told you the dragon was absolutely, completely kind and good, what would you do?"

Ivan inhaled like he was going to speak, but then he let the air out slowly. Once he had finished exhaling, he sucked in a short breath and whispered, "My parents taught us that a fool's true duty isn't to the tsar. It's to the people of Kievan Rus'. The tsar wants the dragon brought to him, but you're telling me the dragon is good. And I think I would be a bad fool to ignore what one of the people says, even if it's not what the tsar says."

A spark of hope warmed Anya's chest. "So you wouldn't tell anyone where the dragon is?"

"No," Ivan said. "I wouldn't even tell Papa. He says we serve the people first, but I've never seen him do that. And even if he did, Dobrynya is loyal to the tsar. Did you know he's the tsar's uncle?"

Anya did not. There was a lot about the tsar she didn't know. She'd never needed to know about him. As the local wisdom went: *God is far up high, and the tsar is far away.*

"I think you're a good fool, Ivan," Anya said, and she pushed the barn door open.

A red, dragony face met her, eyes bright and happy.

"I think he's a good fool too!" Håkon said.

CHAPTER TWENTY-FIVE

"HÅKON!" ANYA HISSED. She shoved the dragon's face backwards, then grabbed Ivan by the arm and pulled him into the barn behind her. She slammed the doors shut, heart pounding. Had anyone seen him?

Ivan stayed pressed against the door, eyes enormous as he watched Håkon coil on the floor before him. Anya put her hand on Ivan's arm, and he startled away from her.

"Oh, it really is here," Ivan said.

"His name is Håkon," Anya said.

Håkon stretched forward and extended a clawed foot. "It's nice to meet you!"

Ivan nodded and brought a trembling hand forward to shake Håkon's foot. "N-nice. Yes. Nice. Too."

Håkon pulled his foot back from Ivan after their handshake, and then he turned to Anya. "Surprise!"

"No kidding," Anya said, ushering the two of them away from the door and toward some hay piles that could hide Håkon if anyone came in. As they rounded the piles, the *domovoi* appeared as a cat, strolling by her leg without looking at her.

"Good job protecting the barn," Anya said.

The *domovoi* slapped his tail against Anya's leg as he continued past. He went by Ivan in the same manner, and the fool startled.

"Whuh . . . cat?" he asked, pointing.

The *domovoi* continued past to Håkon and rubbed against his side before vanishing into smoke. Ivan's face went slack.

"I guess my *domovoi* likes you both now," Anya said.

Håkon grinned. "We talked."

"What are you doing here?"

"I got bored," Håkon said. "How's your arm?" He snaked his head closer to her.

"Fine." She unrolled the bandage and held out her arm as Ivan stood stock-straight next to a hay pile, looking dazed. "My *babushka* put a salve on it. It's almost all the way healed."

Håkon hummed as he inspected the pink slashes. "That's good magic."

"It's not magic," Anya said. "Babulya is an herbalist."

"A magic herbalist," the dragon insisted. He sniffed her arm. "I can smell the magic in it."

"You can smell magic?"

Håkon nodded. "Smell it. Feel it."

"Well, she does use magic in her potions," Anya said. "But she starts with a good potion. The magic just helps it work faster, or something."

"She sounds interesting." Håkon whipped his tail back and forth. "I'd like to meet her."

Anya's chest tightened. "Would you?"

"Very much."

"Maybe you can someday," Anya said. "But first I need to talk to you."

Håkon stuck out his tongue and dramatically turned toward the cellar door.

"I'm serious!" Anya grabbed one of his spines, surprised at how smooth it was. He stopped and turned his head back to her. "It's important. It's about the Varangian."

"Sigurd," Håkon said darkly.

"Yes," Anya said. "And the *bogatyr*, and . . ." She had wanted to discuss the fools as well, but with Ivan there, it seemed rude.

Håkon glanced at Ivan. Too late, Anya realized she had looked at the fool while she thought about them. "And him?"

"No," Anya said. "I mean, yes. Kind of. His father."

"My father?" Ivan squeaked.

"Because of what we talked about," Anya said. "What he'd do to Håkon."

"Oh," Ivan said. "That's right."

Håkon looked between Anya and Ivan. "Are you friends?"

"I think so," Ivan said at the same time Anya said, "Maybe."

"Am I your friend?" Håkon asked Anya.

His question punched the air out of her and left her feeling hollow. Was he her friend? What did that mean, anyway? Anya hadn't ever really had a friend before. Zvezda was her friend as much as a goat and a human could be friends. There were a few other children in the village, but Anya didn't spend time with any of them. She was too busy, and her day of rest was different from theirs.

"Do dragons go to church?" Anya asked.

"What?"

"Church," Anya said. "I mean, I don't know what dragons believe about anything. Your faith."

"Oh," Håkon said. "Um, I don't go to church. I don't see what that has to do with being my friend."

"There are other children here, but they all go to church, and I don't," Anya said. "My Sabbath is different from theirs. So I don't play with them, ever. None of them are my friends."

Ivan said, "Really?"

"Yes." His pitying look was making Anya defensive.

"No friends?" Håkon tilted his head forward. "That's the saddest thing I've ever heard."

"Oh, shut up," Anya said. "Do you have any friends? Ivan and I don't count."

"Of course I do," Håkon said, and he lifted his head toward the open hayloft window. When he opened his mouth, he didn't speak or make a sound Anya expected from a dragon. He tweeted, and twittered, and warbled.

In the span of a breath, birds arrived, pouring through the window, jostling one another for a chance to get inside. Bright songbirds, drab little sparrows, huge black ravens, and a handful of hawks and eagles swooped in, landing on any available surface. The chickens stood around Håkon like a royal guard.

A hawk alit upon the hayloft railing and was unseated unceremoniously when a raven landed nearly on top of it. The hawk screeched, and the raven clacked an impatient beak at it. The hawk found a new perch.

Anya gaped at the horde of chirruping birds all around her, and she whispered to Håkon, "These are your friends?"

"Yep," Håkon said.

"The book was right," Anya said. "Can you talk to anything else?"

"Just birds," Håkon said. "And people."

"Did you tell my chickens to wait outside the house?"

"Well, yes," Håkon said. "I wanted to talk to you. I thought you'd follow them."

"What else can dragons do?" Ivan asked, awed.

Håkon shrugged. "Lots."

"I guess," Anya mumbled. "Sigurd said something to Dobrynya when they were fighting. He said, 'I'll show you what dragon blood can do.' What was he talking about?"

Most of the birds directed their attention at the dragon, who shifted uncomfortably.

"My father told me about Sigurd," Håkon said. "He's known as Sigurd Dragedreper: 'Dragonslayer.' He killed a great dragon a long time ago. And when he did, he ate the dragon's heart. He got some of the dragon's blood in him, and it gave him powers."

Anya swallowed. "What kind of powers?"

"He can talk to birds," Håkon said. "He can see spirits, like I can. And he's stronger. Braver."

"Wow," Ivan said. "So if I drank your blood, I could talk to birds?"

The gathering of birds—every last one of them —turned their heads toward Ivan, watching him with unblinking eyes.

He put his hands up. "I wouldn't! I was just wondering."

The barn door rattled, then slammed open. The birds erupted into a feathery whirlwind, cawing and chirping as they fled toward all exits. Anya spun, knowing it was Sigurd coming through those doors with his battle-hardened, bloodthirsty sword ready to cut all three of them down. She found herself in a panic, hoping he left the chickens alone. Her eyes darted between the numerous pieces of farming equipment around the barn, but none of it would make a dent in the Varangian.

Most of the smaller birds went out the window in the loft, but the others streamed out the doorway around the stone-still silhouette, just as Anya realized the person was too short to be Sigurd. Kin limped into the barn, letting the door fall shut behind him, acting as though a thousand birds rushing past was a normal occurrence. He stopped just inside, his eyes wide as he stared at Håkon.

"Kin," Anya breathed.

He ignored her. The dragon and the blacksmith stared at each other for a heavy moment, and then Håkon tried to run. He went for the hayloft, but a pitchfork ripped away from its spot on the wall and flew at Håkon. He skidded to a halt in time; the pitchfork stuck in the ground just before him.

Ivan and Anya huddled together, gaping at the possessed pitchfork wobbling before the loft ladder.

The *domovoi* leaped to the ground in front of Kin and transformed into a huge black dog, all the shaggy hair of his hackles up as his shoulders bunched. Kin's eyes dropped to him, widening as the *domovoi* snarled and snapped his teeth.

Kin pointed a finger upward, slowly, eyes never straying from the furious *domovoi*. The metal farm instruments hanging on the walls quaked. Then he hooked his finger and yanked it down, and all the tools ripped off the walls and shot straight for the house spirit. The *domovoi* yelped and vanished as metal hoes, shovels, and picks hit the ground where he had been.

Håkon spun and went for where he'd escaped the first time. But Kin whipped a hand up. The pitchfork tore off the floor. It raced at Håkon, and Anya screamed as it hit him.

The pitchfork's tines bent and stretched like claws, grasping Håkon around the neck and yanking him to a stop. He struggled against the trap, scratching at it with his claws. The chickens squawked and flapped around the barn, Håkon's distress sending them into a tizzy.

"Kin!" Anya yelled. "Stop!"

She ran at Kin, intending to shove him or otherwise distract him so Håkon could escape. Ivan ran with her, a step behind. A scythe that leaned against the wall stirred, then skidded across the floor at Anya and Ivan. Ivan shrieked at its charge and tried to dodge it, as did Anya, but it was smart. It followed them as they ducked this way and that, standing guard to keep them at bay.

Anya met Ivan's eyes and pointed at him, then pointed behind him. He nodded. Anya ran one way, and Ivan ran the other.

Something warm and solid grabbed Anya by the ankle, and she tripped. She hit the ground when Ivan did, and they both looked back to see what had snared them. The scythe was no longer a scythe: it had stretched into ribbons of iron, anchored to the ground with the handle the scythe had once been fastened to.

Anya couldn't get away from the metal pinning her ankle. "Kin!" she yelled.

He ignored her again, focused on Håkon. He walked toward the dragon, favoring his right leg, slowly and carefully.

She tried again. "He's nice, Kin!"

Kin didn't pause. He continued on his way to

Håkon, who was still trying to dislodge the pitch-fork from around his neck.

Kin's other hand went up, and the leftover horseshoes from the tack room flew out. They each wrapped around Håkon's legs, and one around his tail, and they held him in place, like he'd been mounted in midair. He couldn't thrash anymore, but Anya could still see him bucking against the restraints.

The blacksmith made a loop with his finger, then tied an invisible bow in the air. He let his arms down, and Håkon remained, his struggles growing weaker.

Kin leaned in close to the dragon, face pulled into a furious scowl, and he muttered two words: "Yer grounded."

CHAPTER TWENTY-SIX

K IN LOWERED HÅKON to the ground gently, setting him on his belly. The metal still
bound him, and Kin lifted a trembling, chastising
finger at the dragon.

"Yer lucky if I ever let ye in the river again," Kin
said.

Håkon stared at Kin, then nodded slowly.

Anya and Ivan looked at each other, then to Kin
and Håkon, then back at each other. "Kin!" Anya
yelled.

Kin opened his fingers, and the metal dropped

off Håkon. It untied itself from Anya and Ivan as well, and the scythe reformed into its proper shape. The pitchfork tines straightened, and all the instruments returned to their original places. The *domovoi* jetted to the cellar door and hid inside.

Kin stood in the center of the barn, Anya and Ivan gaping at him, and Håkon standing next to him with his head lowered.

"I bet ye think I owe ye an explanation," Kin grumped.

"An explanation would be nice," Ivan said.

"Well, tough!" Kin barked.

Håkon sighed. "Da."

Kin rounded on him. "Hmm? What was that? Da, what?"

"'Da'?" Anya crept closer. "Kin, *you're* Jernhånd?"

Kin glared even harder at the dragon on the floor and, through gritted teeth, said, "I suppose I am."

"But . . ." Anya searched for just one question and finally picked the one she thought would explain the most: "How?"

"None of yer business," Kin growled. He headed toward the door. "Come on, son."

Håkon hesitated and softly said, "But Da, I think we can trust—"

"I doubt that very much!" Kin yelled, spinning at Håkon. "I doubt ye think at all! I keep ye hidden for nearly thirteen years, and then ye decide to go play with the locals, and my hard work goes straight in the garbage!"

"It didn't, though!" Anya said. "We won't tell anyone about Håkon. Honest! Right, Ivan?"

Ivan nodded enthusiastically.

"No," Kin said. "We've got to get away from here before those heroes get wise. Or that Varangian."

Anya gasped as a sudden memory surfaced. "Sigurd's people kidnapped you!"

"It wasn't *his* people," Kin muttered, and then said, "It was, but not his specifically. Different village. Doesn't matter."

"How do you know him, then?" Anya asked. "Is that where you brought Håkon from? No, wait. He said you brought him from the south."

"Yes," Kin said, turning an irritated face to Håkon. The dragon sank down to the floor. "The south."

"What were you doing in the south?" Anya asked.

"It's a long story," Kin said. "And it's none of yer business."

Anya furrowed her brow, but before she could snap at the blacksmith, Ivan said, "Gospodin, I think it *is* our business. Håkon's our friend now. We care about him."

The three of them looked at Ivan, surprised. A chicken clucked from the hayloft.

Kin heaved a sigh. "Ye really care about him?"

"We do," Ivan said. "He saved our lives. He's a good person—er, creature. Dragon. He's a good dragon."

Kin said, "Well, if I'm going to tell ye my long story, we might as well be comfortable. Is there anywhere to sit?"

There was. Minutes later they were in the hayloft, with Håkon blocked from the door by some hay bales stacked three high. The *domovoi* appeared on the railing, plucking at his long beard as he listened.

Kin settled onto his bale with a groan. "I'll catch young Ivan up to what ye know, Anya. I was taken from my people when I was a child. Taken by Northmen from across the sea. I told ye I was young when I was taken, much younger than this band usually took. But they knew I had something they could use."

He lifted his fingers up, and the tools shuddered on the walls.

"Magic," Kin said. "Metal magic, specifically. They stole me to do work for them. Mend their weapons. Craft tools. A magical blacksmith at their service. I hated them at first, and especially the man I called Master. He did this to me." Kin patted his knee with a gentle hand. "Broke me the first few days I was with him. Wanted to make sure I couldn't run."

Anya frowned. "That's awful."

"It was my life," Kin said. "But then I got free from that master. The others in the town became my friends. I made a name for myself. I was a great blacksmith. And that's how I met Sigurd."

Anya's eyes widened. "You made his sword?"

"No," Kin said. "He already had it. It was broken.

He said a god broke it." Kin snorted. "But it's a magic sword, and only magic can repair magic. So he wanted me to fix it."

Ivan leaned closer. "Did you?"

"I did not."

"Why?" Anya asked.

"I could smell the evil on him," Kin said softly. "A man like that shouldn't have a sword at all, let alone a magic one. So I said no. Sent him away."

"Then what happened?" Ivan said.

Kin shrugged. "He got angry. Wanted to fight. But it's easy for a metal sorcerer to fight someone who wears metal armor. He was smart enough to leave when I gave him the chance."

"Fighting Sigurd," Anya mumbled. "That must have been scary."

"I wasn't afraid for myself," Kin said. "I would have thrown him from one end of my forge to the other. But I didn't want *her* to get hurt."

Anya almost asked who, but she knew: the owner of the headstone outside the little house. "Yelena."

Kin flinched at her name. "Yes. Another stolen child. A fellow slave. She helped me heal and helped me forgive, and when the time came, she helped me leave." He pointed a finger between Anya and Ivan. "I want to make something clear to ye. Not all Northmen are Varangians. The Varangians are men who left the North for various purposes. Most of them are good men, and most of them go back North when they're done traveling."

Anya and Ivan nodded.

"I wasn't a Varangian," Kin said, "but I traveled with them. Yelena came with me. The Varangians I traveled with were my friends, and we went south down the rivers. We were on our way to Istanbul when we found . . . the woman."

Kin peered over at Håkon, who rested his head on a hay bale. The dragon looked down at his own snout.

"Yelena found her, really," Kin said, "in what was left of a ragged boat. Not even a boat. A raft. The woman spoke the tongue of the Northmen, and she wouldn't let go of a bundle in her arms. Yelena came and got me, and we sat with her, and finally she handed the bundle to me."

He swallowed thickly and pressed his knuckles against his mouth. "I think she knew she was dying. She handed me wet rags with this tiny dragon inside." He nodded at Håkon. "I nearly dropped him out of surprise. We could barely understand a thing she was saying. She said his name, though. We got that. Håkon. Everything else was a jumble until the end. She screamed at us, 'The city, he'll die, the city, Istanbul, Istanbul.' And then . . ." Kin shook his head.

Anya was leaning so far forward, she almost lost her balance and fell onto the floor. "Istanbul? He was going to die in Istanbul?"

"That's what Yelena thought," Kin said. "The woman was fleeing Istanbul with a tiny dragon, but for what reason, we'll never know. Yelena said we couldn't go there. We couldn't leave the baby dragon, either. She was fierce about him. Told me she'd go raise him by herself if I wouldn't go."

To Håkon, Anya said, "Do you remember any of that?"

"No." Håkon shrugged. "I was just a baby. Do you remember things from when you were a baby?"

"I guess not," Anya said. "So, Kin, you left with Yelena and Håkon?"

"I did," he said. "Yelena grew up around here. Not in this village, but close enough to know about the valley. About how quiet and secluded it was. The rivers. The distance from Kiev. We brought the baby dragon here, but soon it was obvious he'd get too big to live inside the village and not be noticed. So I built a house in the ravine by the river, where he could swim and be safe." He sighed heavily. "And he was, until now."

"What happened to Yelena?" Anya asked.

Kin clasped his hands together on the table. "I don't know. Ten years ago, she went out in the morning, and she never came back."

Anya frowned. "I'm sorry," she said, and then she noticed the *domovoi*. He was still on the railing, but he was stiff, eyes wide, head cocked. Like he was listening to something.

Anya stood. She had seen the *domovoi* act that way when a storm was coming. The last time he had listened like that, a blizzard hit that trapped them inside for close to a week. That was his disaster stance.

But it was summer. There wasn't a blizzard coming, for sure. And earlier that day, the sky had been clear. What kind of disaster could the *domovoi* be hearing?

The *domovoi* looked at Anya then, his wide eyes full of terror. Desperation on his face, he pointed a gnarled finger at Håkon. His mouth opened, but he said nothing. He never did.

"What?" Anya asked, skin crawling.

Ivan and Håkon noticed the *domovoi*, and they came closer to Anya and the agitated spirit.

"What's he saying?" Ivan asked.

Kin stood. "Who's saying?"

"My *domovoi*," Anya said. "I don't know."

One of the chickens flapped her wings, and as she did, the barn door slammed open. Anya startled away from it, and the *domovoi* vanished from the railing as Sigurd rode his giant horse into the barn.

CHAPTER TWENTY-SEVEN

ANYA TURNED to Håkon. "Hide!" she said.
He did, ducking behind the hay, but it was too late. Sigurd fixed the hayloft with his cold eyes, a snarl on his face.

"Give me the dragon!" he bellowed.

"No!" Anya yelled, leaning over the railing to punctuate her words. "Never!"

Kin hobbled to the railing. "Ye'll only get to him stepping over my cold body!"

Sigurd drew his sword. "My pleasure." The fury in his eyes was enough to make Anya's belly drop, and a sick feeling spread through her. She swallowed hard, and then the *domovoi* appeared in the air over Sigurd's head. He raised his arms, and the tools on the wall shuddered as his magic pulled at them.

Kin grabbed Anya's shoulder. "Get out of here. I'll distract Sigurd."

Anya nodded and stumbled back from the railing as tools flew off the walls, rocketing for Sigurd. Anya retreated from the railing and Ivan followed her, dashing to where Håkon cowered at the back of the loft.

"You have to run, Håkon!" Anya said.

The dragon shivered. "Where? He'll just find me."

"How did he even find you here?" Anya wondered aloud.

She hadn't expected Håkon to answer, but he did. "The birds. They told him."

"Those traitors!"

"It's not that," Håkon said. "The little ones aren't smart enough to keep it to themselves. It's my fault. I never should have called them here."

Anya sized up the window. "Can you fit through here?"

Håkon darted for it but stopped short. He put his head up, cocked it back and forth, and snorted. "No!"

"Well, run out the door while Kin and the *domovoi* distract him!" Ivan said.

Anya looked down to the barn's main floor. Sigurd had dismounted and was using his sword to whack away the objects that the *domovoi* threw at him. Kin's fingers struggled in the air, and whenever he would grab hold of a thread, Sigurd would swing his sword at Kin with a snarl.

Kin huffed for breath and looked sideways at Anya. "Ye've got to get Håkon out of here."

"But—" Anya said, and then Sigurd let out a roar that shook the walls. He grabbed the wriggling, screeching *domovoi* out of the air, and his roar turned into a triumphant laugh. He flung the *domovoi* into the cellar and slammed the door shut.

Her mouth was dry. How could he grab the *domovoi*? How could he even see the house spirit? Then she remembered. *Dragon's blood.*

"He's too strong." Kin's words came out like

someone was sitting on his chest. "And he can . . . I don't know how he's doing it. He's cutting my threads. Every time I grab one, he cuts it. I can't control him. Get Håkon out of here; keep him safe."

"What about you?" Anya asked.

Kin limped to the ladder. "Don't worry about me." And then he was gone out of the loft to the floor below.

Kin reached a hand up, and the scythe he had used against Anya earlier flew to him. He hobbled across the barn floor toward Sigurd, and the Varangian smashed his sword against the scythe, knocking it out of Kin's hands. "I took the liberty of removing my weapon from your forge!"

Sigurd lifted a foot and kicked Kin in the chest. The blow launched Kin backwards, and as the blacksmith flailed for balance, Sigurd charged after him.

Kin managed to stay on his feet. He balled the horseshoes up and threw them at Sigurd.

Sigurd slashed his sword past the misshapen horseshoes, and they both jerked to a stop. The Varangian flicked his sword at Kin, and the horseshoes spun back around, like they were tethered to rope that Sigurd had caught on his sword.

Anya gaped. The tether was magic. Sigurd could manipulate magic threads with his sword.

Sigurd whipped the sword hard at Kin, and the horseshoes rocketed at him. Kin moved his hands, trying to pull threads, but the horseshoes didn't change trajectory. The metal hit Kin's head, and he fell backwards.

"Kin!" Anya yelped. He didn't move.

Sigurd looked up with a face like a thunderstorm, and he crossed to the hayloft ladder.

Anya ran back to where Ivan and Håkon were clawing and kicking a large hole in the barn wall to escape out of. The loft vibrated with every heavy footfall on the ladder's rungs.

"Go, Anya!" Ivan said, motioning to the hole.

Anya ducked for it but stopped when a loud *thump!* came just before a strangled cry from Håkon.

Sigurd's sword had him pinned against the wall by his tail. Blood dripped around the blade, and Håkon tried to bend back to claw at it. But every movement made him cry out more, and he collapsed against the floor.

"Håkon!" Anya screamed, and Sigurd grabbed her by the back of her dress. He snatched Ivan as the fool tried to run, and the Varangian threw them both out of the hayloft.

Anya yelped as she fell, but the sound *oof*ed out of her when she hit the packed ground. Ivan lay on the floor, not moving. She pushed herself up, dazed, as she heard the dull slam of Sigurd's boots on the barn floor. A moment later, he yanked her up again, holding her by the front of her dress.

"Little brat," he growled, reaching for a dagger at his belt.

Anya screamed and flailed, but his grip was like iron. As the dagger flashed in the light, something hit the side of Sigurd's head.

Sigurd bellowed as the *domovoi* latched his cat claws into the side of the Varangian's head and gnawed at his face. The dagger flew out of his hand. Sigurd managed to keep his grip on Anya while he swung at the house spirit. The *domovoi* vanished and then reappeared a moment later on the other side of Sigurd's head, where he resumed his attack.

Sigurd whipped Anya around as he flailed. He swung her toward Ivan, who was pushing up off the ground with what looked like a lot of effort. She yelled, "Ivan! Help Håkon!"

Ivan stumbled to his feet and nodded, heading toward the hayloft.

Sigurd grabbed the *domovoi*, his giant fist squeezing the house spirit hard enough for Anya to hear a squelch and a crunch. The *domovoi* howled with pain and clawed at Sigurd's hand, but it did nothing to loosen the Varangian's hold. Sigurd stomped to the cellar and kicked the trapdoor up, throwing the *domovoi* in as hard as he could.

The spirit bounced against the floor, then leaped back up. Sigurd brought the arm holding Anya back, and she realized what he was doing a moment before he did it.

She screamed as he threw her at the *domovoi*, barreling him backwards as they both tumbled across the floor and hit the well. Anya knocked stones into the rushing water, and her legs went frigid as she fell into the well.

"Ah! No!" Anya yelled, scrambling for a handhold. She gripped the remaining well stones, holding herself from being swept away by the water. It pulled too hard for her to climb out.

The *domovoi* flickered as he lay on the floor, transforming from dog to cat to old man. He climbed to his knees, his kippah sliding off the side of his head.

He shook his head, gaining his bearings, and went to charge up the stairs again.

Anya yelped, "Wait! Help!" Her legs were numb, and the cold was creeping up her body.

The *domovoi* froze, then turned, and his eyes popped wide when he saw her. He vanished and reappeared in front of her, tugging at her arms to get her out of the well.

A shadow passed over the cellar door as Sigurd stood before it. Anya watched the shadow linger there, terrified that he was on his way down to kill her like he'd promised to.

A pair of feet stepped on the top step, but they

were too small to be Sigurd's. Ivan stumbled down a moment later, tripping down the stairs, and he landed hard at the bottom. He looked up as the cellar door shut, and something scraped the outside, jiggling the handles around.

The *domovoi* finally pulled Anya out of the water. She lay on the floor, gasping. She couldn't move her legs. She was so cold.

Ivan cradled one arm against his chest, face wet with tears. He sat on the floor, hunched over his arm, shoulders stooped.

"Ivan," Anya said, shivering on the floor. "Håkon. Is he—"

Ivan bit his lip, looked away from her, and said nothing.

CHAPTER TWENTY-EIGHT

T HE *DOMOVOI* WAVERED between Anya and Ivan, then looked up at the ceiling as heavy boot steps clunked down on the floor from the direction of the hayloft. A moment later, something heavy dragged after the boot steps, and liquid leaked through the wood slats of the barn floor into the cellar.

The leaking fluid spattered over the floor in front of Anya. Blood.

"Håkon," she whispered, and then she screamed, "Håkon!"

The dragon didn't answer, and neither did Sigurd. The boot thumps and the sound of dragging dulled as they moved from the hollow barn floor to the solid earth outside. Anya put her forehead down on the floor, trying to hold in her tears. She succeeded, mostly. A few escaped to fall onto the dirt, but most of them she kept inside. Crying wouldn't help Håkon. She could cry later.

She managed to move her heavy, cold legs closer to her body so she could sit up. "Ivan, you have to open the door! Get back up—"

She stopped when the *domovoi* grabbed his own beard and yanked hard. He shrieked and ran up the steps, gesticulating frantically at the top.

She smelled something: smoke. Then the unmistakable dancing of flame winked between the floorboards.

Anya struggled to her cold feet, eyes wide as smoke began to seep through the floorboards into the cellar.

Ivan gawked at the smoke and flickering light on the far side of the cellar, then ran up the steps to join the *domovoi*. Using his back, he pushed against the doors and screamed, "Help! *Help! Let us out!*"

Anya hobbled to the door with him and also pushed. But Sigurd had done something to the outside, and the door gave only a tiny bit before it wouldn't go any further. They shoved at the door as the smoke continued to billow through the floorboards, and the fire spread wider, roaring as it went.

"Kin!" Anya turned to the *domovoi*. "You have to get Kin out of there! He got knocked out. He'll die."

The *domovoi* vanished. His footsteps thumped across the floor above them, and then came the sound of something else heavy dragging toward the door.

Anya and Ivan kept pushing, and then the *domovoi* was back. He hammered at the door with them, his kippah askew on his head.

"Is Kin outside?" Anya asked.

The spirit nodded.

Ivan looked at the house spirit. "Get out there and unlock the door!"

The *domovoi* bared his pointy teeth at Ivan and vanished, and Anya heard his pitter-patter on the other side of the door. He huffed to himself, paced around, and then whacked the door a few times.

"Open it!" Ivan yelled.

The doors heaved up but didn't open. They slammed back down, then heaved up again, and then the doors buckled. With a tremendous *crash!* a section of barn floor collapsed into the cellar. Sparks shot out, and flaming pieces of debris scattered across the floor. Anya and Ivan yelped and cringed, and the *domovoi* reappeared. His kippah was smoking, his jacket was singed, and his hands were blistered.

He shoved Ivan and Anya away from the door. They reached the bottom of the steps just before the cellar doors fell in, consumed with flames from the outside.

They huddled by the well, watching the barn above them go up in an inferno that nearly scorched them where they stood. Anya shut her eyes against the heat, coughing with every inhalation.

Ivan had his good arm around her, and he shuddered rhythmically. He was crying.

"Ivan," she said, "can't you . . . Your fool magic. Shouldn't that . . . save us somehow?"

He shook his head, face twisted with anguish, and said, "I don't . . . I don't *have* any fool magic."

Anya squeezed her eyes shut against the smoke. "Can't you just try?"

"No, I can't try!" Ivan yelled over the fire's roar. "If I try, it will backfire!"

She sniffed and wiped her face, not sure of whether the tears coursing down her cheeks were from despair or the smoke.

Ivan coughed. "I'm sorry, Anya." He coughed again, choking as the smoke thickened in the cellar.

She cracked her watering eyes open, and through the haze and the smoke, she spied the well. "Ivan, what about water magic?"

"Water?" He looked at the well. "I . . . I don't—"

"Please!" Anya said, motioning like she was scooping the water from the well. "You can put the fire out! At least enough for us to get out of here."

Ivan hesitated, and then his eyebrows met. He nodded. "You're right! If Dobrynya can use it to beat up Sigurd, I can use it to put out some fire!" He put his hands up, grabbing the air, yanking toward himself with a grunt.

He cringed, holding his hurt arm, and the well splashed a little.

"Ivan." Anya coughed. The smoke was too thick.

He clenched his teeth and balled his fists in the air. He pulled again. Still just splashes. The heat on Anya's skin was making her faint. She watched the cold water run past and wondered if they just got into the well, would it protect them enough? They'd just have to make sure not to let go and get . . . swept . . .

The water in the well. It was just an underground arm of the river, coming from the Sogozha and . . . *going back to the Sogozha.*

Anya grabbed the *domovoi*'s shoulder. "Go warn Babulya to get out of the house, in case the fire spreads!" The spirit clung to her, shaking his head, and she said, "Don't worry. I have a plan. We'll be okay."

The *domovoi* scrunched his face but obeyed, vanishing as another section of floor crashed in.

Ivan yelped, and Anya grabbed his uninjured arm. "Hold your breath!"

"What?" he said, and then sucked in a huge lungful of air as Anya jumped into the well, pulling Ivan into the freezing water after her.

CHAPTER TWENTY-NINE

T HE LIGHT WAS GONE immediately, and Anya was swept away from the well opening in the breakneck darkness of the river. She still held on to Ivan's arm, praying the underground river wasn't full of debris and roots to catch and hold them until they drowned.

A few little roots smacked Anya as she went, and she scraped her legs and feet on the bottom of the river a few times, but she mostly continued unobstructed.

Until she hit a large, hard something. She was stuck against it for a moment, and Ivan slammed into the back of her, which knocked her loose, and she barely managed to keep ahold of his arm as she started moving again.

The current ripped at her, attempting to drag her onward, but now Ivan was stuck on the whatever-it-was. Anya raised her free hand, trying to figure out what had him snagged, and he grabbed her.

She couldn't see him in the pitch-blackness, couldn't see what held him. The coldness numbed her fingers, and she could hardly even feel him.

Then Ivan dislodged her hand from his arm. Too fast for her to resist, he squeezed her hand—and let go. Anya released a blurt of bubbles as the current carried her away from Ivan, leaving him alone in the darkness.

The underground current spat Anya out into murky light, and her lungs screamed for air as she clawed toward the surface. Her head broke the water, and she sucked in a loud, desperate breath that caught a few water droplets and sent her coughing and choking.

She looked toward the shore as the slower current carried her downriver. The flames of her barn were taller than the trees, a titanic torch licking at billowing smoke in the sky.

Anya struggled to the shore, shivering and aching all over. She heaved herself onto the muddy grass slope and set her forehead against the wet ground.

Ivan.

He had pushed her away.

She stayed on the shore, watching the water, waiting for him to come.

Minutes passed. They stretched out as her barn groaned and collapsed, shooting sparks up to illuminate the black clouds like fireflies in the night.

Then the water bubbled.

Anya perked, sitting up, eyes wide. Her heart jumped, so hopeful that Ivan's dark head would break the surface.

The hair that emerged was red. A *rusalka's* empty eyes peered up at her.

Anya's heart still jumped, but with despair rather

than hope. She wasn't even afraid of the *rusalka*; that emotion had been overshadowed by her overwhelming guilt.

The *rusalka* remained where she was, but she brought her head up farther out of the water. The expression on her white face was one of concern.

"Please," Anya said. "The underground river . . . there's a boy trapped in there." She shivered and huddled in on herself. "Help him. Please."

The *rusalka*'s concerned expression remained unchanged, and she vanished under the water. Anya didn't dare hope the *rusalka* would find Ivan and bring him to safety, but she remained on the shore just in case.

As she waited, she thought. Sigurd had taken Håkon somewhere alive. Why hadn't the Varangian killed Håkon in the barn? That would have spilled too much blood, perhaps. Sigurd might have needed a special place to do his bloodletting. Maybe Anya had time to save Håkon.

But how could she do that? She didn't have any

backup, or weapons, or even know where Sigurd was. Without some kind of help, Anya was never going to find him in time.

"No," she said aloud to herself. She couldn't think like that.

Babulya had quoted part of the Talmud to Anya on Shabbat: "Whoever destroys a single life has destroyed the entire world." But there was another part to that. If she saved one life, she would save the entire world.

Anya held her breath until she couldn't anymore. The *rusalka* didn't come back.

She had already failed to save Ivan. She wouldn't fail Håkon, too.

Anya crouched in the trees off the road by her house. The barn's roof had fallen in, and some of the sparks jumped to the house just as Dyedka arrived with the goats. She watched the *domovoi* shoving the goats into a messy herd while Babulya stood nearby with her shawl clutched around her shoulders and Kin sitting at her feet, coughing. Dyedka trundled in and out of the smoking house, carrying books and a handful of Babulya's plants. Anya was glad she had told the *domovoi* to get Babulya out.

Voices echoed up the road from the village. People must have seen the smoke and were on their way to help. She had to get away before they showed up.

Sigurd's mount had left deep hoof prints in the dirt of the road, heading north. She followed the prints until the road forked, and then they went west. After the prints crossed the bridge over the Sogozha —the bridge with the fisherman trail beside it that led to Kin's secret ravine house—they took a sharp left on a meager path, directly south into the forest.

The sun dipped low in the sky, sinking behind the trees as Anya came to a shivering stop on the road. If the northern forest was dangerous, the southern one was even more so. The farther south the forest went, the more dry birch and pine would give way to the swampy shores of the messy, meandering Sogozha.

She stopped at the path's mouth, fear slowing her. The Varangian wasn't the only dangerous thing in the swamp. The local *leshy* would get her lost, which was something she couldn't afford right now. *Vodyaniye* and *bukavac*s prowled the waterways, hungry for people foolish enough to venture in. And besides them, she had to worry about plain old wolves and *zmeyok*s.

Fear slowed her, but a different kind of panic got her started again. She could be hurt or killed in the swamp, but that wasn't for certain. Håkon would definitely die if she did nothing to stop Sigurd. She wouldn't be able to live the rest of her life knowing that her cowardice was responsible for the death of one of the last dragons, and knowing that Håkon had saved her life and she hadn't returned the favor.

Anya licked her lips and clenched her fists, and as the red of the setting sun lit the forest, Anya plunged into it.

CHAPTER THIRTY

I N THE FOREST, Anya followed the path as it
wound south, at first between enormous mossy
trees. As the forest became wetter and swampier,
she had to avoid stepping into still, black pools that
looked like shadows. The sun's dying red glow vanished, replaced with the rising full moon's pale light
through the skeletal trees. Anya wished desperately
for a lantern.

She stumbled along, careful to stay on the path
so she could find her way back if she needed. Every
few minutes, she would pause to get her bearings
and listen for any sounds in the swamp.

The third time she stopped, she thought she heard rustling. It stopped just after she did, and she told herself it was her imagination.

The fourth time, the rustling was still there, and she heard the distinct sound of footfalls on the wet ground before whatever was following stopped along with her.

Anya took a deep breath, attempting to steady her panicking heart. It wasn't a *leshy*. *Leshiye* were silent in the woods, and they rarely harmed people. The *leshy* would confuse her and send her wandering. Since that's what she was doing anyway, she doubted more wandering would hurt.

A *bukavac* made a lot of noise—after all, that's what its name meant. Dyedka had told her about a *bukavac* he had driven away from the village before, and how the monstrous little creature had made such a ruckus, it had caused Dyedka to go nearly deaf. It had also killed a man and maimed another before they had successfully exorcised the thing. She didn't know if they were noisy the entire time they hunted, though, or if they were smart enough to be quiet if they wanted to. Anya hoped whatever was following her wasn't a *bukavac*.

That left a *vodyanoi*, and Anya shuddered. The fishermen in the village would trade stories at the end of the day as they unloaded their catches and set their boats up for the night. Anya had heard stories of *vodyaniye* attempting to capsize smaller boats or drown people who got too close to the river. They rarely ventured into the water near the village, preferring to stay in the area near the swamp, so only the foolhardy were at risk of being dragged into the Sogozha's depths.

Anya's eyes flicked to the swamp around her. She felt pretty foolhardy at the moment. She didn't know how far out of the water a *vodyanoi* would come for a victim.

She searched her pockets, scrambling for anything metal. More often than not, spirits of any kind didn't like metal. If a *vodyanoi* was after her, she could scare it away with iron. Maybe.

Her pockets were empty of anything metal, populated chiefly by small pebbles and assorted scraps of yarn. She stuffed the trash back down into her pockets, scowling.

The footsteps trailing her hadn't started up again yet, so she stood still, waiting, searching the darkness for some kind of monstrous shape. The swamp's stillness was disturbed only by the croaking of a frog and the splash as it leaped into a puddle nearby.

Anya decided she had wasted enough time on a creature that might not even be real. The footsteps might have been in her imagination, and while she was standing there scared, Håkon was potentially having his heart cut out. She steeled herself and turned, ready to find the Varangian.

She hadn't moved yet, but a wet footfall squelched from behind her.

Anya froze, heart hammering in her chest. She was cold all over.

Another step.

She turned. She knew she should run away as fast as she could, but she had to know what was stalking her in the darkness.

Off to the side of the path, a pair of eyes reflected

the moonlight at her. The creature they belonged to was tall and skinny, like a horse that had been pulled until its limbs stretched into spider legs. It was covered with scraggly, long ropes, like vines or tree roots. They dripped swamp water on the ground. It hunched over, standing on six legs but using the front two to feel the ground in front of it. Uneven horns jutted from the sides of its head.

A huge *bukavac*.

As Anya stared at it, it opened its black mouth and groaned. Then another mouth opened beside the first, teeth flashing in the moonlight. The second mouth emitted a different noise, a high-pitched squeal that made Anya's toes curl. The sounds got louder and louder until they bored into Anya's brain, tearing at her sanity.

She ran.

The creature behind her ran as well, and it started bellowing. The sound vibrated in the air and into Anya's ears, making them ring as she fled.

She ran, concentrating only on not colliding with anything that would slow her. She could hear the *bukavac*'s steps behind her, the scuttling rapid-fire of six feet punching the ground as it chased her. It screamed without taking a breath; beneath the screeching, Anya could hear slobbery licking, like the second mouth had stopped howling in anticipation of another use.

The cold swamp air burned Anya's lungs. Every breath she took stabbed pain into both sides under her ribs. Her shoes were soaked from stumbling through puddles. She hadn't fallen yet, but she couldn't see where she was going, either.

And then . . . the path was gone.

The ground wasn't where she anticipated when she stepped. She lurched, uttering an ungraceful "Hurk!" as she pitched forward. She dropped a few heart-stopping feet into a puddle. Her face hit the water, and she scrambled up and back, gasping for air as she tried to claw her way out of the mud.

The creature's screaming and slobbering intensified, growing louder as it approached. The mud around Anya vibrated with every step the *bukavac* took. She waded closer to the shore, then pulled herself out of the mud and onto more solid land.

She got one step into a run when the monster whipped out a long, spindly leg and swatted her feet out from under her. She hit the ground hard, the air rushing from her lungs all at once.

The creature screamed with both mouths again, different discordant pitches that rattled the marrow in Anya's bones. She clutched her ears with both hands and rolled away from the mud pit, chest tight and breath hitching. Her head felt like it would explode at any moment; through the buzzing in her ears, she could hear one of its mouths smacking loudly.

Anya kicked out at it, but it swatted her feet away. Hot spittle dropped on her, and the *bukavac*'s corpse breath washed across her face. Its screaming was louder, closer, and the noise filled Anya's brain with agony.

In a final act of desperation, Anya flailed her arms and legs, hoping she would catch it in a vulnerable spot and shut it up for five seconds so she could regain her sanity. Her feet hit its legs, but it didn't buckle. One hand swiped at nothing but empty swamp air.

The other hand hit something cold and wet.

The wet thing held on to Anya's arm.

The *bukavac*'s screaming changed. It sounded angrier.

Whatever held Anya's arm pulled her away from the screeching monster. She opened her eyes to see what was saving her—or more likely, what was trying to eat her before the *bukavac* could.

Dark spots clouded Anya's vision. She made out the wispy outline of something vaguely humanoid, and then her eyes focused long enough to recognize it.

"Ivan . . ." she mumbled.

The *bukavac* snarled and bellowed with both mouths, and Ivan's cold grip on Anya's arm went away.

Angry roars changed suddenly into pained squeals and yelps. Anya dared a look at what it was yelping about. Ivan stood, feet planted in the mud, before the creature. One arm played strings in the air; the other was swathed against his chest. Whips of water slapped at the *bukavac*'s face, snapping and cracking as they hit. Then Ivan heaved his arm from one side to the other, like he was throwing a bale of hay over his head, and the pool's water rose up in a muddy tidal wave. It crashed into the monster, knocking it over in a tangle of legs and ropy appendages. Anya's ears rang and buzzed from the *bukavac*'s screeching, and then it turned and fled.

Anya rolled to her back, gasping as the silence of the swamp became deafening. Her mind was fuzzy and dark, vibrating against her skull in a frenzy, like it was trying to escape. Her chest was still tight. She felt like she couldn't get a breath, and she sucked at the air as her arms and legs roiled between burning and numbness.

It felt like someone was sitting on her chest. The dark spots expanded, filling up the outer edges of her vision.

Ivan was at her side then, eyes wide. His cold,

cold hand was on her arm, and his mouth moved. She couldn't hear him. Why couldn't she hear him? Why was his hand so cold?

Oh no.

He had drowned. He was a *rusalka*. She hadn't heard of a boy *rusalka*, but drowned men had to go somewhere. Anya tried to suck in a breath to speak, to apologize for leaving Ivan to die, to beg his forgiveness. She couldn't, and the dark spots rolled across her vision like thunderclouds.

CHAPTER THIRTY-ONE

T HE DARKNESS ROLLED OUT as it had rolled in, leaving a splitting headache and sore muscles in its wake. Anya groaned and flopped toward where Ivan had sat, succeeding in rolling to her belly before her strength went out of her.

She lay face-down on the wet ground, puffing in and out of the side of her mouth. Her arms wouldn't work to push her up.

Cold fingers grasped her shoulder and tugged, rolling her to her back again. Anya stared at her dead friend above her, and tears started pouring down her face.

"I'm s-so sorry!" Anya sobbed. Her own voice sounded muffled and far away.

Ivan shushed her and pulled her to him awkwardly, hugging her one-armed. He was damp, and his skin was cool like the *rusalka* that had grabbed Anya in the river. He wouldn't speak. He still had his eyes, but maybe that was something he would lose over time.

"Please forgive me!" Anya continued to cry. She wanted to hug him back, but there was no way. Anya's arms felt like challah dough: floppy and damp. "I would have tried to get you out, but it was so dark, and then you pushed me away, and, Ivan, I'm so sorry I *let you die!*"

His eyebrows shot upward. "What?" His voice sounded muted and distant, like he was speaking with a pillow against his face, but she still heard him.

She gaped at him, and then shouted, "You can talk!"

"Yeah?"

"You're not a *rusalka*!"

"I'm not a—" He shook his head. "Of course I'm

not a *rusalka*. But"—he lifted a finger—"a *rusalka* did pull me out of that tunnel."

"Really?" Anya wondered if it was the same one she'd asked for help.

"I used my water magic like I did when Sigurd threw us in the river." Ivan pointed to his broken arm. "But this arm was stuck in a bunch of roots, and I couldn't pull it out. And I couldn't use my other hand to pull myself out, or I'd lose the magic. The *rusalka* saved me." He stared off into the distance. "I was wrong about them."

"You were wrong about dragons, too," Anya said.

He rubbed his swathed arm. "And your *domovoi*."

"You'll have to edit your book," Anya said.

"I guess." He looked around. "So where are we going?"

"Ivan, you're hurt," Anya said. "You shouldn't come with me." She turned back into the heart of the swamp. "I have to find Sigurd before he kills Håkon."

Ivan swallowed hard. "Anya—"

She spoke, interrupting him before he could try

to talk her out of finding the Varangian. "I've already made it this far." She lifted her arms, indicating their surroundings. "I didn't fight a *bukavac* and get lost in a swamp so I could run away before I even found Sigurd! So you don't have to come, Ivan, but I'm—"

"I'm coming with you," Ivan said.

Anya paused. "Really?"

"Yes," Ivan said.

"What about your arm?"

Ivan shrugged. "I don't want to leave you alone."

"Aren't you scared?" Anya frowned.

"I'm terrified. But . . ." Ivan shifted on his feet. "I want to be a hero. And heroes don't abandon their friends."

Anya smiled. "Thank you."

He tapped his injured arm softly. "Well, I don't think I'm going to do much good against Sigurd with a broken arm."

Anya shrugged, and they walked back to some semblance of a path on the swampy ground. She didn't want to tell him that she didn't think a good arm would make a difference against Sigurd.

CHAPTER THIRTY-TWO

ANYA DOVE DEEPER into the dark swamp, Ivan following carefully behind her. She stayed on the path, anxious to reach the end. She wasn't sure what would be worse when they reached it: finding Sigurd and fighting him, or finding nothing at all.

"I can add a *bukavac* to my compendium," Ivan whispered from behind Anya. "With not one but *two* firsthand accounts of battling it!"

"Lucky you," Anya said. They crossed over another little bridge, and the path wound around a large tree.

Anya came to a halt, and Ivan nearly ran into her. The path abruptly ended at the edge of a clearing. In the center of the clearing sat a hut with smoke wafting out of the chimney. A waist-high fence made of swamp-wood posts stretched around the hut's perimeter. The hut had no door.

Ivan whispered, "Anya, that's Baba Yaga's hut."

"Baba Yaga isn't real, Ivan." But her mouth was dry, and her heart was beating fast. "We should leave."

Anya moved to continue past the hut, and Ivan grabbed her arm with trembling fingers. "Wait. We should go in."

"That's crazy," Anya hissed. "We don't have time for that. Håkon—"

"She could help with Håkon!" Ivan argued. "We don't know where he is, or how we're going to get him away from Sigurd. In the stories, she helps sometimes."

Anya pulled her arm from Ivan's grip. "In the stories, she also eats children sometimes."

"Still."

"Baba Yaga isn't *real*," Anya repeated. "It's probably just a hermit's house or something."

"There's no door," Ivan said, as if that explained it.

"Maybe it's on the other side," Anya said.

Together, they followed the fence around the clearing, searching for a door until they came across one. Two windows on either side glowed like jaundiced eyes in the darkness. A gate in the fence hung open on crooked hinges.

"See?" Anya said. "There's a door. It's not Baba Yaga's hut."

"She's tricking us," Ivan whispered.

Anya rolled her eyes. It was just a swamp hermit's house, and they were wasting time. She moved to continue past the house, but something caught her eye. At the top, a carving of a dragon stretched from one side of the door to the other. The dragon was familiar.

Anya looked back at Ivan, who was shaking in his boots. He wheezed out nonsensical words, and Anya said, "Ivan, that dragon matches the one on Yelena's grave marker. That can't be a coincidence."

Ivan nodded slowly. "Do you think we should go in?"

"I think *I* should," Anya said, "but your arm . . ."

Ivan's wide eyes were locked onto the hut, and though he continued to wheeze, he shook his head. "If we're getting eaten, we're getting eaten together."

Anya took Ivan's good hand in hers, and they started toward the gate. But before they could pass through it, the door to the hut swung open, and heavy orange light spilled out. Ivan and Anya both jumped and clung to each other as a figure silhouetted against the light stomped to the doorway, halted just inside, and jammed its hands to its skirted hips.

"Don't just stand there!" the figure snapped. A woman. An *annoyed* woman. With a lilt to her words that was kind of like Sigurd's and kind of like Kin's. "If you're going to save Håkon, we have to hurry!"

And the woman spun and marched back into the

house, leaving the orange-lit doorway empty. Anya looked at Ivan, and he looked at her, eyes wide and popping. They scrambled through the gate, across the small yard, and into the little hut.

CHAPTER THIRTY-THREE

THE HUT WAS WARM—almost too hot— after the coolness of the swamp. It was a single round room, and bookshelves covered every wall from floor to ceiling. The shelves were stuffed with books of all sizes, shapes, and colors. The windows flanking the door had benches in front of them with poofy pillows on top; the yellow glow Anya had seen from the outside came from hanging lanterns dangling on thin chains, casting light over the window seats.

Anya and Ivan hurried farther into the room, their dirty boots sinking into a plush carpet that covered the floor. Small tables dotted the room, with more books stacked on top of each one. More books were stacked under the tables and teetered on the fireplace mantel. Anya tried to guess how many books had been crammed into this one room, but the only thing she could think was *Every book in the world is here right now*.

The room's hearth crackled on the opposite side from the door, and a pair of great big chairs sat before the fire. The woman was nowhere to be seen. The room was silent except for the fire's grumbling.

Anya swallowed hard, peering up at Ivan. He was breathing loudly through his nose, searching the room with wide eyes.

"I think," he said softly, "that was Baba Yaga."

"She's not Baba Yaga," Anya said.

"She could be," Ivan argued.

"But she isn't!"

Anya and Ivan jumped as the woman spoke from behind them. She bustled past, books stacked high in her arms. She wasn't very tall, maybe coming to Ivan's shoulder, and she had long auburn hair braided to her waist, with a white kerchief over it. She dumped the books into one of the chairs by the fire and began pawing through them as she said, "I'm *not* Baba Yaga. Her hut has chicken legs on it. And I don't eat children. I just enslave them."

Ivan choked a little, and Anya backed up, ready to kick the door open so they could escape.

The woman turned with an impish grin on her freckled face. "Just kidding."

Anya had wasted enough time being lost in the swamp, and she wasn't going to waste any more. "You said that to save Håkon, we had to hurry."

"We do." The woman checked book after book, tossing each rejected tome onto the other chair. "But I have to find the right—Aha! Finally!"

She snatched up a red book and flipped it open, coming toward Anya and Ivan. She looked about Mama's age. The white apron over her white dress had blue waves embroidered along the top.

The woman rustled through the pages, then thrust the book at Anya. "Read that page. You'll know when to stop." She pointed a finger at Ivan. "You. Come here. Bring that broken arm with you."

Anya and Ivan stared, wide-eyed. "What?" he said.

The woman sighed and pinched the bridge of her nose. "You can't fight the Varangian with a broken arm. Now, give it to me."

"Why?" Ivan leaned away.

"Because I'm going to heal it!" the woman snapped.

Ivan remained where he was. "Are you a witch?"

"No." The woman glowered at him.

Ivan narrowed his eyes. "A *vila*?"

"No."

"*Kikimora*?"

"What?" She frowned. "No."

His eyes got wide. "An *upyr*!"

"I'm a person!" the woman said. "Just a person, and I died, and I'm trying to help you."

Anya said, "You died?"

"Yes," the woman said. "It doesn't matter. We need to hurry."

"Why are you trying to help us?" Anya asked.

The woman groaned, exasperated. "Because."

Anya almost asked what that meant, but then she realized she already knew. A person who had died but remained in order to help others. A nice ghost. She pushed Ivan's shoulder gently toward the woman. "Go, Ivan."

He balked. "But what if she—"

"She won't hurt you. She's an *ibbur*." Anya looked at the woman. "You are, aren't you?"

The woman held her breath and nodded. "Yes."

Ivan shrank away from her. "Don't possess me."

"Please." She rolled her eyes. "If only this could be that easy."

Anya clutched the book to her chest. "I'm . . . I'm sorry you died."

The woman shrugged. "I'm lucky, all things considered. Now, Ivan, get over here. And Anya, read that page."

Anya looked down. The words inked on the paper were old and faded. In some places, they weren't even Russian. But she tried anyway: "'And here begins the tale of mistletoe, that most unassuming and gentlest of plants. For though it has always been soft and kind, it was once used to kill. Three brothers: one beloved, one blind, and one wicked. The wicked brother, through trickery, coached the blind brother to kill the beloved one with an enchanted dagger of mistletoe.'"

Ivan's pained squeak made Anya look up. He grimaced and held up his broken arm, tears leaking from the corners of his eyes. The woman stood by him, fingers plucking at the air, head cocked like she was listening to something.

The woman peered up at Anya and said, "Keep going."

Anya watched a tear roll down Ivan's face. "But—"

"He'll be fine," the woman said, gritting her teeth. "Keep going."

Anya hesitated, then started again: "'The dagger, thrown by the blind brother, pierced the heart of the beloved brother, and he died. The mistletoe was so distraught, it vowed never to be rigid enough to form a dagger again. But the existing dagger could not be destroyed, and so it promised never to harm another through trickery, or by accident.'"

The paragraph ended at a drawing of a sprig of mistletoe, and Anya looked up at the woman. She flicked her eyes at Anya. "Good job."

Ivan sucked in a high gasp and clutched at his arm.

"Are you hurting Ivan?" Anya asked, reaching for her friend.

"No!" the woman said. "Maybe. Yes. Don't touch him. I'm almost done. It's been a while since I practiced."

Anya pulled her hand back and watched Ivan suffer through the woman's healing. "Why did you want me to read that?" Anya asked. "That was a sad story."

"So you'd understand." The woman let her hands drop and said to Ivan, "Move your arm."

Ivan stopped grimacing and gingerly tested his

arm's range of motion. He moved it in every direction, his careful wince turning into a broad smile. "Anya, look!" he said, torquing his arm back and forth. "She fixed me!"

Anya squinted at the woman. "How do you know Håkon?"

The woman snatched the book from Anya. "That's not important. Not now, anyway. Later, probably. But not now." She spun and returned the book to the pile on the armchair, tossing it on top. "Anya, I need your help to keep him safe. I can't do it myself. Will you help me?"

Without hesitation, Anya said, "Yes. Of course."

Ivan swung a hand between Anya and the woman. "Wait! What does helping entail? Are you going to possess Anya?"

"No one is getting possessed," the woman snapped.

"It doesn't matter, anyway!" Anya swatted Ivan's arm again. "I'd agree to be possessed. It's helping Håkon!"

"That's so sweet, but I can't possess you," the

woman said. "This isn't that easy." The woman took a breath. "I see the futures. There are a thousand endings to every story, and only by the telling does the ending become clear."

Anya swallowed hard, and Ivan asked, "You see the future?"

"*Futures.*" The woman sighed. "We're wasting them. The new sun. He is dying *now*."

Ivan opened his mouth, but Anya smooshed her open palm against his face, pushing him back as she said, "Håkon is dying? What do we do?"

"You won't like it," the woman said, now hurrying to the nearest bookshelf. She rummaged through the shelf, pushing books this way and that, removing small wooden boxes and grunting when she opened them. Then, finally, she pulled a box off a shelf, flung back its lid, and stopped. She reached one hand toward Anya and said, "Come here."

Anya ran to her as the woman pulled a sharp stick out of the box. It was longer than Anya's hand, a dark, dark wood. It looked relatively unremarkable, but it made the air around it shiver.

The woman offered it to Anya, but she didn't want to take it. She was sure the wood would feel cold under her fingers. "What is that?"

The woman continued to hold it to her. "Don't you recognize it?"

"Why would I—" Then she realized she *did* recognize it. "The mistletoe."

The woman nodded.

Anya raised a trembling hand and grasped the wood in unsteady fingers. It wasn't cold. It was uncomfortably warm, like a beating heart.

The woman balanced her finger on the long blade of the wooden dagger in Anya's hand. "I see two ends, two futures for this story. This dagger is the fulcrum, the point on which both ends balance. Death, but only if you want it. Use it. Blood is best in the new sun." She peered past Anya at Ivan. "Now is the time for action, fool."

Ivan was silent, and the woman left Anya to sweep past Ivan on her way to the door. She stopped there, hand on the door's handle, and she said, "Do not fail him. Strike when the time comes. Be true."

She pushed the door, and a dark, packed-earth landing stretched before them.

"Strike?" The mistletoe felt hotter in Anya's hand. Maybe that was because she was gripping it so tight. "Strike Sigurd? But the mistletoe in the story didn't want to kill anyone again."

"Yes," the woman said. "But it will. Not through trickery. Not by accident. Only if you want it."

A cold feeling settled in Anya's chest. "I stab him. And if I want him to die, he'll die?"

The woman answered with a slow nod.

Anya's hand quaked. Sigurd had tried to kill Anya and Ivan twice each, three times if she counted when he had thrown her into the river near her barn, but she still didn't think she could . . . "I can't. I can't kill someone."

"Because you will destroy the world, hmm?" the woman asked. "If you commit this sin to save a life, have you destroyed the world, or have you saved it?"

"I . . ." Anya felt unsteady everywhere. "I don't know."

The woman's face fell into a sad frown. "Do not fail him. Please."

The pain in the woman's voice scraped at Anya's heart, and she blurted, "Who are you?"

The woman took a deep breath, like she was going to answer, and then an invisible force shoved Anya and Ivan toward the door, through it, out of the hut, and into the night.

CHAPTER THIRTY-FOUR

ANYA AND IVAN stumbled out into the darkness. As they turned around to look at what exactly they had stepped out of, the door slammed shut and vanished.

Ivan shuddered and said, "What happened?"

Anya stared at the empty night, clutching the mistletoe in one hand. She knew what she thought had happened, but it seemed too crazy to be real. There was a mistletoe dagger in her hand, though, and they were no longer in the swamp, so it had to be real.

Anya registered the dull roar of a river. They

weren't standing in a wooded swamp but rather on a cliffside lookout, halfway up the path that wound its way to the top of the ravines north of Zmeyreka.

The moon was gone, but it was light enough to see. Dawn approached.

"'Blood is best in the new sun,'" Anya mumbled, repeating the mysterious woman's words. "Do you think . . ." She trailed off, understanding lighting her brain. Sigurd needed Håkon's blood for his powers, and if blood was best in the new sun, then dawn would be the best time to spill it. She looked skyward, where the sun was making the horizon rosy. The new sun would be there any moment. "The sunrise! Ivan, we have to hurry!"

Anya ran up the path with Ivan behind her. As they neared the top, the day grew closer; Anya had never before dreaded the sunrise.

They neared the top of the cliff, both wheezing and gasping for air after trudging the last few hundred feet of the steep path. The river ran at the base of the ravine behind them, its roar bouncing up to them at the top. The valley behind them slept in darkness, but an unwelcome glow was descending.

At the top, Sigurd stood by a huge dead tree, sword pulled. A stack of wide, flat rocks had been built near the tree; a large stone bowl rested on top of it. Sigurd's horse was on the other side of the flat area, tethered to a live tree that grew beside the river that roared over the cliff's edge. Håkon was secured in a net on the ground before Sigurd, eyes shut. Not moving.

Anya's heart thumped to a stop in her chest. They were too late. Håkon was dead.

Then he moved his tail the tiniest bit, and Anya released a held breath of relief. But as Sigurd shifted the sword in his hand, she realized they were barely there in time.

She picked a small stone off the ground and turned to Ivan. She whispered, "Hide! I'll distract him, and you get Håkon out of here!" She waited for Ivan to nod and hide on the path over the cliff, and then she threw the stone at Sigurd. It bounced off the back of his head as she yelled, "Hey! Sigurd!"

Sigurd turned slowly, face curled into a furious grimace. When his eyes focused on her, he uttered what were probably several Varangian swears and bellowed, "Why won't you die?"

Anya felt much less brave when Sigurd was glowering right at her, but she didn't want him to know that. She did her best to square her shoulders and grip the mistletoe in her fist as she paced away from the path.

"Let him go!" she demanded.

The Varangian's snarly face tightened. He brought the sword up, twisting it in a wide arc, and said, "None of your heroes are here to save you now. You'll die at the end of my sword this time."

Anya kept pacing as Sigurd stepped in huge, menacing strides toward her. Behind him, Ivan snuck up the path and padded past the tree toward Håkon.

Anya did her best not to watch Ivan, not wanting to draw Sigurd's attention to him. In her mind, she was planning her escape route: She could follow the cliff-top plateau north for a way, and then there were rock jumbles and trees she could hide in.

By the time Sigurd gave up chasing her, Ivan would have Håkon away safely, and . . .

And Sigurd would chase them. He'd kill Ivan, kill Håkon, and none of their efforts would have mattered.

The mistletoe felt heavy in her hand. *Strike when the time comes.*

Could she? If she did, would she destroy the entire world, or save it?

Ivan was picking apart knots in the ropes that tied Håkon down. Without realizing it, Anya glanced their way as the sun crested the hills and splashed its first waves over the valley. Sigurd followed her eyes back to the dragon.

"Sigurd!" Anya screamed, trying to distract him again. He ignored her and charged back toward the fool.

Ivan tried picking one more knot, but Sigurd was approaching too fast. Ivan stood and backed away, stumbling toward the cliff edge, where he teetered as Sigurd closed in.

Anya ran toward them, knowing there was no

way she could get there in time. She wouldn't be able to cross that gap before Sigurd shoved Ivan off the cliff and stabbed Håkon. They were dead. Ivan was dead. The last dragon in Kievan Rus' was dead.

Sigurd bellowed as he raised his sword at Ivan. Ivan tried to dodge to one side or the other, but Sigurd lunged in every direction he tried for. Håkon was struggling in his ties, trying to flop toward Ivan, but the knots bound him up too well. His tail was caked with blood, and his struggles made new blood flow from his wound.

As Sigurd swung his sword, Ivan lifted his hands, clenching his fists. Then he ripped his hands down, and a huge ball of water shot out of the river. It slammed into the side of Sigurd's head, exploding and raining water in a wide arc. Sigurd stumbled to the side, his swing going wide and slicing nothing but air.

The fool took his opportunity to escape from the cliff's edge, heading away from Håkon and yelling as he pulled more watery missiles out of the river.

Anya ran to Håkon, sliding to the ground next

to him. She sawed at the rope frantically with the mistletoe dagger, but it made slow progress.

Håkon watched Ivan. "I didn't know he could use water magic."

"He didn't really either," Anya said, sawing through the first length of rope. "Can you try chewing this rope or something?"

"I could, but I can't reach—"

She shoved some rope in his mouth, and Håkon gnawed on it while Anya kept slicing at the hole she was making.

Ivan whipped ball after ball of water at Sigurd's face, forcing the Varangian to keep his head down and his eyes shut. Ivan moved to the side, arcing around so he wasn't a still target for Sigurd's mounting fury.

"Almost," Anya grumbled, and the rope finally frayed enough for her to yank it apart. She had cut three consecutive pieces of the net, and that was enough space for Håkon to wiggle his long body out.

As Håkon pulled his bloodied tail free of the net,

Sigurd roared. Anya looked up in time to see him charging in their direction, Ivan forgotten.

"Run, Håkon!" Anya shoved him toward the river, but he resisted. His face darkened with fury, and he whipped his tail up. A ball of water shot out of the river like a cannonball, and just before it hit Sigurd, it crunched into ice. The ice ball shattered as it hit Sigurd's face, knocking him down. Pieces of ice littered the ground.

Sigurd fell and didn't get back up. His face bled from cuts. A steady trickle of blood seeped out of his nose. His sword lay on the ground a few inches from his outstretched hand.

"Is he dead?" Anya asked.

"No." Håkon nodded toward the Varangian. "He's breathing."

Anya let out a sigh of relief. "Let's get you out of here before—"

Heavy footsteps pounded up the path, and Anya turned as Dobrynya and Yedsha appeared at the top.

CHAPTER THIRTY-FIVE

ANYA SHOVED HÅKON behind the dead tree, hoping he wasn't seen. He crouched down, coiling himself into as small a ball as he could, and Anya ran to where Ivan stood. If she could make sure Yedsha and Dobrynya's attention was away from the tree, hopefully Håkon would go unnoticed.

Yedsha came up the path first, and he sprinted to Ivan and Anya. He grabbed them both, smooshing them together in a bone-cracking hug as he yelled, "You're alive!"

Ivan and Anya wiggled, trying to squirm out of

Yedsha's grip. Of course she was alive. Why would he think she wasn't?

Then she remembered. The barn. The fire. It was strange to think her barn burning down wasn't the most unbelievable thing that had happened to her that night.

"Uh, yes," Anya said, managing to dislodge herself from Yedsha's hug. "We're alive."

Dobrynya came toward her, sword pointed at Sigurd. "What happened?"

Concentrating hard on not looking toward Håkon, Anya said, "What happened? Um, you know, that's a long story."

Yedsha pointed to Sigurd. "We have to do something about this one. The blacksmith said he's the one who started the fire in your barn."

Anya grinned. Kin wasn't hurt! Or if he was, he wasn't hurt too badly to speak.

"He was," Anya said, just as Sigurd stirred. He grunted as he opened his eyes and rolled over. He spat blood onto the ground.

Dobrynya leveled his sword at Sigurd. "Put your hands on your head!"

Sigurd didn't acknowledge Dobrynya's order. He grabbed his sword and got to his feet, unsteady, but not unsteady enough for Anya's taste. He would still be formidable.

"Drop your weapon!" Dobrynya ordered.

Still, Sigurd ignored him. He faced the enormous tree where Håkon sheltered, frowned, and charged at it. He stabbed his sword through the trunk, then heaved the sword through one side. He shoved the half-felled tree hard, and it crashed to the ground. Dead wood plinked as it snapped and shot off in every direction.

From behind the tree's remaining stump, a red head peeked out, blue eyes huge and terrified.

Sigurd roared and grabbed for Håkon. The little dragon dodged backwards, scampering over jagged branches in an attempt to escape.

"Come here!" Sigurd yelled, crashing after Håkon through the wood.

"The dragon!" Dobrynya gasped, then took off after Sigurd.

Anya watched Håkon flee, slithering as fast as he could go. He was moving erratically, panicked, not thinking. She had to help him.

The river. He could hide in it and use his magic to ride down the waterfall and get away. It was his only hope.

Yedsha grabbed Anya and Ivan and pulled them down the path.

"Wait!" Anya yelled. She struggled out of his grip.

"Stay back," Yedsha said. "If you get caught between them . . ." He shook his head. "We already thought you both were dead. I won't let it happen for real."

Anya heard Sigurd bellow, and she yanked her arm out of Yedsha's grip. She ran back to the plateau, ignoring his cries for her to stop.

She reached the top of the path as Sigurd swung his sword at Håkon and missed, barely. Håkon squeaked and pulled his tail tighter to him, pushing off to try to gain some ground as his blood spattered the rocks behind him. Every step brought Sigurd closer.

Håkon changed direction as Sigurd stabbed his sword down. The blade missed Håkon's tail by a hair's breadth, driving into the rocky ground instead. The sudden stop made Sigurd trip, and Dobrynya slammed into him.

Håkon raced toward Anya. He got closer, and Anya could hear him saying the same word under his breath: "Help. Help. Help."

"The river," Anya said, pointing.

Håkon nodded, and they both ran to the riverbank. Håkon nearly dove in, but at the last moment, he hesitated.

"What are you doing?" Anya said. "Go! Hurry!"

"And then what?" Håkon said. "They'll both come after me no matter what. I can't go back home and put my father in danger. So I'll be on the run for the rest of my life, alone, and that's not a life I want to live." He sighed. "I'll never be happy that way."

Anya wanted to shove him into the water, but he

was completely right. He was a fugitive, and Sigurd, Dobrynya, and Yedsha would hunt him until the end of his days.

The mistletoe dagger in Anya's hand throbbed, and she remembered the mysterious woman's instructions: *Death. Only if you want it.*

But what if she didn't want it?

Across the plateau, Sigurd shoved Dobrynya away and heaved himself to his feet. He turned, snarling as he set his eyes on Håkon and Anya.

Strike when the time comes.

She imagined she could feel Sigurd's footsteps on the ground as he charged toward her and Håkon. Maybe it was just her imagination. It didn't matter. The time the woman had spoken of had come.

Anya turned to Håkon, throat tight and nose stinging. "I want you to be happy." Her voice cracked as she said the final word, and as soon as she did, she lifted the mistletoe dagger and stabbed Håkon in the chest.

CHAPTER THIRTY-SIX

ANYA HEARD SIGURD SHOUT and Ivan scream, but both of those sounds faded into background buzzing as Håkon's mouth dropped open with surprise. He looked down at the piece of wood embedded in his chest, and then back up at Anya.

"Anya?" he asked. She didn't hear it over the buzzing, but she could tell that's what he said.

Her vision blurred with tears, and she bit down hard on her lower lip to keep it still. She yanked the dagger back, pulling it out of Håkon's scaly chest with a wet smack. Blood followed the dagger, splattering on the ground and the front of Anya's dress.

"Go home," she whispered, and she shoved him backwards.

Håkon fell into the river. He didn't swim against the current, and in the time it took Anya to inhale, he was gone over the waterfall's edge.

The roar of the waterfall was all she could hear for a moment. The dagger in her hand was sticky with blood. Her friend's blood.

The thundering of Sigurd's feet was louder, and then he grabbed her by the arm. He yanked her around to face him and screamed in her face, "What have you done?"

She didn't have an answer. She hadn't thought he'd bleed like that. The woman said the dagger would kill only if Anya wanted it to. Had she lied?

Sigurd shook Anya hard and screamed at her some more. Then he stopped, and he said, "Give me that dagger."

Anya pulled it back. "No."

"The dragon's blood is on it!" Sigurd swiped for

it, and Anya felt the subtle crunch of the dagger's sharp tip piercing Sigurd's palm.

He didn't act like he felt anything at all, and he grabbed the dagger from Anya. He lifted it to his mouth and licked once, twice, and then stopped. He dropped the dagger to the ground. His arms went limp at his sides. Blood trickled anew from his nose, and more from his ears, and then he fell forward without putting his hands up to catch himself. He slammed into the ground, taking the impact full in the face.

Dobrynya limped up, holding his side with one hand and his broken sword with the other.

"Are you hurt, Anya?" Dobrynya asked.

"No," she said, and noticed blood seeping between his gloved fingers on his side. "Gospodin, you're bleeding!"

"I'll be fine," he said. "Just a little nick, is all." He hooked the toe of his boot under Sigurd's chest and kicked him onto his back. The Varangian didn't move. He stared at the sky with frozen-open, bloody eyes.

Dobrynya winced at the sight. "Good God. What happened to him?"

Anya glanced at the mistletoe dagger. "I think it was the dragon blood," she said, not really thinking that at all. The dagger had poked Sigurd's hand, and just like the woman said, it killed him. "He licked some off that stick I stabbed the dragon with."

"I heard dragon's blood gave a person special powers," Dobrynya said. "I never heard about it killing someone."

She didn't say anything. Ivan stood at the top of the path, staring at Anya with disbelief. She'd explain herself to him later, maybe. If he let her.

CHAPTER THIRTY-SEVEN

ANYA FOLLOWED DOBRYNYA down the road toward the village. Ivan walked close behind her, with Yedsha bringing up the rear, leading Sigurd's horse by its reins. She kept checking around for Håkon's red head peeking out at them, but she never saw it.

To break the silence they traveled in, Anya asked Dobrynya something she had been wondering. "How did you know where we were?"

Dobrynya smiled. He had his hand pressed against his injured side. "I didn't know you'd be there. I thought you were dead. But I knew Sigurd would be there."

"How?"

"Yedsha and I have been all over this valley, between the two of us," he said. "He mentioned this plateau to me, and the altar. I knew Sigurd planned to use the dragon's blood to make himself more powerful, and . . ." Sheepishly, he said, "I admit. I have looked into the ancient rituals. Not for myself," he added quickly. "Just to understand. The greatest magic in the world is an open mind. So when Kin told us Sigurd had been there, I thought maybe he had found the dragon somehow. If he killed the dragon, he'd need to do it at sunrise, and he'd need a way to make sure the blood didn't get lost."

Anya shuddered at the thought of her friend's blood in the stone bowl. "I'm glad you figured it out. I guess Ivan was right about how smart you are."

Dobrynya's smile faded. "Smart, but not fast enough. I'm sorry we didn't realize he had taken you two as well. Do you know why?"

Anya tensed. He thought Sigurd had kidnapped them. Of course he did. What other reason did they have for being there?

"I don't know why he did it," Anya said, and Dobrynya didn't press.

They came out of the woods onto the road north of town. The wood smoke still smoldering from the barn fire made Anya's eyes water, and her stomach clenched.

Dobrynya turned onto the drive to Anya's farm, and the rest of them followed. The entire village was gathered in the field between the river and what remained of the barn and the house. Most of the villagers were smudged with soot and dirt, and others were all wet. They all looked exhausted and heartbroken.

The *bogatyr* cut a path through the crowd, with Anya following close behind him. The crowd gasped and murmured as they saw Anya and Ivan.

Near the riverbank, the crowd thinned. The house and barn were gone, and smoking piles of ash and charred wood were all that remained.

The villagers nearer to the remains of the house held buckets, and a few were patrolling near the ash, looking for embers that still needed extinguishing. The goats were milling behind the ash pile that had been the house, bleating every now and then, like they were confused. Zvezda had his head lowered, gazing toward the river. If goats could be forlorn, Anya thought Zvezda looked very forlorn.

Someone sobbed, and when Anya peered around Dobrynya, she stopped cold. Her mother was on her knees under the willow tree, hands over her face, bawling as Ivan's mother, Marina, knelt beside her. Marina also cried and had her arms wrapped around Mama's shoulders.

Mama and Marina weren't alone. Dyedka and Babulya huddled together, foreheads touching, silent, with eyes shut. Babulya clutched the Torah, wrapped in its mantle, in her arms. Ivan's brothers stood in a tight gaggle. All but two had their faces turned down, and the two with their heads thrown back were openly wailing.

Ivan stopped beside Anya, and he murmured, "Mama?"

Zvezda trotted over from the herd, turned his eye to Anya, and then let out a loud *"MYAH!"*

One of Ivan's brothers looked up, and his brilliant blue eyes widened. He pointed at Ivan and screamed, *"Vosya!"*

All of Ivan's brothers looked up now, and the two who had been wailing silenced abruptly. After a heartbeat's pause, they all ran at Ivan, shouting his name.

Ivan took a step back, hands up, and said, "What's the—*grk!*" as they barreled into him, knocking him to the ground. Each one tried to hug Ivan.

"Vosya!"

"You're alive!"

"We thought you were dead!"

"I'm not dead, Pyatsha! Get off!"

"But you *burned up!*"

"I'm so glad you're not dead! I would have been the youngest!"

"You're not a ghost, right?"

"I'm alive, Semya! I'm fine, Shestka! Get off!"

Anya smiled at Ivan's brothers' enthusiasm, and then she realized Yedsha was gone. She looked up the drive in time to see him disappearing around the trees onto the road, and then Mama gasped, "Anya?"

She turned as Mama stood, eyes wide. Her mother said nothing as she ran to Anya, and the hug she enveloped Anya in was nearly rib crushing. Anya wheezed under the force of Mama's hug, and then she returned the embrace.

Mama cried against Anya's kerchief. As she looked past Mama's head, Anya spied Dyedka talking to Babulya, and the old woman wiped tears from her face with one hand as she smiled. The *domovoi* in his cat form sat beside her, and his tail whipped back and forth behind him against the ground. He glared at Ivan's family with his ears flattened back against his head.

"Mama," Anya whispered, "I'm sorry."

Mama sobbed. "I'm so happy you're not hurt."

"But the house—"

"Oh, the house." Mama released Anya and wiped

the tears from her face. "The *domovoi* got Babul-ya out before the fire spread. He even managed to get out our clothes and all the books." New tears streamed down her face. "We can rebuild a house, Annushka."

Anya's heart sank. What good would be rebuild-ing a house if their land got taken away?

Ivan's mother ran up to Mama then, her beauti-ful smile brightening the day.

"Masha, they're back!" Marina yanked Anya into a hug, pressing Anya's face against her dress bodice. Ivan's mom smelled like the river after a thunder-storm, and a handful of salt crystals, and some kind of flower that Anya couldn't place, and an ice-cold winter night. She was warm, and soft, and Anya leaned into her.

Marina released Anya long enough for her to get a breath, and then she hugged her again. "Oh, I'm so happy you're not hurt, Anya! We all thought you were . . . Well, never mind what we thought. We're so glad you and Vosya are here!"

She swept her arm toward Ivan, who was still being hugged and petted by his brothers.

Marina threw her arms around Dobrynya then, and he winced against his injured side. "Thank you for bringing them back, Dobrynya."

"Of course," he said, then laughed. "They didn't make it easy."

"No," Marina said. "My Vosya never does."

Yedsha returned, and he wasn't alone. The magistrate followed, perfectly clean and looking incredibly irritated that he'd been disturbed and dragged to the farm. When he passed the burned place where Anya's house and barn had been, his eyes bugged.

"Gospodin Ivanov," the magistrate said softly as he halted in the field, "why—"

"You told me no one lived here," Yedsha said.

The magistrate observed the burned home, the sooty villagers, and said, "You don't understand."

"I understand you lied," Yedsha said. "Because you wanted to, what? Force these people off their land?"

Mama moved to Anya's side and put her arm around Anya's shoulders. "He told them what?"

The magistrate's face got red, and he stammered, "I said . . . What I said was, er, I said there *would be* an empty house, and . . ." He trailed off, mouth curling into a furious grimace, and he spat, "They're *Jews!*"

Anya's mouth dropped open, and Mama sucked in a strangled sob. Everyone in the crowd was silent.

"I was doing this village a favor!" the magistrate continued. "We don't need a family of Jews here. We don't need them in Kievan Rus' at all!"

Mama clutched Anya closer and sobbed. "Oh God," she whispered. "Oh God."

Frenzied, the magistrate screamed, "And I know you all agree with me! This is a Christian village. Jews are a *blight!*"

The magistrate stalked toward Mama and Anya, waving an accusatory finger at them. He turned to the fishermen in the crowd, panning over each in turn as he spoke. "This family is the reason the river is low! They poison the water!" He pointed at the nearby river.

Anya wanted to ask him what sense that made; if they poisoned the water, they'd be poisoned with everyone else. But she couldn't speak. Her palms were cold and sweaty, and she was dizzy. Her heart slammed against her lungs, knocking the air out so she couldn't catch her breath to ask any of the thousand unanswered questions in her head. Did they really agree with the magistrate? Did the village hate Anya's family? Would they be glad when they were gone?

The magistrate was still ranting. He spun to another side of the crowd. "They're why there are so many demons here! They're cursed! It's *them!*"

Anya grabbed Mama's arm. She realized several people had moved closer to her and Mama, and her heart pounded.

Dusty old Bogdana Lagounova—the chandler who Dyedka thought was terrible—stepped forward. She held a bucket in one wrinkly hand. "I think you should go," she said.

Anya felt Mama shudder as she sobbed, and Anya went cold inside.

"Yes!" the magistrate trumpeted. "Throw them out!"

Bogdana threw her bucket to the ground. "Not them. *You!*"

The magistrate's triumphant cry died in the air. "What? Me? What possible reason—"

"I think you should go too." Father Drozdov joined Bogdana.

"And us." Sveta Mihaylova said. Her sister, Zlata, stood at her side, silent, but she held a piece of charred wood like a club.

The magistrate watched with mounting disbelief as the other villagers voiced their agreement.

"You stupid peasants," the magistrate growled. He panted, sweat glistening on his forehead. "Miroslav Kozlov would have been a Christian if not for *her.*" He jabbed a finger at Mama, who recoiled away from it. "She tempted him away with . . . blood sacrifice, and converted him! That's why I had him sent away! Jews aren't supposed to be conscripted. The tsar *doesn't want them!* So I told the conscription officers he was Slavist!"

Mama gasped. She trembled and whispered, "Miro . . ."

"You *what?*" Dyedka shouted from behind the crowd. He stormed forward as best he could on his wooden legs, eye fiery with hatred. "You sent my boy away to die!"

The magistrate sneered. "I sent him away so he could be free from her influence. Not that a heathen would understand salvation." He faced Dobrynya. "I had to get him out of the village. I have to get *all of them* out. You understand, don't you?"

Dobrynya's mouth tightened, and he shook his head. "What you did was wrong."

Anya watched Dyedka's fingers twitch, then swim through the air, reaching for threads she couldn't see.

Every goat in the herd turned to look at the magistrate.

The magistrate noticed Dyedka's movements, and he went from pleading with Dobrynya to glaring at Dyedka. "Don't. You. *Dare.*"

"Or what?" Dyedka spat, bringing his hands up. The goats took a step toward the magistrate, Zvezda in the lead. "Or you'll have *me* conscripted?"

The magistrate pointed to Dobrynya. "I'll have you executed!"

Mama moved. She stepped forward, hands up, yanking threads. Her eyes were hard, shining with fury and grief.

The magistrate's threats died in the air as a slender willow branch snapped around his arm, tightening as another snatched the other arm. The magistrate wailed as Mama pulled more plant-magic threads and more branches wound around other parts of him. She stepped toward him as the tree dragged him back toward the river.

Anya watched with awe as Mama wordlessly followed the magistrate to the riverbank. With a flick of Mama's wrist, the willow's graceful, slim branches jerked the magistrate, tossing him a few feet offshore.

The magistrate went under and surfaced seconds later, gasping and sputtering. His meager hair was plastered to his forehead and the back of his neck, with small pieces flopping this way and that as he floundered in the shallows.

"You thought you were in trouble before this!" the magistrate shrieked. "There's a *bogatyr* right here! He'll throw you in prison, where you belong! You'll rot there! *Die there!*"

Anya's stomach turned sour, but Mama didn't seem to hear the magistrate's threats. She finally spoke, her voice smooth and calm: "Gospodin *bogatyr*."

"Dobrynya Nikitich, Gospozha."

She nodded. "Dobrynya. You may take me to prison. But please let my husband's regiment know what happened. Please bring him home."

Dobrynya put a finger to his lips, thinking. "I think you've suffered enough because of this man's ignorance. If you promise me not to use your magic to throw him into the river again, I'll forgive your trespass this time."

"And my husband?"

"As soon as I leave here, I'll speak with the proper authorities to have him sent home."

Mama nodded, a curt single shake. "Thank you."

"What?" the magistrate shrieked from the water. "No! She broke the law! She deserves to go to jail!"

Anya stomped closer to the river, her words ripping out of her: "You broke the law too! Don't you deserve to go to jail?"

The magistrate screamed nonsense as he flopped toward the shore. The water behind him bubbled.

A head surfaced, but it wasn't the red of a *rusalka*. A *vodyanoi* rose up, his green hair matted with algae, tiny black scales clustering here and there on his sickly green skin. He looked froglike; his eyes were wide on his face, his nose was flat, his mouth was lipless and wide.

The *vodyanoi* grinned, needle teeth flashing.

The magistrate was oblivious to the danger behind him. He continued ranting about Mama going to jail and ignorant children and respect for elders.

"Behind you!" Anya yelled.

"Do *not* interrupt me!" the magistrate screeched.

Dobrynya bellowed, "Get out of the—"

The *vodyanoi* leaped forward, hitting the magistrate from behind. They both went under the water. The magistrate surfaced, floundering, sputtering, gasping for air.

"*Help!*" he screamed, then vanished under the water.

A willow branch whipped over the water, then plunged into it where the magistrate had disappeared. It strained as it tightened, then withdrew and hauled the magistrate out by his ankle, still screaming, with the *vodyanoi* clinging to his back. As the branch dragged him out of the water, the *vodyanoi* howled and leaped back into the safety of the river.

The branch released the magistrate once the *vodyanoi* had fled, and he collapsed onto the ground in front of Mama with a wet squish.

Mama stood over him, her shadow covering his face. "You're a terrible, wretched man," she said. "But I didn't throw you into the river so you could die." She pointed a finger at the road. "Now get off my property."

The magistrate glared at her, then pushed himself off the ground. He straightened out his wet, dirty shirt, marched stiffly to the road, and vanished around the trees.

Bogdana yelled, "Good riddance!" then picked up her bucket and went back to scooping up debris.

Anya started toward her mother, but Father Drozdov beat her there. He wiped his robe's sleeve across his forehead and said something to Mama that Anya never expected from the priest.

"So," the Father said, "what are you making for Shavuot?"

CHAPTER THIRTY-EIGHT

ANYA HAD NEVER EATEN so many bliny in her life.

The village square was decorated with a hodge-podge of greenery, flowers, and leafy garlands, plus a small birch tree the villagers had moved from the forest to the square. The tree was decorated with ribbons and beads, and the villagers danced around it while they sang old Slavist songs.

Many of the villagers provided Mama with milk and cheese, and she made dozens and dozens of bliny for everyone. Every family brought a table, some chairs, and a dish to share. Old Andrei Vasilyevich strummed a *gusli* on and off all afternoon, and Ivan taught Anya to dance the way he learned in Kiev.

The magistrate didn't come. His house was empty.

No one ever saw him in Zmeyreka again.

Exhausted from Ivan's energetic dancing, Anya took a break with two bliny and went to sit by the bridge to her house. She ate slowly, watching the water. Did the river seem higher? Or was she just being hopeful?

A raven landed on the ground in front of her as Ivan came to sit by her side. They watched the raven strut back and forth across the road, and then the bird hopped closer, eyeballing the food in Anya's hands.

Ivan stared at the bird with squinty eyes. "Do you think Håkon sent it?"

"It just wants food." Anya tore off a piece of the blin, tossing it to the raven.

The raven flapped its wings and gobbled up the morsel, then croaked at Ivan.

Anya sighed. "If only Håkon sent it. Then I'd

know he's alive." She hadn't seen Håkon since he had fallen off the cliff the day before. Kin had been absent from the village as well, so she couldn't even ask him. When she went to Kin's house, no one answered the door. His smithy was dark and cold.

The raven croaked again and bounced forward, flapping its wings. This time when Anya threw blin at it, it didn't eat.

Anya threw another piece of food. The raven cawed again, ignoring the treats being lobbed at it. It looked at Anya, head twisting side to side.

"Do you know where Håkon is?" Anya asked in a low voice.

The raven tapped its beak on the ground. *"Caw!"*

"Is that a yes?" Anya asked. "I can't tell."

The raven ruffled its feathers and glared at Anya. It picked up the blin but, instead of eating it, tossed the piece over its feathery shoulder, north, toward where Kin's house hid in the ravine. Then, with huge exaggerated steps, it marched to the blin piece.

Anya's heart raced, but before she could ask the

raven anything else, it snapped up the blin and flew away over the bridge.

"So weird," Ivan said.

Anya wasn't sure if it was weird or if it was a message. She and Ivan went back to the celebration.

Dobrynya lurked near the tray of bliny Mama had made, sneaking one after another until Mama approached him.

"You like my bliny so much that you're staying, Gospodin *bogatyr*?" Mama asked.

Dobrynya stopped mid-bite. "Well, I can't leave now, Gospozha. What if the magistrate decides to come back? I have to be here to defend you."

Mama nodded. "Of course."

"Besides, if these get left out, I'm sure they'll spoil."

"They will," Mama said. In a quieter voice, she said, "Thank you for sending for Miro. I think, after all you've done for me, you could call me Masha if you'd like."

Dobrynya just smiled and stuck the rest of the blin in his mouth.

Anya glanced toward Kin's smithy again, and she saw the door crack open. Kin peeked out, and when he caught Anya's eye, he motioned for her to come over.

"Ivan." Anya pointed to Kin, and they both hurried to him, passing by Dyedka and Yedsha making plans for the new Kozlov house and barn. Before she made it past, Yedsha looked up and saw her.

"Anya!" He put a hand out, stopping her. "Look at our plans. What do you think?"

She studied the drawings they had made and noticed one of the sleeping rooms had a tall loft in it. She pointed. "What's that?"

Yedsha thumped her on the back. "Well, your *dyedushka* and I figured a girl brave enough to stand up to a mad Varangian probably deserves a space for herself. Don't you think?"

Anya didn't dare believe it. Her very own loft? It would be in the same room as Mama, but somehow being a few feet above her seemed like such a huge thing. "Yes. I think that would be very nice."

He grinned, then nodded behind her. "I think Vosya is waiting."

She turned. Ivan stood by Kin, motioning for Anya to come over. As Anya approached, Kin said, "So I guess this is some kind of flowers-and-cheese holiday, huh?"

"It's Shavuot."

"The day ye eat cheese?"

"It's remembering when we received the Torah," Anya said, and after a pause, "and when we eat cheese."

He smiled, and a shiver of guilt chilled Anya's skin. "Where have you been, Kin?"

"Busy," he said. "Sigurd's horse needed attention. I've named him Alsvindr."

"Oh," Ivan said. "That's . . . nice."

Kin laughed. "Alsvindr is the horse that pulls the moon across the sky. I think it's a good name." He shrugged, then said softly, "I've got something for ye. Come inside."

Anya and Ivan followed Kin into the smithy. Anya looked around, hoping Håkon's ruby head would poke up from behind an anvil. Kin pulled a long, cloth-wrapped item from one of his workbenches. He handed it to Anya, and she unwrapped the cloth to reveal a shining sword beneath.

"Kin," she breathed, barely whispering.

"It's Sigurd's sword," Kin said.

Anya frowned. "What?"

"I helped Dobrynya and Yedsha bury him," Kin said. "And I asked for his sword. Neither of them wanted it. I melted it down and made ye yer own sword, Anya. And Ivan . . ." Kin disappeared behind his forge for a moment, then came back with a long staff. Either end was capped with gleaming metal. "Ye're taller. I think ye've got the skill for a staff, as well."

Ivan took the staff from Kin, eyes wide. He ran his hands down the smoothed wood, then lifted it and bounced against its weight. "Thank you."

Kin nodded. "The metal's magic, and ye can use it for magic. Yer both well deserving of such weapons. But . . ." He lifted a finger. "Ye can have them only on one condition. Ye leave them here until I've trained ye to use them."

Anya grinned. "You're going to teach us to be fighters?"

"No. I'm going to teach ye to use yer weapons," Kin said. "Yer already fighters."

Anya was fine with that. She imagined being older, wielding the magical weapon, and going on adventures with Ivan and Håkon. He'd be a *bogatyr*, and she could be a different kind of hero, and Håkon could . . .

The fantasy fell away as reality intruded. Anya rewrapped the sword and handed it to Kin. "Thank you for the sword, Kin." She took a deep breath. "Have you seen Håkon?"

Kin fiddled with the magical sword's cloth wrapping for several long seconds, saying nothing. He took Ivan's staff and the sword into the ember-lit depths of the smithy, and then sunlight spilled in as the front door opened wide.

Anya and Ivan turned. Dyedka hobbled in. Zvezda peered around one side of him, and another goat shoved on the other side, both trying to force their way into the smithy. He swatted them back and said, "Annushka, you'll never believe it!"

He turned back to the village square. Ivan trotted after him, pushing the goats out as he went. Before Anya left, she peered back into the smithy's darkness, where Kin lingered by a forge, quiet.

"Kin." She had to know. "Have you seen Håkon?"

Kin said nothing. Then, so quietly she barely heard him, he said, "He'll send for you when he's ready."

Her breath caught on its way in. "Annushka!" Dyedka hollered at her from outside, and she went to see what was so unbelievable.

An enormous brown hawk perched on Dobrynya's arm, its claws digging into his leather bracers. The huge bird wore what appeared to be a leather vest, with a solid cylindrical case attached to the vest on the hawk's back. Zvezda stood at Dyedka's side, neck stretched up as far as it would reach to sniff at the bird's tail.

"It's a messenger hawk." With his free hand,

Dobrynya uncapped the case and teased out a stack of rolled papers. "I've never seen this many papers, though."

One of the papers fluttered out of his fingers, and Anya stooped to grab it before Zvezda ate it. As she did, she read the writing on the top of the paper: *To my darling Masha.*

Her mouth dried up, all the moisture apparently being converted into stinging tears. She would know her father's script anywhere.

"It's . . ." she mumbled. "It's from Papa." She turned to her mother, who stood frozen by the bliny tray, one hand clutched over her heart. "It's for you."

Mama's face trembled, but she didn't cry. Stiffly, she hurried to Anya and eased the letter from her. She read the letter, eyes darting back and forth so fast that Anya was sure she couldn't actually be comprehending the words.

But then Mama smiled, laughed, and said, "He wrote it a week ago." She kissed the letter, hugged it to her chest, and murmured, "Oh, Miro."

"There's one for you, Borya," Dobrynya said to

Dyedka, handing him a paper. "And more pages for Masha. And . . ." He held out the last paper to Anya. "One for you."

Anya did her best not to snatch it, but she felt like she did anyway. She held the letter in numb fingers, unable to bring herself to read it in front of everyone.

Dobrynya recapped the case, stroked a thick finger down the hawk's back, and said, "I'll keep him here, so you can write a letter back. Hopefully he'll return to where he came from." He set the hawk on the top slat of the fence in front of the church, tethering the bird with its leather leg straps so it wouldn't fly away.

After Dobrynya walked away, a raven flew overhead, cawing loudly. Anya looked up and watched it circle the celebration. It made eye contact with her —she swore it looked right at her—and then flew north.

He'll send for you when he's ready.

With the letter clutched in one hand, and Zvezda on her heels, Anya followed.

CHAPTER THIRTY-NINE

ZVEZDA'S LITTLE HOOVES clacked on the bridge out of the village as he chased after her. When she looked back at him, he bleated loudly. Ivan trotted abreast of Anya halfway to Kin's house. The three ran in silence until they crossed the rickety little bridge over the ravine river. Marching around on the ground in front of Yelena's headstone, pecking at bugs and worms, was the raven from before. When it saw Anya and Ivan crest the path's top, it cawed and flapped its wings again.

A moment later, a familiar ruby head poked out

of the fast-moving river. Håkon pulled himself out and shook tiny diamonds of water off his scales. Zvezda bleated, and Anya ran up to him.

"Håkon!" She hugged him around his neck. "I was afraid you really died!"

He used one of his clawed feet to mimic her hug, patting her awkwardly on the back. "I didn't. Amazingly."

"I'm so sorry," Anya said. "I thought, because the *ibbur* said the dagger would kill someone only if I really wanted them dead, and I didn't want you to die, that if you *looked* like you were dead they might stop chasing you, and then you bled so much and . . ." She heaved a huge breath. "I'm so sorry."

He continued patting her. "What's an *ibbur*?"

"Long story." She squeezed him.

His hugging arm tightened. "So you meant what you said? You want me to be happy?"

Anya sniffed. "Yeah."

Ivan approached then. "I thought she was crazy at first! And then she explained, but you never came back, so we thought you were dead."

Håkon laughed as he released Anya. He indicated his smooth chest. "I fell down the waterfall, and by the time I got to the bottom, it was all healed up."

Anya hugged him again. "I'm glad you're alive."

Håkon smiled his dragony smile, and then he saw the letter in her hand. "What's that?"

She lifted it up. It had come out of the hawk's case so smooth, but now it was wrinkled and a little damp in places. "It's a letter from my papa."

"What does it say?"

She shrugged.

The dragon watched her, then said loudly, "Ivan, I can make a spider out of water. Come over here and see." Off Håkon slithered, and Ivan followed, with the raven soaring after them around the other side of the house.

Anya was alone. Except Zvezda. But he couldn't read. She sat on the steps in front of the house, and Zvezda plopped down next to her. With trembling fingers, she opened the letter and read Papa's graceful, smudged words:

My beloved Annushka,

I feel as though it's been years since I've seen you, though I know it's been only a few weeks. We arrived at the southern border in March, and, boy, is it warm! I think it will get very hot here once the summer comes.

It's not so bad here. The real soldiers have given us weapons training, so now I know how to use a sword better. The men in charge said that since I work with animals at home, I should be in charge of caring for the cavalry's horses. Horses aren't as interesting as goats, but it's a better job than cooking or digging trenches.

Did you meet my friend who brought the letters? His name is Germogen. He uses magic to fly to your dyedushka, *and to fly back to me. He'll always be able to find the two of us, so I can send you messages this way. There's no post in or out of the camps otherwise.*

I know you're being very good for your mama and dyedushka *and* babushka. *I miss*

*you so much, and I can't wait to get home and
see you again. When I get home, we'll race goats
to the bridge and go up to the waterfall! Keep
working on your reading and writing. Germogen
can bring your letters back to me. I'd love to see
something from you.*

*Tell Mama you love her every day, because
she deserves to have someone say it, and since
I'm not there, you have to take over for me. Can
you do that?*

*I love you so much, Annushka, and I
know this is hard for you. I'll see you again
soon. Happy birthday, and I'm so proud you're
becoming a bat mitzvah! I'm sorry I'm missing it. We'll have double celebrations next year.
Promise!*

Love,

Papa

Anya wiped away an errant tear that ran down
her cheek as Zvezda leaned in and nibbled on the

edge of the letter. She pushed his mouth away. "You're a bad goat."

She didn't mean it.

Anya tucked the letter into her dress pocket, and Zvezda leaned against her. They sat on the steps of the house for a while, watching the river water rush past as she patted him, and then Ivan and Håkon returned to Anya's side.

Ivan put his arm around her and said, "Good letter?"

"Yes." She nodded. "Good letter."

Håkon bumped her shoulder with his snout. "Want to watch me and Ivan have water wars?"

Anya smiled, and Zvezda bleated. She still didn't have any magic, and maybe she never would, but that didn't matter just then. She had a home to live in, and a family that loved her, and two new best friends who were foolish and brave and wonderful. And that was all the magic she needed.

THE END

ACKNOWLEDGMENTS

Writing a book is a blast, but it's not something you can do by yourself. There are so many people who helped me write this book—not directly, but whose little contributions to my life made this book possible.

First, Rena Rossner, my incredible agent, who had faith in Anya and her story even when I didn't. You made that winter the best, busiest one I've ever had, and I'm eternally grateful for your encouragement and tough love (and the apple challah recipe you gifted me!).

The hugest of thanks to the team at Versify! To

Erika Turner, my editor, for reading my manuscript eighteen thousand times (at least) and pushing me to make it better than I ever imagined it could be. To Margaret Raymo, for taking a chance on me and my story. To Kwame Alexander, for making me feel like a member of the Versify family. To the whole team at HMH: Mary Magrisso, Jessica Handelman, Margaret Rosewitz, Kristin Brodeur, Erika West, and Alix Redmond. Every time I turn around, one of these wonderful people is doing something great with my book, and the enthusiasm from everyone warms my heart.

Jeff Langevin, the cover you illustrated literally took my breath away, and I can't imagine anything more perfect for Anya's story. Celeste Knudsen, your wonderful, flowery chapter art surprised me in the best way, and an extra thank-you for your extra-hard work!

Alex Ott, my Pitch Wars mentor, and Kim Long, my almost-mentor: you two get a special thanks for being simultaneously the very first (non–friends or family members) who told me you liked my story and my characters. That small gesture on your parts, plus Alex's huge efforts during PW with my manuscript, did worlds for me.

To Nevi, thank you from my entire heart for being my first middle grade reader. To Sophie and Melissa for being my first adult readers, and not being afraid to give me honest feedback (in the middle of the night, no less).

Lindsay, thank you for always being available for my out-there messages, and for your honesty and bravery with critiques, and for your unfettered fangirling of my characters.

Thank you so much to the Salt Lake City Writers Group: Shauna, Stephanie, Lori, Rebecca, Zach, Sean. I grew so much as a writer because of you all. I still have a long way to go, and I'm so grateful I'll have such wonderful people by my side.

To Lisa, Boris, and the gang at that language place I live near. *Spasibo* to you all for helping me with the Russian language and some Russian culture and having lengthy discussions about what the deal is with all those Ivans anyway. Thank you, Ben, for nerding out with me about Jewish history.

To my husband. Thank you for being patient and being present even when I wasn't. For supporting me. For letting me take over the office and buying me that really awesome trunk-desk. For buying me cupcakes and celebrating every little thing. For reading my drafts and doing your best to answer weird questions about dragons and root vegetables and the climate of Russia in the tenth century during June and "People know what the *Völsunga saga* is, right?"

My kids. Thank you for being my inspiration. I wrote this book for you. If you love it even a fraction as much as I love you, I'll be happy.

And finally, I want to thank you, reader. For giving my book a chance to be a part of your life for a while, and for believing in nice dragons.

Sofiya Pasternack

TURN THE PAGE
FOR A SNEAK PEEK OF
ANYA AND THE NIGHTINGALE.

The warmth faded, and Anya looked up. The *ibbur*'s hut was gone, replaced by an unfamiliar road with trees on all sides; half of the trees had decided to put on their fall colors, but the other half stubbornly clung to summer green. The sun shone into Anya's face out of a clear blue sky. Ivan stood next to her, likewise blinking away the brightness, and he mumbled, "What happened?"

Anya looked around. "I think she brought us to the Pecheneg territories."

"Patzinakia," Ivan corrected. "It's called Patzinakia."

"Fine, Patzinakia," Anya said. "I think we're there."

"How does she *do* that?" Ivan yelled.

"Be quiet!" Anya hissed. "Håkon, hide."

She realized then that Håkon wasn't there. She spun, her heart seizing in her chest, and almost tripped over a pile of coats and bags on the road next to her. It was a hodgepodge of their clothes, but also new coats and hats that didn't belong to them.

She pointed. "There's your coat . . ." She bent closer, staring.

A foot poked out from under the pile. A *human* foot.

"Ivan," she gasped, and knelt. She threw his coat at him and pushed the bags away. Underneath it all, a boy lay face-down on the road.

Oh no. When the *ibbur* had let them out, they must have landed on top of someone. She rolled the boy over, grimacing, hoping he was alive.

Ivan pulled on his coat as he bent to peer at the boy. "Does he look familiar to you?"

Anya shook her head. She had never seen him before in her life. He had deep golden hair, curling around his ears and at his neck. His clothing was too big for him, threadbare, and he wore oversize, scuffed boots. A smattering of freckles colored the rosy skin at the tops of his cheeks. She reached out to touch his face. Then his eyes snapped open. They were a familiar shade of brilliant blue.

Anya jerked her hand back. "Håkon?"

He looked up at her. "An—Ayn . . ." He ground his teeth together and a look of panic crept across his face. His lips moved like he had a mouthful of honey. "An. Ya."

She couldn't speak. She just stared at him with her mouth hanging open. Ivan stood by, equally agape.

Håkon—was it really him, though?—looked back and forth between them. His panic was plain on his face, and mounting. "I f-feel . . . strange."

"You look strange," Ivan mumbled, and Anya swung her fist at his leg. "Ow!"

Håkon's breath hitched and it took him a few tries to get out "Wh—what did she do?" He tried to roll off his back, but only moved from the waist up.

He swung his arms up, and then froze. He brought his hands back, trembling, in front of his face.

Then he screamed.

"Håkon!" Anya slapped her hand over his mouth. His breath blasted against her palm as he continued screaming. She shook his head back and forth. "Stop! Stop it. Someone's going to hear you."

Finally, he quieted, and Anya took her hand away from his face. His mouth was still twisted in a silent scream. He didn't blink.

"What," he squeaked finally, looking down at himself. At his human body. His breathing got faster and faster the longer he looked. He kicked one foot and started keening, like he was going to scream again.

Anya put her hands on his arm. "It's okay."

"Okay?" He crossed his eyes, looking down his face at where his dragony snout no longer stuck out. "Whuh-whuh-where is my *face*?"

Ivan pointed to his own. "You've got one like this now."

"I hate it!"

"You haven't even seen it," Ivan scoffed. "It's not a bad face."

Håkon still lay on his back, hands up in front of his face with the fingers curled in. Anya hooked her hands under his shoulders and tugged him, trying to prompt him to sit up. "Come on, Håkon."

He was dead weight as she tugged him forward. Sitting up, legs straight out in front of him, wasn't a good position. He started to lean to one side and did nothing to stop himself from falling over.

He let his arms flop against the road and wailed, "I don't have a tail!"

"Humans don't," Anya said.

"How am I supposed to walk?" Håkon said. "Why would the *ibbur* do this to me?"

Anya almost said she didn't know why, but then she realized she did. "I bet the Pechenegs are just as hostile toward dragons as the tsar is. We couldn't bring you here as a dragon. They'd kill you. So, she changed you."

Ivan crouched in front of Håkon and studied him. "How did she do it? Where'd the dragon parts go?"

Håkon glared at him, looking miserable on his side, with his face in the cold dirt. He was much more expressive as a person.

"Magic, obviously," Anya said. "Håkon, come on, stand up." She reached down to help him stand, but he remained in the dirt of the road.

"May I have a moment, please?" he asked. He curled his arms in close to his body.

"Are you cold?" Anya asked.

Håkon grumped, "My skin is tingly."

"That's goosebumps," Ivan said. He grabbed the remaining coat off the pile the *ibbur* had left with them. "It means you're cold." He wrapped the coat around Håkon as tightly as he could while the dragon-turned-boy lay on his side.

Anya felt bad for rushing him, but they couldn't afford to just sit there. They needed to figure out where they were and find the door that fit the key the *ibbur* had given her. But Håkon looked so miserable and lost, and Anya decided that letting him find himself for a minute wouldn't hurt. "Um . . . take your time, Håkon." She caught Ivan's eye, looked pointedly at the other side of the road, and walked a few paces away to stand there.

Ivan patted Håkon's shoulder and joined Anya. They stood, arms crossed, heads together, and Ivan said, "I wasn't expecting that to happen."

"What *were* you expecting?"

"I dunno." He shrugged. "Not that."

"This doesn't change our plan, right?" Anya said. "Rescue Papa, bring him back to Zmeyreka."

Ivan looked unsure. She cleared her throat.

"I mean, clearly," Ivan said quickly. "But Håkon—"

"Håkon is fine," Håkon said. He pushed himself uneasily into a sitting position, pulling his legs up in unsure, jerky motions. He clutched the coat around him like a blanket. He tried to get his feet under him, but he couldn't figure out how.

Ivan darted to him and fastened the coat shut over Håkon's meager clothing. Then he sat by Håkon's side. "Like this." He tucked one foot under his behind, then leaned forward, balancing himself as he brought his other foot up and straightened out.

Håkon tried to do what Ivan did, but he got his feet tangled and fell forward onto his hands. He grunted with frustration.

"Or you could try . . ." Ivan mimicked Håkon's position, on his hands and knees, and he walked his feet up and used his hands to push to standing.

Håkon did better with this method and almost stood, but then stumbled as he tried to straighten up. His knees buckled and he went down. Anya and Ivan ran to him, each grabbing an arm and helping him up.

Håkon laughed. There was something grim in it. "I need my tail back."

"At least you're getting better at talking," Ivan said.

"You'll figure it out," Anya said. "Let's find somewhere safe to sleep before it gets dark."

Anya and Ivan searched up and down the road. It was packed earth, much more heavily traveled than the roads in Zmeyreka. The trees crowded close to the road, their leaves rustling in a breeze that sounded like the whole forest sighing. That sigh and birdsong were the only sounds that disrupted the forest's quiet.